PRAISE FOR *THE ASKING GAME*

'a real page turner,' *Bookseller & Publisher*

'a teaser of a novel,' *The Age*

'intelligent and curiously affecting,' *The Canberra Times*

'impressive ... no tentative beginner's piece,'
The Australian

'an unexpected treasure,' goodreads.com

'*The Asking Game* is serious play – an interrogation
of realism and the real, of the rip tide of memory, of
the riddle of identity – in writing that is lyrical, edgy,
intellectually provocative, and sly.' Janette Turner
Hospital

'I was thrilled when I first published Rose in *Best
Australian Stories* 2004 . She has gone on to write with
great flourish – to quote one of her characters, her
writing is like chilled gin "as thick as syrup, as sticky
as lust".' Frank Moorhouse

Born in England, based in Melbourne, Rose Michael is a writer, editor and academic who has been published in *Griffith Review, Best Australian Stories, Island, Muse, Cultural Studies Review, Review of Australian Fiction* and has won a number of short story prizes. Her first novel, *The Asking Game* (Transit Lounge, 2007), was a runner-up in the 2002 Allen & Unwin/Vogel award for an unpublished manuscript and received an Aurealis Award honourable mention.

THE ART *of* NAVIGATION

First published in 2017 by
UWA Publishing
Crawley, Western Australia 6009
www.uwap.uwa.edu.au
UWAP is an imprint of UWA Publishing
a division of The University of Western Australia

National Library of Australia Cataloguing-in-Publication entry

Creator: Michael, Rose, author.
Title: The art of navigation / Rose Michael.
ISBN: 9781742589213 (paperback)
Subjects: Speculative fiction.
Gothic fiction (Literary genre).

Printed by Mcphersons Printing Group
Cover design and typeset by Carolyn Brown www.tendeersigh.com.au
Cover image by Wyman H www.unsplash.com

This project has been assisted by the Australian Government through the Australia Council, its arts funding and advisory body.

ROSE MICHAEL

THE ART *of* NAVIGATION

'What seest thou else
In the dark backward and abysm of time?'
Prospero, *The Tempest*

Back then I had no idea – a grown up might've, maybe; but I was six, after all. Seven. Crouched before the narrow gap between my mother's door and the floor, posting my drawing into the darkness.

The first magician I ever drew was in 1995 – lead-grey beard and hat coloured in black. She always said, with that slight shake of her head, watching the pictures my pens conjured, that I was born a listener. Her stories were my world: soon, she promised, I'd go to school, but for now I could amuse myself among her books. That morning, I remember, I'd been looking for a picture of her favoured chess-piece Queen when the polished pages – the sound of their turning slicing the quiet room – drew a red thread from my bub thumb; but who was there to tell? I sniffed a breath. Inhaled our house. Stopped flipping on and instead turned back to two men who were made to look 3D by the parabola of paper when all the other prints were as flat as their original portraits: no depth, no shadows.

Face-out in full light the rest of Elizabeth's court stared back at me, but those two looked at each other instead. I dug out my favourite 6B pencil and began to copy. Faithfully. Curving a skinny arm about my drawing and bowing low over the page – almost as close as when I pressed my forehead to Nat's so our lashes brushed and eyes on either side were wateringly wide.

One white corner disappeared under her bedroom door. I pushed the whole sheet in, pulled my hand back to suck the stinging cut. On the other side I sensed Nat's dreams crowding in that dark room, which smelt of something medicinal, and mothers.

I realised it was up to me to free her from the sleeping spell. I stood on tiptoe, the better to turn the porcelain knob – with two hands, which I did. Carefully, so it didn't catch. And saw for the first time what everyone had always said. How very small she looked, lying down. Not like a mum at all.

I beat a retreat holding in my hand the notebook that'd fallen from hers. Flushed with pride – now she would wake and open curtains and windows and doors and arms. Shake off the curse that had made her forget *I* was the love of her life. Her little man. When she saw my drawing she would smile and tell me there'd never been any magic, only ever science. That there was no such thing as a potion, only prescriptions like hers. And if I ever heard her talking it was just inside her head ('not yours,' she'd promise – a finger pressed to my kiss – the words would never be in mine). But I had never. Not a murmur. Until, unpacking, she came across that diary covered in a collage of cut-out rock stars.

'An old journal,' she said: 'an odd journey.'

I fingered the peeling tape that had pinned the paper men down my lifetime long. Rifled through pages I couldn't read – her teenage script was hieroglyphics: running-writing recognisable, but indecipherable – wondering at the story her words spelled.

I knew the perfect place.

I hid Nat's old diary – paper crinkled as the soft skin around her eyes, ink faint as the veins appearing there – at the bottom of one of the leaning towers that walled in our new home. Not intending for *me* to never find it again. Though now I'm not so sure: she always said I was smart.

'Jo,' she'd say, 'you're sharp enough to cut the pair of us.'

1987

10.00 pm

The year of the Slippery When Wet Tour, Di and Nat took to hanging out at Lizzie's house and never leaving. The three of them said they were orphans, had only each other to rely on. 'There's only us,' they swore, and promised to love each other forever – even if they killed each other first – and die together if everything ever got too much. Or, as Di pointed out was probably more likely, life turned out not to be enough. Though surely she was joking.

It was 1987, the year cock rock crossed into the mainstream, and in the Yarra Ranges one night in May our trio were belting out 'Livin' on a Prayer'. Lizzie might've said they sounded like choirgirls from a religious school that'd buried its virgins alive out there, but Nat secretly – sacrilegiously – thought chipmunks described them better. The rock anthem, sifted through their private girls' school soprano, came out sounding too perfect, prissy: neither the hit single of the year (not that they knew it'd be that), nor ghost girls singing. But it was, for the moment, their song. They liked it because they'd discovered it, because it wasn't whatever the rest of their classmates were tuning in to. Because it wasn't U2.

'*Wo-ah, we're a pathway there!*' The lyrics echoed their own desperate fixation on the future.

And they were in love – *sooo* in love – with glam metal's self-conscious pose. They had no idea grunge was waiting in the wings, no inkling of the gritty guitars and angst-filled lyrics already rising from the Seattle streets – the indie attitude that would define their generation. They didn't know they *were* a generation, one that'd be labelled by a letter for the first time that year. As far as they were concerned they were alone and unique, probing their parents' lies with X-ray eyes. Seeing, they thought, right through society's façade: searching for answers, seeking identity, singing themselves into being as they mixed romantic lyrics into mashed-up messages. A cryptic kind of code.

Even if you could've warned them of the massacres that year would bring – named after the city streets where two twenty-something boys went on separate shooting sprees – they'd have acted unsurprised. Hoddle Street might make history by winter's end, its clippings inspire the Queen Street copycat come summer, but back then there'd only been the Russell Street bombing a year before. And – they were teenagers, remember – the fact that a cop shop had been targeted made it a meaningless move in a grown-up game that didn't concern them…no matter that the nutter had come from the nearby town of Kallista.

Foreknowledge of those shooting sprees might not have had the effect you would've expected; it'd take other unimaginable events to turn that year into a mercurial amalgam of wrong times and right places.

But while Nat and Lizzie, and Di too, may've been naïve, their cynicism could make them seem world-weary – almost wise. If you'd told them the Cold War would end before the decade was done, the Berlin Wall fall, they'd barely have cared. It wasn't that they were apolitical, or not exactly; they just knew they were powerless. Seventeen and stuck in the sticks. There. Then. In an outer-suburban upstairs bathroom, light filtered through a creepered window. In a not-so-modern mansion on the edge of

Sherbrooke Forest, above a cellar jackhammered into a green hillside. A lonely walk from the end of the line.

There they were then, that night when three girls pushed something to breaking point – and someone broke. The self-styled misfits watched themselves being best friends in an amber-tinted mirror. Nat teasing Lizzie's hair into a pink–gold mane as they sang their hearts out, riding the high of those days and – Nat's skin constricted as she surfed a feeling she didn't dare describe – a wave of preemptive nostalgia: cresting, crashing, with the conviction that their youth was almost over. And they'd done nothing with it except try to ditch it. Being away, and coming back, made some things clearer than any crystallised cliché: this golden scene was an unreal moment; these girls were no fixed triptych. Nothing was solid and no one was sure, certainly not unstable Nat.

'*We gotta sol-dier on, ready or not!*' Di's alto barely made it. Was Nat the only one finding it forced? As though the girls were acting out how they thought they were supposed to be.

'We could row out to the Bermuda Triangle and wait,' Lizzie said abruptly, pulling her hair out of Nat's hand. The image fitted Nat's feeling that the three of them were floating: unhinged, adrift. The only set thing the pyramid of their friendship – or the solid line joining the other two, anyway; she wished she were more sure she was part of it. No one, she knew, had ever felt such sympathy, such synergy. It was everything: worth living for…worth dying without. That, and Bon Jovi!

'When we're thirty, maybe,' shrugged Di, swinging her foot so her heel hit the side of the bath: hard flesh on harder tiles. That seemed a lifetime away, a lifetime again from seventeen to then. So Nat thought, anyway, as she returned to Liz's hair, teasing it into knots as the other girl dug through a nearby drawer, picking out a pale lipstick. Then a bright-blue eyeliner that she handed to Di. The two leant side by side over the basin, peering speculatively into the darkish mirror. Nat drew back.

'*An angel's smile is how you fool*,' Liz pouted to the mirror, leaving her faithful friends to finish…

'*You promised me hea-ven then put me through schooool.*'

'If we don't burn up before then,' Di said, screwing up her face. Her tanned features throwing Liz's into pale relief. 'Man, thirty.'

'*I* feel about to explode,' Liz declared. 'I might spontaneously combust, right now, so only my fingers are left.' She stretched her eyes. 'Don't I look witchy?'

'You know what they would've done to you,' said Di, reaching for the brush to fluff up her own unruly mullet, 'last century? A dirty virgin dreaming of hairy men?'

'You know what *we* would've done?' Liz retorted. 'Been mediums, like the Fox sisters, communing with angels and falling into trances. Touring the country turning tables – cracking our toes in code.'

'Like *who*?' Nat asked – which was all Lizzie needed to launch into what she'd been learning at the esoteric Belgrave bookshop they'd passed on their way here. A coterie of homegrown Goths hung out there, making it the closest thing to the city in this hippie shire of towns that sounded like they'd been founded by flower fairies – Olinda, and Sassafras – or foxes, for that matter, and only lately overrun by rogue rednecks.

Di snorted into the mirror as she opened and closed her aqua-rimmed eyes, handing the brush to Nat behind her, who absent-mindedly picked their hair from it: strawberry-blonde and Lady Di brown. She added some of her own more mousy strands to the pile then quickly – surreptitiously, superstitiously – swept the tangle to the floor. Something about the night was pulling Nat's nerves tight.

'We wouldn't have *been*,' Nat said, channelling her most matter-of-fact tone, 'not who we are, anyway. No school for girls —'

'No BJ!' shouted Di as Lizzie pushed her out the bathroom door and towards the stairs that led back to the heart of the house.

'I would've spoken in tongues,' Liz continued, 'worn a white nightie with nothing underneath – hidden behind a curtain before wafting out.' She gestured to demonstrate, exposing the shadowy hollow of her armpits and the sparse hair growing there. Bringing Nat back to the here and now of them, the where and when of then, as she wondered whether maybe her friend didn't use deodorant because she was *proud* of the musky odour that – Nat breathed in – wasn't actually that bad. Though it certainly wasn't good. Maybe Lizzie wanted to be teased. Maybe she thought standing out for the wrong reasons was better than not standing out at all.

Lowering an arm in a faux-regal wave, Lizzie directed them out. And down.

'Covered in KY, so they felt your ectoplasmic coolness when they groped you in the dark!' Di grabbed at Liz's acid-washed crotch, but missed.

'Was it all a con, then?' Nat asked, trailing after. 'No real ghosts – ever?' She ran her hand down the banister as she followed the others to the ground floor. 'I guess no one would've known...'

'Yup, one huge hoax,' Lizzie kicked a strut. 'Exposed a hundred years ago – A hundred years ago *exactly*, actually.'

She stopped short, looking back up at the others for a hung moment before jumping the last step.

'What happened?'

'The sisters? Alcoholics. Seriously though,' as they entered the kitchen she raised her voice above the sound of Di rummaging through the pantry, 'why don't we give it a go? Hypnotism, mesmerism…Precognition.' She rapped her knuckles against the pine bench behind her: rat-a-tat-tat.

'Nat?' Tat-tat.

Nat shifted from one foot to the other as Di stacked the kitchen table with a box of Cheezels and bag of Smith's chips. Their perpetual gourd of Diet Coke. 'How d'you know about this anyway, Liz?'

'I've been reading up on séance shit since we moved out here. The Dandenongs is like a nexus for weirdness: first in the twenties, then the seventies. This forest is so ro-*man*-tic.' She shrugged so her white T-shirt slipped off one shoulder, shaking out her Petra-pink-streaked hair: 'What else is there to do at the arse end of the world but commune with the dead?' The others knew neither of her parents were ever around. 'You got any better ideas?'

'You just said the Fox chicks were phoneys.' Nat watched Liz's eyes slide between the pair: careful not to stare at the odd one out, no doubt.

'Then it doesn't matter, does it?'

'Now now, ladies,' Di interrupted, loading her friends up with snacks and propelling them towards the couches at the far end of the room, where the open-plan living area was separated from the back deck by large glass doors. 'Leave her alone, Liz.'

'The theory is,' Liz continued, and Nat was listening, even though she wasn't looking, 'there isn't a single heaven or hell but a series of spheres.' She dumped an armful of food and gestured a universe with her hands.

'And God communes with the living through the spirits of the dead.' Not until the silence became palpable did Nat realise she'd spoken aloud. She wished she hadn't; Liz was getting her going again.

'Right on!' Di snorted, as though some old Nat were on her way back. Di dropped to the ground and leant back against the couch, stretching out denim legs: kicking off sneakers and flicking on the TV. Stuffing her mouth as though she couldn't see that something was going wrong. As though she didn't know that anything was going on.

'Or,' Liz stared at Nat with shining eyes, 'we could try the Wicca rite Drawing down the moon. That's when the High Priestess enters a trance, after a ritual bathing, and requests the Goddess – the moon – to *enter* her.' She raised her arms high above her head so her T-shirt, thin with wear, revealed ribs beneath barely-there breasts. Lizzie closed her eyes: '*If I command the moon, it will come down; and if I wish to withhold day, night'll linger over my head.*' She spun on the spot, spun once around again. '*If I embark on the sea, I need no ship; and if I want to fly, I'm free from my own weight —*'

'Ri-ight,' repeated Di, pointing the remote at Lizzie and miming changing channels. 'Whatever you say, *B*-itch. Personally, I think we should do like those Fox chicks and get toe-pop-ping-ly drunk.'

'Or that,' Liz agreed, unoffended, as she crashed onto the couch and reached for the bag. She made a grab for Nat's hand. 'Come on, Nattie, don't be afraid of Big Bad Lizzie because I can call on the Goddess Trinity. I'll let you be the god within? The spark of life divine!' Laughing, she pulled the shorter girl to her so they sprawled together, limbs mingling. Surely she too could feel their separate hearts keeping the same time?

Nat tried to push herself up, pull herself away. 'Forget about it, Our Nat, I never meant…or not much anyway!' Quick as a trick Lizzie licked her finger and slipped it into the other girl's ear – 'The small straight pin is mightier than the pen!' – so Nat squirmed to be free of that feeling: a wet hole in her head. Laughing all the same. Finally, losing, letting herself go limp.

'In red voodoo the Queen Priestess or Doctor Priest serves the spirits, drawing them near by binding hair into the heart of some form with a thorn,' Lizzie whispered, pulling a strand from Nat's scalp and winding it tighter and tighter around her own finger till the licked tip turned purple.

These two, Nat thought, almost as though she'd slipped outside herself to look down on them: we interchangeable three. Was the ache she felt recognition that what they had wouldn't last? Or was it fear that the symmetry and perfect harmony weren't real? She wondered if the others felt that too. Was she only outside it now, or had she always been and it was just that she'd forever feel it from now on?

Now that most days passed as though she were living someone else's life.

'Another time, maybe?' Lizzie whispered just as the stillness seemed about to settle, so they started laughing again and were soon crying so hard the whole couch shook beneath them. The world rocked and rolled, and good old Di thumped her head back in camaraderie as she channel-surfed with the remote.

At last the chaos subsided. The background sound and shifting light of the flickering TV finally only interrupted by an occasional comment from one or other of the girls in the room, the rare response.

There they were then, our three teens: seemingly so similar – even if two of the girls were following their more forthright friend, and one was wondering if she weren't on the outer of this trio of self-professed outliers. Nat sighed, gave a brief half-laugh and wriggled into the cushions, burying her face in the back of Lizzie's cotton tee, its Radiant soap smell achingly familiar. She curled around the other girl, closer: clung. And finally felt herself relax, her softness cleaving to her friend's sharper angles. There might be only this, she thought – no more, no forever (she trusted nothing now that everything was at once the same and so, so subtly different) – but there was this.

Is this; Nat was almost absolutely sure.

But Lizzie could never stay still for long. When she shifted, which wasn't much later, Nat took the chance to pull down her own top where it was riding up. She shuffled the seams back into place and tried to tuck her tummy in, noticing as she did how day had faded, the last of the light drained from the sky. Evening had wrapped itself around the house, the room growing dark about them while MTV strummed on.

Lizzie sighed – did she too sense the moment's passing? And sat up to speak, but before she could make the suggestion that would determine the evening's direction, Di turned to the others from her seat on the floor and offered her rare two cents' worth. Which made what she said all the more surprising.

'I know,' she grinned, turning off the TV. 'Ghost stories!' Billy Idol's pouting pose contracted to a single pixel and the screen went black.

Before Nat had time to hesitate, Lizzie'd seized on the idea. 'Oo-oo-oh yeah!' she sang. Jumping up she began to gather Tim Tams and blankets and – from a kitchen drawer as she swung by – a box of extra-long matches. 'Come on, girls, come *on*. Let's go…Gothic!'

Back towards the stairs they went, this time heading down a flight to the dugout below. Nat put one cautious foot in front of the other on a curved metal staircase that must've come from the garage sale of some tree change gone wrong. And reached rough-hewn rooms that stretched almost the length of the house – from what she could see in the strobe of one swinging globe. Liz's father's last project, started with wine in mind, presumably, or real-estate prices. Or had it just been a way of keeping busy when his wife was leaving? Did he jackhammer it out before or after Liz's stepmum left? Nat'd been too caught up in her own drama then to know, but could see how any activity might be better than an absence, and wondered if an obsession didn't make the best repression.

In the weaving shadows, made more wild by the flare of Liz's match, Nat scrambled aboard an ancient couch. For a moment the room seemed to open out around her: walls retreating into blackness, furniture and bric-à-brac shuffling back. But strange shapes crept from the corners and leapt onto the ceiling.

'Don't be such a scaredy-cat, Nat!' Di said, so Nat untucked her legs and let her feet dangle over the edge.

'Well I already told about the Foxes.' Lizzie threw herself onto the cushions beside her nervous friend. Tweaked Nat's hanging toe: 'Three sisters. A doorway in time.'

'Or not,' Di pointed out, 'since it was just a hoax,' pulling on her fringe so it stood up like Bono's Live Aid do from a couple of years before – a style that'd taken a while to reach their shores, and longer still to sprout among dags like them. 'And wasn't a *story* anyway.'

Liz slid onto the hard-packed floor and threadbare rug beside her and Nat shifted into the space left behind. She leant into the cushioned arm of the couch, coughing on damp dust as she tried to reduce the height that made her feel unfairly exposed. 'Okay,' she forced herself to say, copying one of the other girl's shrugs. 'Sure – shoot.'

Lizzie turned so they were all facing in towards each other and sucked Cheezels from her fingers as they waited: five – four – three – two – one. Di began.

'D'you remember what happened here?' She poked the thin carpet under their feet. 'Right here?'

'What?' One of the others asked.

'It wasn't that long ago…' Di said nothing for a minute. 'I can't remember exactly, but there were some kids…' She chewed her chapped bottom lip, trying to remember the details, or maybe just building suspense: 'A brother and sister.'

Nat searched for her friend's face in the limited light; it could be anyone, any*thing*, over there. Or just a paler patch of darkness, her own eyes playing tricks. She knew enough at least to know what not to trust.

'The last anyone saw was the two of them walking into Sherbrooke Forest,' Di continued as Lizzie broke a line of Cadbury's off the fast-disappearing block. 'That's what everyone remembered – afterwards, anyway.'

'So what happened?'

Now Nat – eyes adjusting to the darkness that crowded out Liz's candles – could see Di's wrists clasped around drawn-up knees. And there was the other head, tipped forward expectantly. They were her best friends, but how much did she really know them? Not like they knew each other, came the quick retort. Nat frowned, digging her chin into the sofa arm as she struggled to recall: dark water, a distant pale reflection. Was it some urban myth? They were way past the urban zone out here. Nat dimly remembered the story of a boy who climbed a tree and refused to come down when his mother called. Who said he wanted to stay up there forever. How gradually his hands became claws, his ears got bigger and fur grew to cover his body. Eventually, when his mum passed right beneath where he was sitting, all she saw was a koala, beady black eyes staring in shocked surprise as she walked – and kept on walking – by.

'Wasn't there a pool?' Nat gave an exaggerated shudder to hide the hint of a real one. 'Didn't someone see a ghost?'

'What made it so weird,' Di went on, 'is there weren't any clues. There was this huge search party. Which turned up nothing. It'd been a couple of days and everyone said there was no way those kids could still be there —'

'And then the girl appeared,' Nat took up the tale, seeing, as she said it, a small figure stepping between enormous trees. Visualising it vividly, though she knew she must be making it up: a pale androgyne emerging into watery sunlight as if passing through a dark doorway.

'It was right here,' Di said again, so the girls turned as one to where the cellar reached back beneath the Belgrave home. And there, in a glass door abandoned at the bottom of the stairs – a blind window, framing a forgotten way – they saw themselves reflected back. Sitting in a circle of sorts.

'She just kind of *appeared*.'

'I don't get it,' said Liz, watching her see-through shadow open and shut its mouth.

'What's to get?' Di shrugged. 'Everyone just thought the teacher did it – whatever *it* was.'

'The girl walked out,' Nat interrupted, 'but the brother...'

Di nodded. 'The sister had a few bumps and bruises, some pretty vicious scratches. She was soaked to the skin.'

The image of the lost girl at the edge of a big wood waned. The feeling of sun on long-chilled skin receded. Nat wondered what it was about the tutor, and then remembered: the young woman claimed she'd seen ghosts. Or one, anyway: a man out of time. A shadow from some other side. Nat's skin crawled with warning.

'That's it?' Liz asked.

'That was it,' Di shrugged. 'Foul play and the dark arts suspected but nothing ever proved. No body found. I'm surprised your new friends at the bookshop haven't filled you in.'

'A *vanish*ment.' Liz shivered with pleasure.

Nat kept quiet about the haunting man – not sure why exactly, just some sense that she didn't want to draw who-knew-whose attention to this. To them, sitting in companionable silence as the story settled: two children entering a forest but only one emerging.

'Maybe time stopped,' Di offered. 'I mean, it isn't real for kids anyway, is it? So maybe it ceased to exist. Maybe they were just, literally, caught in the moment. You know, walking, stopping. Minute by in-the-moment minute. Hour by getting-colder-when're-they-gonna-fucking-find-us hour.'

Her nonchalance made Nat wonder why she'd brought it up at all; it wasn't like Di to fixate on something so fantastic. Maybe the story wasn't actually hers, but otherworldly words channelled through a down-to-earth dummy. Nat tried to give herself a shake…

…but had never been able to resist where a good narrative seemed to lead: 'Maybe the *sister* was never found,' she whispered and felt familiar chills. She could scare herself better than her friends ever would. 'Who're we to say the same girl who went in walked out?'

The others looked across at her, their faces masked in the dark, and she felt a shock of premonition at the pattern they presented: them and her. Two, to one.

'I mean, just because she was the right age, wore the right clothes – looked the same.'

Nat didn't mean it was the brother who'd emerged; she was picturing two silent siblings frozen hand in hand on a deathbed of dank leaves. And an apparition – like this returned her, which was either the realer girl or her erstwhile shade – walking out into the world.

11.00 pm

An hour later Liz pulled herself off the rug, poking Di as she did. 'I'm so bored,' she said, drawing out the 'so' as long as she could. Longer: 'Sooooooo bored.' Lustily launching into Europe's latest power ballad: '*We've seen through this before / in every rhyme / in every re-ea-son.*' When no one said anything Liz circled the room in search of something, ending up at a cupboard in the far corner from which she unleashed a small avalanche of board games and books. The performance was typically Liz: their Drama Queen Teen. Returning to the dusty sofa Lizzie slumped against it, sighing exaggeratedly as she shuffled through the paraphernalia in her hands.

'I know,' she said, perking up, '*I* know what we should do...'

But Nat never heard how the sentence ended. She felt sidelined, and so suddenly that her vision shrank to a pinprick filled with her friends' faces, almost kissing close. How impossible to imagine ever brushing Liz's hair! Swinging from the sweet moment of their togetherness back to her aloneness, Nat sank deeper into the decrepit couch, her worst suspicions confirmed. Of course their threesome was a partnership plus one. Three might be a magic number – uniting mind, body and spirit; synthesising past, present and future – but triangulation was ever a means to measure the distance between two points. She was but a bridge, a route: a way for Lizzie to get to Di. That was the only reason she'd been missed last term – if, in fact, she had.

So Nat withdrew, too caught up in her own emotion to hear what Liz said next. If she had, the evening might've taken a different turn. But if she had – and had managed to steer them in another direction – she wouldn't have been their Nat.

Because something flirtatious *had* crept into Lizzie's voice: a coaxing note, a cajoling tone. At Nat's feet, though as good as ten thousand miles away, the slim girl's eagerness was practically palpable: an intense intimacy, impossible to resist. It was as if those two couldn't see Nat, perched on the couch above them. As though a physical shrinking mirrored her shrinking within, and Lizzie and Di were alone in the underground room. Why didn't they just fucking get it over with? Why didn't they just go ahead and *fuck*? The vehemence of her thinking, rather than the thought itself, shocked Nat, who wished she were anywhere but there.

'I wish I wasn't,' she whispered.

Why was she there, anyway? Why'd she come when she could've been home in her room with the radio on, listening to Casey Kasem count 'em down? Nat didn't belong here. She never belonged anywhere. But before her thoughts had time to spiral further, Di turned and cast a conspiratorial wink. That's all: one quickly glimpsed chink. And then Liz looked over too and grinned with an excitement she clearly expected Nat to share. Thank God thank God thank God, Nat thought, forcing herself to unwind her legs and lean down from the couch towards her dear, dear friends. Thanking, fervently, the heavens and her not-always-lucky stars as she plucked her T-shirt loose and leant.

'So?' Lizzie asked. Obviously not for the first time.

And Nat said yes. Casting her vote 'for' rather than, as usual, 'against'. For what? Who cared! Could destinies be determined by such incidental actions: and even if they were, wasn't it worth it to be caught up in Liz's embrace? All Nat had ever wanted was to be part of everything.

With a shrug that might've meant anything – from 'So be it' to 'It's on your head' – Di picked up a thick black texta and reached across Liz's lap to grab the nearest cloth-covered games board. Quickly she flipped it over. Her gestures had none of Liz's theatricality, yet they seemed somehow significant. Like her maybe-fable that had happened – as the best horror stories start – 'right near here'. Nat was sure she was just nervous, wondering what she'd agreed to, but all about them she could swear time was bating its breath.

She caught one of her own when she saw the characters Di was drawing on the back of the old Scrabble board. Snatched another in a pinch of…not fear exactly, more like fate. An instinctive 'Oh no' followed by an almost instantaneous 'Oh yes'. So this was what she'd agreed to. Oh.

No!

Oh yes.

Trying for a more steadying breath, Nat then happened to look up at the very moment when a second wave of pamphlets slid from the still-open cupboard to the floor. A slow-motion waterfall of paper that made Liz, too, start. The two girls shared a shocked look as the pages settled, and Nat wondered if Lizzie felt the same, as if she'd made it happen. Abruptly she unfolded her legs and walked on pinned-and-needled limbs across the room.

'What are they, anyway?' Nat asked, attempting nonchalance as she reached past the pooled paper to shut the door. Squatting to tidy the flyers from galleries and museums around the world into a sliding pile of DL and A4 souvenirs when one picture caught her eye – held it as surely as if the image had gravity: its own drawing force.

'What?' Liz asked, in a voice that made Di look up.

Slowly Nat extracted the thin brochure – black-and-white pictures from the British Museum faded to a uniform grey, corners curled and paper yellowed – and turned it around so the others could see for themselves the magic mirror in its wooden case covered in tooled leather. And register its uncanny resemblance to the ouija board Di had just finished. Nat fingered the pages, turning the leaflet over in her hands – loath to leave it on top of the pile, reluctant to slip it surreptitiously into the middle as though it were something to be hidden.

'You're not some freak, Natalie,' Di said when Nat rejoined the others. 'Well, you may be,' she laughed, 'but not because of that. You just saw what I was doing and sought it out. Subconsciously,' she added, when Nat remained unconvinced.

Lizzie, clearly thrilled, threw herself onto the collapsing couch and sang out from its sunken centre: '*Can't you free it in my thighs!*' Making Nat realise that that was just what she was afraid of – that their threesome would free something (pre-empting *The Witches of Eastwick*, which would be released that year). That they would pretend, and it'd become real; that they would play, and it wouldn't be a game. Not that Nat could blame her friends for last summer: she'd been the one too stupid to work out that not wanting her current life hadn't meant she actually wanted to die. She and her shrink were working on 'other ways out', a phrase Nat saw in neon, lit up like an exit sign – except that she hadn't seen it yet.

'*Let this night be our fast go-od-bye!*' The chorus to 'Carrie' buffeted Nat's brain and she realised, in one of her rare flashes of real insight, that her friends needed her and her fateful thinking. Oh yes. Her fear was fuelling the night, creating that sense of consequence she recognised from the other party, and the pool. Oooh no. She was the one lending it the edge they were all – yes even her, if she were honest – relishing. The edge of a knife, a cliff, reason. *She*, little old Nat, was the one making things mad.

So be it: Nat decided, surprising no one more than herself when she hooked her hair behind her ears and slid the pamphlet across to Di.

'All right,' she said. 'Better get it right.'

Under Lizzie's direction they made a circle of sorts out of the junk on the floor and shifted to sit inside it. Having selected an old Monopoly piece, a tiny doll's iron, Liz and Nat reached their hands towards it. One lean, one small. One so white it was almost tinged blue.

'Come on, Di, you too.'

'We need three,' Nat agreed. And within a heartbeat that's what there were: three little pinkies; three girlish hands; three almost-women sharing one secret wish for something more, someone to come.

Perhaps what happened next wasn't entirely unexpected. Perhaps it was a bit of a con by one or other of the girls in the room. Maybe Di, maybe Liz. Maybe not. Could it have been Nat – unconsciously wanting to punish the others for leaving her out earlier, for making her feel left out again? Maybe all three, whether they were aware of it or not, tugged or nudged or pushed what the brochure called a make-do planchette. To give it a start: to loosen gravity's hold. It would've made sense, might've seemed part and parcel of the childish game of conjuring that anyone can play and probably everyone has.

Or maybe an alien wind snuck in and eddied about the die-cast miniature until it started to slide across the board of its own accord. A slip, a skip, a slightly sinister sli-i-ide.

'Is anyone there?' Liz asked, her voice a shock in the earthy dark. Electric. Paper rustled in the airless cellar as the toy began to inch its way towards the square marked 'Yes'.

Yes.

'Who are you?' they asked, and the answer came like an echo: *U.*

It wasn't long before Nat was shaking. Excitement, perhaps. Her teeth chattered and skin rippled with goosebumps. She shifted closer to Di, until she thought she could feel the warmth rising from her friend's solid form. At the same time she pressed down harder on the smooth metal object, until the tip of her little finger went almost numb. She wouldn't give in, give up. She wasn't going to be the one to give the game away.

'Are you dead?' asked Liz.

Yes.

'Are you alive?' asked one of the Bon Jovi–mad three.

Yes, came the answer again, making Lizzie shriek and lift her right hand to her mouth. She, at least, was loving it.

Then someone whispered: 'What's your name?'

And Nat leant forward, as though tuning in to a conversation between just her and…*him*?

This time the answer, when it came, seemed less sure. First the token travelled to *N*. But there it hesitated, waited, and stayed a while before making its slow way onto *E* and, quicker then, to *D*.

But Nat only had eyes for the first letter of her own

name: N for No. N for Never – never mind, never fear, nevermore. As she stared intently at that single letter and wondered about a northern hemisphere place – Northwick Hill – that she couldn't remember ever having heard of, she imagined the hastily sketched symbols were a reflection cast on water and she was searching the depths beneath. Were scribbled on a steamed-up mirror and she straining to see beyond.

And then the letters at the edge of her vision began to behave strangely, breaking apart and joining together. Some retreating, others rising to greet her. Inviting Nat in, enticing her until she longed to leap – like a prisoner escaping a castle keep. (What made her think of that?) A final free falling: no longer fearful, no longer afraid, she no longer felt like Nat. She – *not*-she – swam alongside the letters' non-existent height, somersaulted through one-dimensional space towards the very centre of the circle. And what was that, there? Of course! A curtained door.

There was a sense of touching something, touching nothing. There was a sense.

And then Liz gave a gasp, pulling her left hand back as if burnt, so at the very point of dissolution Nat found herself sprinting, limping, back. And back and back. Squeezing into her scrunched-up teenage form, thoughts slipping into place behind a familiar if flushed face. She wanted to say no – to leaving? to returning? – but it came out more like 'woe'.

'Go.' Said a small sad voice: hers, and yet not.

'What?' asked Di, yawning as she stood. Stretching her arms above her head to tap the solitary light so the exposed globe swung. Making the whole room sway seasickly. 'Nat?'

Nat shook her head to try to steady it, blinking: 'I

thought I heard – someone.' A call like a tug: a definite pull. Ah! Yes.

'Who?' Liz asked, intrigued. Ready to believe.

'I don't know. Probably one of you guys. I think I was falling asleep.' Nat spread her hands, stretching her fingers and flexing her knuckles until quite suddenly a joint cracked. Clicked into place, or out of it. She felt impossibly aged.

'Was it Ned?' Lizzie asked.

'*Ned*?'

'Maybe you heard "Ned", not "Nat",' said Liz, pointing to those three letters on the board. N. E. D. Needing nothing more to launch into everything she'd ever heard about Ned Kelly, and how it must be him they'd found – or who'd found them. And how they had to try again.

'We don't *have* to do anything,' Di said when Lizzie begged them to head into the forest behind her house, where a bushranger would no doubt feel at home: 'Go *on*.'

Come *o-o-on*.

And absent Nat – off in another world where letters and numbers kept combining in cabalistic code – for the second time that night, distractedly agreed. Not that it would've mattered: Lizzie was already packing them up, pocketing matches and leading her loyal followers back upstairs. Depositing the leftovers from their pre-midnight feast before heading out through the double doors. Towards the waiting forest.

12.00 pm

Silently the forest closed around them. One, two, three girls left the dark garden and disappeared from sight under the green canopy that, at nearly midnight, extended beyond the bounds of the gully – inched towards the houses on the hill. One by one they left the lawn and passed quickly through the first line of trees until they were shoulder to shoulder with thicker, darker, older ones. Nat, bringing up the rear and already falling behind, put out her palm and found the nearest trunk mossy and damp…at least up to waist height, like some Pan-god with smooth woody chest and wild hairy legs. Quickly she pulled her hand back and followed the others deeper in.

It wasn't long before they came to the clearing. Backlit clouds parted to reveal a bloated moon that bathed everything in a waxy light. Beneath it, before them, a square black rock. And behind that – of course! – a pool. Nat watched from a distance that seemed further away than where she actually stood as Lizzie arranged the homemade ouija board on the centre of the stone. White kitchen candles weighed down its four corners, and the small iron token pointed towards the roughly drawn texta letters.

Darkness quickly resettled after the brief flare of Liz's match; Nat moved closer in. The three girls linked arms and resumed their positions around the facedown board:

'Ready?' Someone asked.

'Ready,' someone answered.

'Here goes nothing,' whispered Lizzie as the witching hour neared, turning from one friend to another as though she could draw out – or in – the two very different girls.

Here goes everything, thought Nat.

'Come on, Kelly,' Liz begged, beckoned, beseeched: 'Famous bushranger, handsome stranger.'

Nat found herself imagining Ned's spirit – if that's what it was – flying to their girl-triangle. Whispering through the trees, whistling through the misty night towards the light, an untapped power, their lust for something *more*.

'Come to us, Kelly. Now, at the hour of our *need*.' Lizzie grinned, grinding her hips to make her friends laugh. But when Nat joined in the sound was thin and snaked away.

Above the girls' heads water collected on leaves that dipped under its weight. Water dripped onto the forest floor below as carefully, so carefully, each of the three lifted their left hand and moved it towards the very middle of the stone with a drawn-out slowness that ensured no one was first – or last – to touch the tiny token.

Time, what was it? Passing or standing still, Nat hardly knew. A world away she thought she heard her name being called: '*N—*' She kept her gaze fixed on the board, ready to deny that in the darkness at the edge of her vision shapes were moving. As if. It was only shadows and, anyway, they were only leaves. She kept her eyes focused firmly ahead, coughing uncomfortably as she fidgeted to ease an ankle pinned beneath her.

On Nat's right Di sighed loudly. She dug deep in a pocket with one hand, eventually extracting papers and a lighter.

'What's that?' Nat asked stupidly, feeling cold, which made sense – and alone, which didn't.

'Nothing,' Di shrugged, awkwardly opening a zip-lock bag.

Nat's defensive 'I don't want any' was drowned out by Lizzie's eager 'I do!' Ignoring them both, Di fumbled a knobbly number that she lit and sucked before passing it to Liz, who took her time inhaling before handing it back. To and fro it went, leaving Nat feeling even more out of things.

The sweet smoke hung suspended.

'I'll pop the other half here, shall I?' Di teased not long later, pinching the unfinished joint between thumb and forefinger. Slipping the butt and lighter into their plastic pouch and then, feigning reluctance, into Nat's pocket. 'For safekeeping? Don't go getting any ideas, Miss Goody-Two-Shoes,' she wagged her finger in her friend's face, as good as daring her, 'that's *wicked* weed.'

But Nat only half heard, too busy worrying about other things, trying not to think on Ned Kelly's death cast – the forever-closed eyes and sensual lips that'd been hidden in life behind his famous, faceless mask. She must've seen it in some history book. Or had he been in one of those flyers that'd escaped from Liz's cupboard?

Nat found herself wondering if it'd occurred to either of the others that maybe no one would come here; someone would go there. (Where?) Who said séances were a one-way portal? It was hardly a science. Nat reined her thinking in: it was hardly real. She shifted her weight, watching the dope fog fa-a-ade, knowing that not so deep down she didn't want whatever it was they were doing to work. Not like Lizzie, on the other side of Di, who wouldn't shut up – as though she could make miracles with words and will alone.

'Come on, you fucking fucker,' Liz hissed fiercely,

clearly longing to be swept up and over a saddle. 'Come thundering out of the past and galloping into our present. Come to us – come here, come now, come *on*. You daring darling Ned!'

Liz's body seemed to sway then, or was it Nat's head that spun? There came that voice again, laying a hand on her. That call, bypassing ears to ring inside her head. Now Nat heard it clearer: not 'N', *no* 'N'…

And gradually – so gradually it was impossible to tell when it began but only to notice once it had – the iron started to move. Were Nat's eyes playing tricks on her? Were the others? Was it some sort of game?! Focusing on the cold and feeling, fleetingly, so sceptical – and safe with it – Nat let her head dip towards the stone. Closer and closer her forehead slipped until the smallest breath misted the metal surface of what was only, after all, a toy. Her fringe hung perilously close to the flames. There was no doubt now she'd hear the edge of the planchette scraping against the old Scrabble board if it moved. Lower and lower, until Nat's temples came to rest against the rock the board was on and then…it seemed…she thought – was that a voice within the stone?

'Alone,' it said, or 'Atone'? Nat tried to concentrate on the cold, the way her skin felt like someone else's that she was shrinking to fit within, but the sound – 'own' – swelled to fill her skull.

And then the piece gave a strange little shudder. And then it began to move. Travelling in startled fits – as though possessed with surges of power or decisiveness – it made its way towards the letter 'E'. And then to 'D'. Nat could've sworn it was alive under their fingers and they were holding it still and definitely not, she was shaking-almost-certain, moving it.

'E,' Nat sighed, blind to the forest of books.

'D,' she whispered, blocking out a library of trees: '*Dee!*'

Nat stared harder at the letters, sensing that if she looked away, if she shrugged her shoulders – if she even thought 'away' or wondered what a shoulder was to shrug – she'd disappear. Exit as silently as she'd so recently returned, sliding sideways from *here* to some *there* the same way she'd slipped from their universal *then* to this singular fucked-up *now*.

'Kel-ly,' Lizzie was chanting – 'Kel-ly' – her voice dark and wet with forest, as though imagining Irish eyes pushed in with a sooty thumb, a horse, a gun, and somewhere brothers. 'We call you Ned...or Ed,' a quick flicked look to Nat, 'our Neddy, Ed Kelly. *We know it's you / coming through...*' she sang.

'One minute,' shouted Di suddenly, lifting her left hand to check the time, 'forty-five seconds...thirty...' But before she could finish counting down, before the distance between hour and minute hands had closed, a sudden wind whipped up the undergrowth, causing leaves from the forest floor to stir and dance. Rushing through the girls' hair and pushing beneath their clothes, almost prising their circle apart.

'Fuck!' yelled Di, smashing her watch against the rock as she pulled away from the other two: 'Fuck fuck fuck!' She struggled to catch the sides of her denim jacket and keep it closed while Nat scrabbled for her friend's hand in vain, horrified that their protective ring had been broken.

And then the heavens opened. And Lizzie – though superstitious Nat tried to stop her – was clambering onto the centre stone, pushing aside the homemade ouija board, the token and candles, screaming with hysteria as she watched the lightning break. Baiting it with head thrown back and throat exposed. She spun on her podium, beckoning Di. Laughing, then laughing louder at each other – though the sound was nearly drowned out by the sudden downpour – the pair dragged each other down onto the ground, getting covered in mud and mouldy leaves before staggering back up. Shrieking.

The night as noisy as it'd been quiet before.

Behind the three the no longer still pool gleamed, moon shining whitely in the centre of its stirred-up darkness. Before Nat could join the other two – hesitating, as always, so she almost missed the moment – they'd stripped off and jumped in. Nat could just make out Liz's pale face below the chopped-up surface: her long hair seethed with reeds, her face was a play of shadows. Di burst up in a fountain spurt, spitting a jet of water as she gargled rain, laughing and splashing and beckoning their more cautious friend to *come on in*.

But still Nat hesitated, trying to clear her cottonwool confusion. From where she stood the roundness of the pool reminded her disconcertingly of the magical mirror she'd seen in the flyer, that had so creepily echoed Di's ouija board – wasn't water used to cast reflections before mirrors were invented? Reluctantly she shed clothes and edged towards the others, toes feeling for a foothold in the soft mud as water, warmer than the rain, crept up past her knees. She didn't want to be left out. She didn't think she could bear to be left out ever again. She stepped, and almost tripped. She nearly sank.

'Come', or was that 'be one'? Nat wasn't sure but thought she heard whispered words when she let her head slip beneath the surface of the pool. The sound seemed to get louder as water filled her ears. She duck-dived through the dark water, away from her friends' kicking legs. Whoever thought the pool could be so big? She crested to snatch a proper breath before diving deeper down.

Toes flexing and curling, Nat reached towards slippery rocks to pull herself under. She thought she felt fish flick between her legs. It was dark in the airless underworld. Gradually a watery weightlessness overtook her and she spun slowly until she was on her back looking up at the luminous moon that appeared rippled and distorted, as though seen from inside – or outside? – a crystal ball. It looked benevolent, but very far away. It was only when Nat reached towards it, her hand passing before her eyes in a mermaid's languid wave, that she had a funny feeling. A waterlogged almost-worry: a very faint flicker of foreboding. Already fading.

Again came the name. Not – this time Nat was sure – Ned.

'Ed,' someone called, as someone had been calling all night. The sound ebbed towards her and flowed away. In the subterranean whirl strange plants wove webs around her legs. Far, far above, the earth's nearest satellite waxed and wept.

The watery world was no more real than the wild wet wood where trunks of trees stretched straight and tall as the masts of a fleet of ships. Than the small purgatorial room she thought she glimpsed where two globes, gifts from the Continent, trembled on their axes.

'Kelley,' came the call – from below, from within. 'Kelly,' echoed above. But her ears were full of water – her eyes, her mouth. Limbs heavy and numb dragged a body down, down, down: sinking towards stray numbers; drowning alongside depthless letters. Of a sudden, as clear as her own reflection in a piece of polished obsidian, Nat saw a direct grey stare that drew her like metal to a magnet. An eye, suspended – in the centre of a glass? Another pool? An imagined I, spying new worlds!

But Nat's body was fighting fiercely – lungs burning, hands and feet churning to propel her up and out. Away. And back. Breaking through the surface, she dragged herself to the edge of the pool to find the forest alive with her friends' laughing screams. There was something else, another sound closer at hand: numbers and letters stumbling over each other in an endless alchemical alphabet. Could it be – surely not? – coming from her? Nat clamped her shivering jaw. Nobody was listening. Her body, limp with another near drowning, purged pond water onto the mud. She gave in to gravity with relief. Curling towards a ball as the last vestiges of the room she thought she'd seen disappeared: the black-raftered roof and smoke-stained walls resolving into tree-fretted sky and rain-curtained wood.

What had she seen? she wondered, as one final word forced itself between chattering teeth…

'Home.'

Nat dragged herself to her feet. 'God!' she begged, shivering, and then again more loudly as she clambered to her knees: 'God, guys – *pleeeease*…You girls are crazy.' Her voice trailed away. Her friends were long gone. Nat sensed she'd seen white limbs flashing in and out of trees as they'd crisscrossed the clearing before streaking away through the glossy wood. Why should they've waited anyway? She might say she wanted to be part of it, but she was forever too fearful to follow through. Wussy-puss Nat, always snapping back, then regretting it and trying to get the others to join her on the sidelines of life.

Nat shook her head, already forgetting how close to panic she'd been. She rubbed her gooseflesh brusquely, stumbling across the glade to grab her clothes from the rock where they lay like a shed skin. She could've cried with frustration, and her face was pinched with failure as she pulled on wet wool. If it'd been Lizzie in the water – Lizzie who'd heard that voice, seen the dimly lit room – she'd still be there. Too wrapped up in her own adventure to notice the others moving on. Or to care, even if she had. Which was why Nat loved her so much: because sometimes Liz made her, too, forget. Sometimes, around them, Nat did let go. Which was also what she was most afraid of: herself, going.

Gone.

Nat shook her head so a halo of rain sprayed out as she circled the clearing looking for the path. It was hard to tell trees from the spaces between them. Hard, in the darkness, to see any way through. Her friends' distant shrieks rippled back, but Nat faced stonily ahead: it was way too late to give chase. Bloody hell, she thought, wishing she could do it all again, and differently.

Nat shivered, wet skin in wet clothes withdrawing, her steps slowing: she didn't want to go up to the house without them; she didn't want to go back down to the pool. Fuck. Nat stopped, hesitating on the edge of the path, in the overhang of a huge tree that'd been hollowed out by age or animals. And on a whim crawled in. She crouched inside, watching sheets of rain descend like so many veils. Hiding on the way to someone else's house. Bloody…

Hell. Nat's limbs spasmed in the after-rush of adrenalin. She began to calm. For once she wouldn't be the wet blanket who went home first. For now, she smiled, she'd stay right there. Exactly. Here. She was just a tiny bit pleased with herself and warmed by that spark of pride. Liz was always buoying her up, jollying them all along –

assuming her friends wanted what she wanted and that she spoke for everyone – but when Nat was alone and got a chance to catch her breath, she saw the madness they were making. She was the one who'd invented that term for their craziness: a 'triumvirate of bitches'. And the others had loved it, screaming with delight as though their cautious friend was finally getting into the spirit of things.

But Nat'd felt just the opposite: somehow so much older and more cynical than them. As though someone else inhabited her skin, and looked out at this future world with ancient scrying eyes.

1.00 am

Pulling her sodden cardigan around her, Nat felt a packet in one of the pockets. Eager to prove something, to herself as much as the others, she rummaged until – success! She found the half-smoked toke. Nat drew out the lighter and, after a few failed attempts to flick a flame into life, brought it lit towards the joint from an hour earlier. Inside a tree as vast as a spar, locked at the bottom of an unhewn tower, it was as though every sense in the universe hovered over Nat's cupped hands.

A spark on the stub hove into view and the night before inched towards a morning after. Light flared as Nat breathed deeply in and what *was* became what *is* – for a fleeting, tipping second – before becoming what would be. Time, she remembered (she was sure she'd known it, once), was a collapsing telescope. Time, she knew, was a fairytale told to fuel the illusion that we're not all statically trapped. Bound in one undivided atom.

She inhaled again, losing herself in the precise specific exactness of that moment – and Nat was not. The question was whether she ever had been.

2.00 am

The noise of a party from down the road travelled up to the house – was it the classic riff and funky synth of 'Dude (Looks Like a Lady)' that Nat could hear as she pottered about tidying up the mess the girls had left behind?

Realising she was still shivering, despite having changed into Liz's clean clothes, Nat moved to the kitchen to heat some milk. Tiny bubbles clustered and disappeared as she tilted the pan this way and that. So, Nat slo-o-owly smiled, this was being stoned. This: sto-o-oned. Waiting for the milk to come to the boil, keeping an eye out for the creamy head that she always thought made it seem – not that she knew – as if it were fresh from a cow and not out of the carton, Nat sipped brandy from a spoon in a newly invented ritual that seemed to soothe. She screwed up her face at the taste, but swallowed again and again like the good girl she was. Tipping up the bottle. Before suddenly remembering the milk. With a care she knew was comical, Nat chose a tiny teaspoon to lift off the skin. She felt warmed just seeing the steam rise from her Milo mug. Which made her realise how dark the kitchen was. The only light was coming in from the window.

There's a party on the hill would you like to come? Then bring a bottle of Rum-tum-tum…

Nat shook her head, which rang from water in her ears or stray words still echoing around in there. Funny how the night that'd been so recently wild and wet was now utterly mild and unbelievably benign; could she be caught in the still eye of a passing storm? The air certainly seemed clear enough: the sound from down the road did, indeed, travel light-like. Nat returned to her milk, reminding herself that the evening was over, her night as good as done. Straight Nat might regret her early exit from the pool but this version didn't mind so much. It was as though she'd left some strung-out self in the hollowed-out tree – *that* adolescent Natalie might be waiting, trapped in an indecisive moment at the fork of a dark path, but *this* more mature her was here now, carrying an empty cup to the sink, carefully. Rinsing it. Dry.

Nat licked her lips, wondering at their sweetness. Already forgetting what'd passed between them, having hidden the empty brandy bottle in the bin. She made her distracted way through the lower level of the house – turning off lights and carefully closing doors as though there was anyone to hear but her. The activity seemed to settle her nerves, at least temporarily, but as soon as she'd done one room and turned away Nat felt she should go back and check it again. Not that she did, reminding herself that she was just really ripped. For the first time: split. This was – she stopped at the top of the stairs that led to the dugout below – *it*. A pity she was alone, but maybe that was why she was so far gone. Had let herself go so far. Nat noticed the smudged white circle of her own face staring in the dark glass of the front door. Which she deliberately double-checked was locked before descending with drunken caution to the underground den.

What now?

'Now?' The sound startled her – she hadn't meant to speak aloud. She picked up Cinderella's *Night Songs* knowing she wanted to take in 'Nobody's Fool', but suddenly unsure how. Oh my, she was tripping now! She looked at the album with its vampish pink type. Slid the record out, and slipped it onto her finger; she knew you didn't lick it. She spun it slowly, watching the grooves oscillate and gravitate. Thoughts were appearing in her head as if words, or words written by someone else – some future *elf* – were directing her thoughts, which were *oscillating*, about a point of equilibrium; *gravitating*, towards an attractive force.

'Indeed. Indeedy-do. Da-da-dah.' That was her humming – not a good sign but one she couldn't control. Nobody's perfect. 'What next, Little Miss Perfect?' Nat asked, as she abruptly stopped gathering up the stray papers that'd drifted into every corner, feeling her fingers tingle. So. She raised an eyebrow in imitation of Liz as she picked up one particular pamphlet, wondering if it was what she'd been looking for all along. God, she felt gone: the slowness of her brain, the doubleness of everything. Nat – or her doppelgänger, if that's who she was – tugged at Liz's sloppy joe and looked deliberately at the brochure in her hand. This time she read the text that accompanied a long-ago exhibition on the radical Renaissance scholar who was scientist and sorcerer both, apparently. Back when magic and maths were flipsides of the same Elizabethan coin.

Nat launched into the prophecy of one Dr Dee: '*As the molecules of metals are transformed, so the emotional elements in human nature undergo an increased intensity of vibrations, which transforms them, making all spiritual.*' She licked dry lips. Mouthing the words as she went: '*In its third and final stage, the secret of the Philosopher's Stone lets a man's soul attain unity with the divine.*'

'Metal molecules,' Nat repeated, unaware that she was standing and walking in circles as she pored over the paper, puzzled. Picking out odd phrases: 'elemental emotions'. She tapped the page, chewed her lip. The dense text made no sense to her spaced-out mind – but the sentences sang out below the garden that, above, sloped away. Nat finished her unintentional laps widdershins and moved towards the stairs. Making her muttering way one slow step at a time.

'Vibrating intensity.' That was them all right: their trinity of teenage furies.

Was it her fault for not believing enough? The thought Nat'd been avoiding swung to the fore: had she done all she could to make sure it – whatever *it* might've been – didn't actually happen? But wouldn't that mean she'd believed? That she believes!

Nat walked through the kitchen and into the lounge with the leaflet still in her hand – noticing only distractedly, on the page facing the magic speculum, a small jewel encased in silver. Some sea float caught in a fisherman's net, but so much smaller. A cloudy marble, in chain mail.

She heard herself say not 'alone', not 'atone', not 'home'…

'The stone!'

It was only when she felt cold and looked up that she realised she was standing before the double doors that gave onto the lawn and, over on its far side, the forest. For all the world as though she were about to reach for the handle, step out onto the deck and descend into the dark garden.

Nat stepped out, smiling with pleased surprise. Turning determinedly away from the trees, she strode off in the other direction. Towards the party that swelled with sound and heaved with light: '*Oh what a spunky shade-y!*'

3.00 am

Weaving around the odd body on the lawn, pressing past a stray one in the hall, fuelled by brandy, skunk and such a mad, mad night, Nat headed into the heart of the house. It was only once she was well inside the faux Revival façade that she realised there were far fewer people than she'd imagined – maybe everyone had left? It didn't look like it though: backpacks and bags stowed in corners suggested that those who'd come this far into the sticks were here to stay, even if they weren't planning on sleeping.

Not only were there fewer people but – Nat noticed – they were all boys. Usually she'd care, but in her present state she just thought how easy it'd be to find her friends.

'Welcome, and well met!' came a languid cry from a pile of pillows. A long form unwrapped itself from the floor and Nat had to laugh at the mismatched get-up: a plaid dressing gown worn like a smoking jacket over cricket whites, topped off with a woman's silk scarf tied in a careless cravat.

'The fairer sex is *always* welcome,' her host said, standing with a slight stagger. Extending a hand and bowing low over Nat's in return, 'expected or *un*expected, invited or not yet invited.' Byronic ironic; he gestured expansively about him, telling her to make herself at home.

'Though I don't actually live here, you know,' he confessed in a more normal voice. 'Home for the hols to find the olds had moved – trying to *find themselves* in the Romance of the Forest,' he finished, keeping up the capitals and italics.

'I got lost,' Nat offered, not shy like she usually was. 'My friends?' The pair laughed unsoberly. Tilting her head to look up at him, Nat guessed he wasn't as much older than them as she'd first thought.

Johnno, as he told her to call him, tucked her hand under his arm. 'First things *first*,' he said, leading her through myriad rooms to an 80s large kitchen, where he introduced her to a huge stockpot that was filled with a steaming sangria punch. 'As if,' he waved theatrically, ignoring the piles of empties at their feet, 'by magic.'

And Nat found she was right: her two friends *were* there, with post-pond-dunked hair and clean boy clothes. A dramatic reunion followed, complete with drunken kisses for their audience's benefit. Between Liz and this new Nat anyway – Di was too busy leaning over the brew, ladling glacé cherries and rough-cut orange quarters into cereal bowls she'd commandeered since there were no cups left. A bevy of boys watched appreciatively as the three girls drank till their lips were berry red and their teeth stuck with pith. It was far sweeter than the brandy, Nat noted, accepting a refill, and then – when proffered, no one pushed her – another. And more fiery.

Presumably some time passed before she found herself back in the front room, Nat hardly knew. No matter, they were there and all firm friends by now. It was, Nat thought, very late and she was…not out of it exactly, but not quite present. She'd read about the room spinning, but this house seemed far more tricksy than that. The room was fading. No, she corrected herself, concentrating, it wasn't actually actively fading, just every now and then she'd realise that for a little while it hadn't been there – and again, not there. Or maybe – a scary thought – it was still there and she wasn't. Either way, Nat only noticed when she returned, so it wasn't really worth worrying about. She let her head drop back onto the couch behind her and focused on the friends beside her: Lizzie, leaning into John. Nat dragged her head up, sensing rather than seeing the room swing into focus.

'So,' Liz challenged, flicking her hair off her neck with long fingers. Johnno lifted a strand from his shoulder, examining its split ends. 'What's it to be, then?' She eyed off the group one boy at a time. 'Truth? Or do you dare to dare?'

'Sure,' Johnno drawled, only a slight slur giving away his state as he spun an empty bottle. 'We'll do what's asked of us – but…what's asked?' He gave the empty a final flick towards where Nat sat.

For once Nat wasn't afraid of going first – her nerves seemed to have taken a back seat (the way they usually made her). She thought she could see so clearly how far gone they were, and knew just where to start. She looked across at Liz and wondered if her friend registered the similarities: the cross-legged circle, the coming questions. But Nat denied the déjà vu: *this* was nothing like *that*. This was a hoot, that's what it was. A lark. Nothing like what they'd done around the ouija board. She laughed.

'The first time,' she started speaking, slowly rolling the anti-planchette, 'you ever…'

The bottle slowed.

'Wanked!' The last word bursting out as the vessel came to rest with its neck pointing towards a boy on her left.

'Can't remember,' he said quickly, 'too young!' Laughter swelled as he chugged back his punch and gave the bottle another spin.

'Last time...you ever...' it turned back to Nat like a compass that only gave one right reading, 'did!'

'Can't answer.' She laughed so hard she toppled over, surprising herself with the admission that followed: 'Never have.'

'No!' Liz joined in the protestations of disbelief. Waves of laughter buoyed Nat up as the room receded. Oh to let go! (To plummet over the edge and be caught in clouds – to know no death but only flight.)

'Seriously,' Nat swore, straightening, licking her index finger and beginning to trace a cross over her heart – but trailing off, leaving the sign unfinished as she reached for Johnno's joint. He passed it over, along with an appreciative smile, and shifted to sit on the other side of her so he'd get a go again before the reefer did the rounds. It didn't matter what she said, Nat told herself, she was among friends: literally, wedged between Liz and John. Nat drew smoke into her lungs until it burst out in a coughing fit that made her lose it more. This time her head hit the floor; the sound of the hard knock on wood ricocheted inside her skull. Fuck!

'Me?' Liz chuckled, looking past Nat to John, 'I remember when I discovered what my finger could do – couldn't get enough. Thought I'd have to duck into public loos on the way to school!

'Of course,' she conceded to the cheering boys, 'that was after years of practice on the poles in the playground. "My turn, my turn," all the girls cried, but *No*! I was the big bully who got there first and shimmied to the top. Not letting go till I was: done!' She gave a big sigh of satisfaction and accepted the joint that'd come full circle, smoking it exaggeratedly like a post-coital fag. Reaching over Nat to pass the burning butt to John, who cupped it expertly and inhaled the last gasp deep into his lungs.

Nat felt herself fade.

A mutter.

' 'K?' someone asked, and answered.

K—

When Nat next noticed they were lying in a loop: everyone's head on someone else's stomach. Playing a wordless game that started with a chuckle, a belly ripple, rose to a guffaw, a roar. By the time their laughter had settled back down – which took some time – they'd started up again. They were, she thought, resting her heavy head on Liz's slim midriff while Johnno lay his on hers in turn, chasing time. Or driving it. It stopped: it started. It flowed forward and back. She could feel it moving through her, along with emotions that swept her up and dumped her dramatically: fear, excitement, anticipation, dread. Desire. She felt alternately trapped and happy, at peace and restless. Can't wait: waiting. Waiting: can't wait. The room receded, and returned. This moment had gone on forever. This moment had only just begun.

Like Johnno's breath where she could feel it on the tops of her feet: it had gone on forever; it was just now beginning. He'd rolled her socks off gently, so slowly she'd thought she would melt and peel away with them – once she'd noticed what he was doing, that was. Now his warm tongue pushed in and out around toes until her sole trembled in his palm. Her skin flinched when he took his mouth away and the wet patches turned cold. She lay deathly still, aware of his weight where he lay across her legs, and reached behind her head for Liz's hand. Her own palm was sticky with sweat, fingers strangely numb.

But her feet were so alive! Johnno's sucking was so

soft and subtle she wasn't sure where he was nibbling and where he wasn't. Tongue and finger merged and converged. Pulses of pleasure raced up the insides of her legs, tightening the skin over her buttocks and inner thighs so she wanted to clench her hips and rock her groin towards the ceiling. He was turning her inside out, that was it: outside in. Nat licked dry lips, opening her eyes to the darkness and wondering who else was awake and if she cared. Did she move? Was she about to or had she just? She lay still, barely daring to breathe, gripping her girlfriend's hand so tight she could feel Lizzie's bones. Begging Johnno to keep going with every fibre of her being. Willing him to never ever stop.

He was on his side, and she on hers. Nat could feel the heat of his mouth above her knees, and when he slid his hand between her thighs, upwards, she let him separate one leg and bend it up so she could feel the fabric of her jeans press into flesh where the weight of her thigh rested on his hand. She remembered the recent touch of his fingers against her feet and her mind brought the two sensations together: fingers here, tongue there; skin there, wet here.

She felt his heat and teeth through the denim and almost against her will thrust her pubic bone out as he bit against the cross where the stitching of Liz's borrowed jeans came together. When he laughed into her she grabbed his head between her thighs, loving the feeling of it: the weight, the substance of his skull.

Lizzie rolled over and stood up.

Nat followed her friend to the bathroom. She waited, perched on the edge of the porcelain tub, hanging her head and swinging her feet, smiling sheepishly. Staring into the woven pattern of the bath mat and wondering how on earth they'd managed to find the toilet and whether they'd ever make it back to the boys.

'You're fucked,' said Liz, not completely unkindly, as she finished, flushed, and flicked on the light.

'I know,' Nat rolled back her head, eyes closed.

'D'you know what was in that punch?'

'Nope.'

'You okay?'

'I dunno.' Nat tried to right her head, aware how she must look but guessing her awareness meant she was on the way back. The room, returning. She tipped her chin up and opened bloodshot belladonna eyes: 'It's like I keep waking up – like I'm surfacing through all these layers of me, layer upon layer of all the different Nats of all the various ages —'

'What-*ever*,' Liz cut her off, considering the two of them in the small mirror of the medicine cabinet. Turning back and bending down to stare into her friend's face so she was only millimetres away when Nat kissed her. An unplanned, unprecedented pash.

A minute or hour later Lizzie wiped her hand across her mouth. 'What're you doing?' she said.

Nat smiled, Lizzie always liked to be surprised. 'You wanna —'

'What?' Liz shot back, 'with that boy out there? You sure you know what you're doing?' she asked.

'Nope,' Nat shrugged her shoulders like Lizzie might, 'but one of us is gonna do it anyway!' She stuck out her punch-pink tongue, laughing hysterically when Liz popped half a tab on it, keeping the other half for herself. Oh it was a most auspicious night all right! Innumerable first best times. Nat swallowed.

She felt so very not-Nat she couldn't believe Liz still

recognised her. Or maybe – Nat wasn't going to stop to think about that – Lizzie didn't. Swallowing, she waltzed them both back to the boys.

4.00 am

'*Come on* – this way!' Lizzie's voice rippled back as she darted ahead, leading Nat deeper and deeper into the dark forest.

'Follow me,' she called again, pressing into the undergrowth, quickening the pace.

And Nat did, wondering whether John would keep up, weighed down as he was by bedding and booze. When she turned around he peered past her, as though he'd caught sight of a will-o'-the-wisp. Nat swung her torch in a wide arc.

'What?' Her question was quickly swallowed by the wet wood. 'Are we nearly there?' she whispered to the figure flitting in and out of the foliage. All she could make out was a mass of close-pressed trees. Or was it the opposite? Columns of matt-black sky? She shivered, flipping from claustrophobia to agoraphobia, the dope in her system unleashing bubbles of paranoia that threatened to pop. Pop!

'Yes,' Liz hissed, so close it sounded as if she were inside Nat's head. 'Shhhh,' she whispered, appearing out of nowhere to run a finger up her friend's arm, pressing it to her own lips before darting away.

'Thirsty?' Nat gasped as Johnno dramatically dropped what he was carrying, opened his dressing gown and pulled her to him. Briefly he tied the belt around them both – tilting her chin up to land a kiss before she ducked away.

'Thirsty,' he agreed, bending to the bottle at his feet. But Nat grabbed his hand, drawing him towards two trees that grew so close together she'd almost missed the narrow opening Liz'd slipped through a bare breath before.

She heard it before she saw it, but as soon as they were through the gap they both spied the small fall of water that dripped over a slippery outcrop of stone. Quickly Johnno crossed the damp ground, making Nat wonder if he'd seen Liz, but he just leant in delightedly to lick the glossy rocks where they shone silver and black. When she reached his side he twisted around and – holding her by the waist, leaning into her for support so she couldn't help but feel his hard-on – tilted his head back till the trickle ran over his forehead and into his eyes and then his open mouth.

Wondering aloud where the water came from, Johnno pulled himself upright and sprang up the rocks in search of the source, all trace of his earlier camp manner gone. Was that an act, thought Nat, or this?

'Ace!' she heard him yell from what she suddenly guessed – suddenly *knew* – was the clearing. 'Bulk ace!' Of course: the pool!

A second later he'd jumped down and ducked back for their things, clambering with them to where she'd been – was it hours? only hours! – earlier. Wheels within wheels, Nat thought; spheres she'd set in singing motion once upon a twilight time. Back at the start of this wild night that was driving them all towards some unimaginable end.

'*And the night woes lie so very low…*' she hummed under her breath, telling herself unsympathetically that it was a bit late to think that now.

'What?' It was his turn to ask, not recognising her mangled version of Heart's power ballad. Or not wanting to.

'*And now it wills me to be home…*' Nat broke off, noting

how the pool waited glossy and slick as a well of ink. And, on its far side: the rock. The perfection of the setting was obvious and even – no! – Johnno had found the girls' candles and was lighting them delightedly. Lizzie was nowhere to be seen. What'd made her friend bring them here? Nat wondered. Did Liz think he was the hero they'd summoned? And she some sacrifice?

Johnno patted the sleeping bags, looking pretty pleased with himself and the bed he'd made atop the rock. Well, Nat told herself, running hands through reedy hair: the room had gone for good. Time might seem a maze you could get lost in, but really it was a labyrinth with only one twisting turning path through. Was she even on her way out the other side? Or still heading deeper in? The night had doubled back to dump her here because this place was not yet done with her. (Was she in a tree tower, too – lighting a smoke, or sighing her whole life out in one infinite exhale?)

Trying to act as if this were what she'd all along intended, Nat walked over to John, carefully avoiding the churned-up mud at the edge of the water where earlier prints might've been.

Shyly, Nat climbed up.

'Did you ever…' She started to ask, trying to break the uncomfortable silence that made her want to jump up and run. Knowing the timing would never get better than this, the choice never better than him.

'Ever what?' He grinned down at her.

'I dunno. Believe in magic?' Nat tried to laugh, wishing she knew how to dispel the seriousness that'd settled.

They shifted, sat up and reached for cigarettes, and somehow, instead, kissed. Clumsily. One of them keeping eyes open. Mouths exploring each other ineptly and the kiss lasting a little too long; they didn't know how to move on and didn't want to start again. Until Nat muffled a sound that seemed to cue Johnno to lie back on the bags. They made awkward eye contact, prompting Nat to grab the bottle and sip from its slippery neck while Johnno lit two cigarettes.

'I guess I did once,' he answered eventually. 'I had this imaginary friend?' Flipping his fringe out of his eyes, he blew a practiced smoke ring that hung above them perfect as a porthole.

'What happened?' Nat asked, thinking how it should be so obvious what was real and what wasn't – what was possible and what was not – but maybe once upon every lifetime it wasn't. She stared at the billion stars that stared unblinking back.

'I grew up, I guess.' Johnno said. 'I remember one afternoon Mum asked whether *he* wanted anything.' He dragged on his fag, their makeshift bed rustling as he shrugged. 'I thought she was so stupid not to know.'

'Or maybe you thought she thought *you* were stupid,' Nat giggled, wriggling a little against him; she'd never seen anyone so close-up before. The pores of his skin were like pinpricks in wax. She lifted a hand, ran it up his jean-clad thigh and along his side.

She was trembling before he even touched her. To lie so close to a boy was somehow dirty and divine. Nat shifted on their bed–stone, stretching arms and legs into a peace symbol that invited Johnno to explore her. She – slut! – quivered with nerves and pulled his head to her chest to hide her face. Over his tousled hair she looked boldly around the circle of trees, daring them to see…what? Two about to become one: the most mystic meeting. She felt herself moisten at the thought of herself moist.

Pushing aside Liz's borrowed Bonds top, Johnno bunched up Nat's bra until the thin elastic stretched under her arms and front fastening came undone. He flicked her cold nipple with his hot tongue so she gasped and gripped his hair – harder. He sucked Nat's swollen flesh so her reactions came on strong: that's good, that's bad; too little, too much. When John slid an icy hand beneath the waistband of her jeans, popping the button and working at the fly so she wriggled her hips to help free a leg – when his finger, just the tip, finally reached between – everything in her was ready to recoil: Nat almost pushed him away and had to remind herself that she was the one who'd wanted this. She…wanted. This.

Her nails dug into his skin. He withdrew his hand and licked fingers before going back.

Nat took his cock where it crested his jocks and tried to caress it like he said: harder. She guessed she was doing it right when he ate a gasp and the skin in her grip tightened. A bead of moisture, Nat sat up to get a better angle. And John slid his finger fully in: her turn to bite and grip her thighs together. Squeezing him hard in turn. She was shocked by the sensation – so strange, so brutal – and at the same time thrilled – so brutal. How strange.

It was when Johnno pulled back onto his knees, so his lean form and curved prick were silhouetted by the sudden moon, that Nat saw Lizzie on the far side of the clearing.

How long had her friend been there? Nat heard John suck in a breath; he'd seen her too. Wearing only her thin white tee, Liz danced towards them, pulling herself up onto the rock where they waited. Smiling broadly she straddled Nat. Kneeling on all fours – so her flamingo-pink hair, dark in the wet, hung over her friend's face – she kissed Nat full on the lips. Behind Liz's arched back

Nat could just make Johnno out; presented, there was no doubt, with two alternatives.

Her tongue still in Nat's mouth, Lizzie reached behind to grab Johnno's hand and pull it down and back into her friend. Nat gasped, arching hips almost against her will as his fingers – surely many more than one? – dipped in and out of her as Liz thrust his forearm forwards and back between her own legs. Then Nat felt another vicious sting: Lizzie had bit her neck and was sucking so hard it hurt.

Everything was slipping, sliding. Nat wriggled on the rock beneath the two of them. Writhed. Blood racing between pinned cunt and pierced throat.

'Come,' Liz commanded, her teeth at Nat's nipples. She rocked further forward on her knees and reached further back behind to peel apart a thigh, a buttock, or perhaps to guide him fully in. 'Go on…

'COME!' she threw her voice. Rocking even further forward – arching even further back – she turned to look at John, giving Nat the chance she needed to squirm out from under the two of them. Stumble damply down and stagger away.

No idea which way she was going, or where she'd come from, abruptly Nat arrived back at the glade, having circled the clearing she couldn't seem to leave. Arriving from the other side to catch the couple at the very moment when their effort paid off and he was no longer pushing at her. She had closed around him.

Nat saw Lizzie staring across the clearing, as though she could make the moment theirs, but Nat was miles away, centuries ago: caught in a stoned reverie; paralysed with pity for the poor fools they all were to think they could connect when nothing would come together that wasn't separate. Didn't they know? Everything was already…

One!

She broke away, suddenly seeing the forest for the in-between realm it undoubtedly was – the waiting wings between worlds. How would she find her way back? Could she swim through the leaves? If the wood were an ocean and she a ship skimming its surface…

N— (who was she again?) bethought herself of the Doctor's good work: '*By the shortest good way, by the aptest direction – and in the shortest time.*' The last words read recited themselves rote-learnt. '*A sufficient ship – between any two places in passage navigable.*'

Floundering through night, clinging to the idea of dawn, Nat began to run. Half-buried roots tripped her up, half-hidden branches caught on unfamiliar flesh: looking down she saw bare legs that seemed not hers. Hovering on the brink of some fucked-up place from which she knew – with that tiny part still apart – she might not return, Nat ran. She told herself to find the straight way and the true path and the one road. The house, she remembered, putting one foot in front of the other. Push on, she willed herself: push through. Get back to that – home! – where some things at least made sense.

But Nat knew the truth: that nothing did.

Now she was scaring herself. Now Nat was afraid. How could she be in the wood and running, still? Shouldn't she have made it out by now? Could she have been turned back and back again? Doomed to follow that poor fairytale boy to his sad storybook end? Why hadn't dawn come? Her jerky jogging slowed.

'Come along, Nat.' There was that voice again, clearer now. Was it, Nat tried to reason, the voice of reason? It sounded like that other her, the one she pushed down only to have him sometimes spring back up, Jack-out-of-the-box-like.

'You're nearly home now, Nat,' someone said. (How long had she been…not thinking in words, but thinking about those words? Writing, reading these thoughts of – *not* – hers?)

'But how to make sure the points you visit are those you pick and not some other two? To neither of which you'd ever sail a ship?' Nat muttered as some aspect of self slipped away. Suddenly glimpsing the real meaning of the Doctor's manifesto: the 'perfecte arte' was – of course! – the possibility, the reality, of *other* types of travel. Not over oceans, to newfound lands, not guided by dead reckoning and the downward shift of a ship, but betwixt times.

Pop! Nat's brain about burst.

Nat rose and began to run again. She didn't remember falling down. The body was preserving itself, propelling her onwards through green curtains. What was this self? She tried to hold the thought: what, beyond it, and who, before or after her?

Finally Nat stopped thinking, stopped talking, stopping talking thoughts and thinking words and ripping at leafy hair and hirsute leaves in her desperate haste to be free of a forest that, she now knew, was inside her. Nothing more – and nothing less – than the monstrous mess of her own deranged imagination.

5.00 am

'Di?' Nat called, stumbling through the door to the house they'd left so long ago. But she regretted it almost as soon as she said it: if their friend wasn't around she didn't want to call her down. The moment of reaching out had passed an age ago – in the stone heart of a dark wood, the empty belly of an ancient tree.

When no one replied Nat fell into the nearest easy chair with relief, pulling a rug up and over herself. Sinking into the cracked vinyl cushion as she tried to hide from the coming day. She was dreading the morning now, with its freshly scrubbed sheen.

Flicking between five channels on TV, Nat longed for her exhaustion to resolve into sleep but found herself unable to settle. As video clips strutted their New Romantic stuff, all Egyptian eyeliner and poetic ruffs, she thought she might remember this drawn-out moment as much if not more than all the excitement of before. It was taking at least as long to pass: longer. Idly, Nat tuned in to the test pattern that kept no-time better than any true clock could.

Her head rocked, dipped forward and jerked back up once or twice before coming to settle at an acute angle. Not that Nat cared: dreaming she was still at the party as she was.

Only it wasn't the same – more like the masked ball from *Labyrinth*, the girls' favourite film of the year before – where David Bowie played a Goblin King based on his own ultra-vivid childhood nightmares. And fell for a teenage girl.

Nat sighed, vaguely aware that she was already too old, ageing way faster than anybody knew. Wishing she too had a crystal ball that could show her her dreams. And what would she see? Tarot faces flipped before her fast-shut eyes: the Magician, master of creation; the Lovers' duality; the paradox of a Hanging Man. What did she know about such esoterica? Had those flyers featured Renaissance sketches of the Catherine wheel of fortune? The circle of life: destiny, fate. But the dial in the sky was there to remind that the seeds of every death were present in its birth. And in all endings was a new beginning. '*Once we know that everything is connected,*' the voice of some One whispered into her eardrum, '*the universe opens up to us.*' Someone's downfall was essential if another were to ascend.

'Everything we did, we did for you,' Johnno was saying as he swung her through a crowded court, one arm around her waist and the other cupping – Nat gasped, in her dream and the empty room – her *mons Venus*.

'We've reordered time,' he said, waltzing her on. 'Turned the world upside down, brought your Down Under to the fore.' She should've been more careful what she wished for.

They swayed to stand still in space. Nat, concentrating on not cowering – on *not* wanting him to be frightening – offered up a laugh that had a manic edge. She recognised the hollow ring a beat too late. She got angry with him then, but couldn't escape and dared not move – caught as she was. So frustrated, she cried, and felt the plaid wool of Johnno's dressing gown rough against her cheek. The threads were so clear she could see where they crossed over each other, and peer into the gaps between. The dark squares that, as she looked, switched from negative to positive space so they seemed like buildings and the woven grid the streets.

She was flying above Melbourne's CBD. Or was that the fucking forest far below? Trees lining up along old ways, fauna following some hidden order.

Nat gave herself over to the vision of the two of them, now moving serenely through the fixed firmament – a dancing constellation, trapped within a crystal prison. Spinning, spun, she caught the echo of an earlier scene: an Escheresque tower – stairs stepping into nowhere – that taunted with the idea of escape, teased with the threat of entrapment. And there, upside down, crawling on the underside of a fallen tower, a squalling baby boy.

She was trying to tell Johnno something, but couldn't speak. Her mouth might've been open, but the only words she heard were Bowie's lyrics, twisted: '*Cal-ling / as the girl falls do-o-own...*' Nat wanted to say that she shouldn't be here, and in a way she wasn't, or soon wouldn't be. That someone was coming, but she couldn't remember who. And no one knew when. She grabbed a nearby chair, waking only then to find herself scratching at tear-streaked cheeks with the remote, still gripped in her fist.

Throwing it at a curved glass wall.

FUCK! Nat jerked upright as the French doors slammed back. Cold air rushed in, driving Liz before it just as Di emerged from the main part of the house.

'Fuck, Lizzie! What happened?' Di asked – in a normal enough voice that made Nat realise how very far from normal she felt. Lizzie, semi-naked, rolled over, scratching her back against the carpet. Smiling slyly, she grinned up at them.

Nat stepped over Liz's outstretched hand and walked

across the room to the banging doors. She rammed in the bolts and dragged shut the floor-length drapes before returning to her still-warm chair. Tucking knees up and the blanket tight around her again she sat back, watchful and on edge.

Di looked from one to the other. When no one spoke she chucked a rug in Lizzie's direction and headed towards the kitchen, switching on lights and turning off the TV as she passed by.

'Fuuuuuuck,' Lizzie might've been saying, but Nat wasn't listening; she didn't want to hear. Fuck. Hugging her arms around herself she scratched at the skeletons of leaves pressed into exposed patches of skin. Raising a knee to keep Liz away when their friend crawled over and tried to push her head into Nat's lap.

'I…' Nat started to say when Di came back. I am indeed an *I*, she thought self-consciously or, rather, the other who'd taken over thought for her: an eye. Aye! Nat shook her head, taking the proffered cup and holding it tight.

'Me, me, me,' she whispered: not Dee. Or – the letters of his name inverted themselves – *E.D.* Nat felt hysteria like a fatal tightness in her chest, and whistled in a shaky breath.

'I never saw,' she whispered, closing her eyes. 'Such a forest!' Smooth grey trees that creaked like a royal navy set to sail the seven seas and four rivers in one great act of global circumnavigation.

'Shhh, Nat,' Di soothed, a hand on her arm, 'shhh.' She turned up the gas heater and dragged Nat's chair closer to it. 'Just wait while I grab Lizzie some dry things.'

Staring at the flickering flames – vaguely aware that she was rocking in time to a heartfelt beat – Nat concentrated on not humming or keening or in any way letting on how far away she really was. The voice in the prompt box inside reminded her to breathe, and she did. *Breath*ed. She counted to ten, breathing once in the middle and then again at the end: bre-e-eathe.

From the kitchen, snippets of Di's monologue could be heard, saying that she wouldn't be a second and to just sit tight: '— sugar for shock, I think,' she finished, returning with dry clothes and a box of Arnott's choc-chip cookies.

'Now,' Di munched comfortably as she gestured to the others to hoe in, washing a mouthful down. 'What's the damage? Someone'd better tell me what the hell happened tonight – *last* night. You guys,' she peered into bleary eyes, 'you guys look totally burned.'

' 't's okay,' Nat whispered – unsure whether she was reassuring them or herself. 'It's okay *now*.' And suddenly it was, as if the saying made it so. Relieved at the momentary mental quiet, Nat sipped, registering then her burnt tongue. It seemed an aeon ago that she'd made Milo in one of these mugs. Or another mug in the same set, she corrected herself. Or a completely different cup but from the same kitchen. Nat sat straighter, snipping the neurotic spiral, reminding herself that she mustn't be afraid if she didn't want fearful visitations.

Carefully she placed her cup on the floor and crossed to the pile of wet clothes in the corner of the kitchen. Digging in the pocket of her cardigan, Nat pulled out the small Monopoly piece and brought it back to the hearth. When she put the iron down in front of the fire its base scraped across the ceramic tiles. She knew they all recognised it.

'That flyer,' she said, searching around for it, 'you know, the one with the speculum in it? And crystal ball?' She skidded it towards Liz. 'I read all about your Dr Dee. And his scrying glasses.'

'Dee?' Lizzie echoed. 'Oh! That exhibition…Elizabeth

the First,' she explained to Di. 'Her adviser, this occultist – him and his henchman, Mr Kell-*ey*.'

But Nat was silent: something in her had stirred at that name and she veered away from saying it. Avoided the other girls' eyes as though *he* might stare out at her – or was it fear that he'd peer at them through *her*? That mad thinking again. Already she was regretting her attempted confession: she'd hoped her friends would help, that talking about the black-beamed book-lined room she'd seen when she floated in the pond – sank, in the pool – might make it go away, but suddenly she was terrified the speaking-out-loud act might send her back. She worried she wasn't really there. *Here*. An icy wind licked the far side of the big glass doors.

'Kell-*ey*?' repeated Di, finally getting the connection. Watching Liz watch Nat.

Who remembered almost drowning. The flying feeling of freefalling. She gave herself a shake: 'I feel okay now – kind of okay, anyway – but for a moment there…Fark! I was completely out of it.'

'It's okay,' Liz murmured, reaching for the other girl's toe the way she had a millennium ago – but Nat pulled her feet away. Tucked them up under herself.

'It was a fucking crazy night,' Liz said. 'That skunk – and booze. *Boys*.'

'We pushed your superstitious buttons with that séance crap,' Di added.

'Don't say that!' interrupted Nat. 'Just,' she lifted a finger, let it fall, 'don't…I nearly died,' Nat tried. 'In the pool – I felt that whole falling-asleep thing. And there was a light: I was floating above my body, drifting towards it.'

'Ri-i-ight.' Di would probably have snorted if it weren't for her friend's history.

'I was slipping, sliding. Someone was calling.'

Di shifted.

Lizzie tried to take Nat's side: 'Don't, you know, make reality only what *you* can imagine.'

'And not – what? *Un*imaginable?'

'Please,' Nat held up her hand again. 'Just shut up. This is me we're talking about: me, *mad*. Losing the plot, my marbles – my mind.' She offered the words like a trail of breadcrumbs, begging them to follow and find her. But she also kept her eyes on the fire, hoping feigned fascination might mesmerise the man within. 'I just felt,' she stared at the base of the flames where blue jets burst into orange leaves. Fucking forests everywhere. '*Feel*. So small and evil and alone. It's like,' Nat whispered, as if she didn't want anyone to hear, 'I'm this different girl: an alien imposter, utterly other – a changed thing.' She laughed strangely, pulling the blankets in. 'A changeling.'

There it was, that ill wind whistling in.

'And at the same time this, *this* is the real Nat.' Gasping a lungful of air like a drowning man bursting up from the depths, knowing he was only going to be dragged back down, or maybe swept away, she gulped as much as lungs allowed. 'I could barely remember you guys,' she sensed that the door that night had opened wouldn't be easily closed. From subterranean depths icy waters were rising: an epic flood tongued beneath the curtains of her mind. 'And when I did it wasn't with love – it wasn't with anything. You were just a memory.' Nat sat absolutely still, resisting rubbing her skull or pulling on where ears should be, afraid any movement might disturb her hands so carefully cupped around…nothing. Ned, for the moment, leaving; Nat, for another minute, left.

'You weren't there,' Lizzie told Di. 'Nat and I went back to the clearing. Later.'

Di waited.

'We saw Ned,' Liz said defensively. 'Didn't we, Nattie? *Ed* Kelley? It was him.'

'Yeah. Right.'

'Fuck you, Di, *you weren't there*. It was him – the right time and place. We did it, Di, whether you wanted to or not, whether you believe or you don't, we did it.' But Nat – spying with her inner eye a bedroom wall beyond an overturned stool – thought even Lizzie didn't know what it was they'd done.

A time away in worlds Nat was waiting, still: squatting on her haunches in the burnt-out hollow of a tree; mesmerised by the receding night. Her senses preternaturally alert to the air against her skin and breath tickling the tip of her nose before filling her lungs.

She reminded herself every minute – but it might've been more often, since she had no way of knowing and there was no doubt her mind was playing tricks on her – that time moved in a straight line. She'd been here before, but then she left. She was back at the pool, and then back at the house, but now she was here again. It was as if this place had been forever waiting. Time, it seemed, wasn't an arrow after all – travelling from bow to target in a meteoric arc that could be calculated mathematically, given known factors, if you knew how. Time was boomeranging back.

A world away in time Nat waited, still as a statue about to be brought to life. Outstretched arms resting on knees, palms rotated outwards offering up lifelines.

'I am not afraid,' she observed, watching her reactions

rear and disappear as the only universe she knew imploded into a real event horizon.

'I am nought to fear,' he concurred, as two travellers going in opposite directions recognised they were neither opposite nor separate. And space, impossibly, expanded.

6.00 am

When, finally, the girls slept, it was with the help of the Valium Johnno'd given Lizzie as a parting present. A couple of pale pills pressed into a palm to ward off the comedown that waited on the other side, or to add another dimension to their hallucinatory high. Meant to soften the edges of the night, not dissolve them entirely. Nat pictured it so clearly – heart-shaped holes in candy – she almost couldn't believe he hadn't given them to her.

Like she wasn't sure that she and John hadn't, actually, fucked. Did they really just do everything but? She ached, but whether that was desire or its fulfilment, she hardly knew. Her pubis was bruised and swollen from grinding, her lips sticky and sore. Raw.

Rearranging her position on the hard floor Nat worried, typically, about the drug's side effects – hadn't she heard talk at the clinic of anterograde amnesia? What were the odds no more memories would be made? And where was the harm in that, Nat thought with a snort, given what they'd lived through this night: times enough for all her life, lives enough for all time. She was so tired – *so* tired – she shouldn't need the chemical help, but her mind was ricocheting away. And Liz'd been so intent on doing everything together that Nat'd swallowed the diazepam along with Di, not asking why Lizzie had left John. Had she been so eager to get back and boast about how far she'd gone? Stupidly proud to no longer be their Virgin Queen, her hymen ruptured as surely as the invisible membrane binding teenage friends?

Nat shifted as much as she could, tight-packed between the other two as she was. Her body growing heavy. A comfortable numbness crept over her as night lifted. She tried not to leap on signs of encroaching sleep, knowing that only made it retreat. Her body really was unbearably heavy. Nat sank through the carpet and floor and foundations to settle into the earth far, far beneath the house.

As she touched down an arm on her left flung over her...to find another limb there, reaching from the right. Unable to open her drunk and much-drugged eyes, Nat sensed her friends holding hands over her almost-asleep form and wondered if they were really there with her, or if they'd gone off and left shucked shells of their former selves to stand guard. A mind wandered: what would've happened if tomboy Di had followed Lizzie into the bathroom at that party? If it were their new friend John, here, who thought he was not where he was or who he'd always been.

A restless brain, too fried to hold a proper thought but revving too fast to unwind into sleep, spied on the three from above: arms interlinked like the famous graces in their maiden forms. Breathe – as the garden shrugged off night and light peered in the window at the one, two, and then – *breathe* – three sleeping girls.

Nat woke.

Into a lucid dream.

Nat dreamt she was a man called Edward, lying on plaited rush matting. The roof overhead, Ed knew, even from behind closed eyelids, was fretted wood with plaster in between. Oh! A scream was building. No! What time, what place was this? Not now, not then again. He sat up, rubbing eyes filled with tallow light, wicks in need of trimming telling him time had passed.

What'd made him hide out here, among the boxes and books? Ed knew from experience that, much as he'd have liked to slide a knife between uncut parchment pages, he couldn't read most of the languages in which the Doctor dabbled. Any secrets here were safe. He crawled out from under the trestle sensing, suspecting, *seering*, that in the middle of it, resplendent on its own throne, sat the lodestone. He didn't look, but even so a potent undertow lurched to the fore, making him spew into the nearest ewer.

So that was it: not slumber, but stupor. An action, and its ending. He poured the last of the water from the pitcher so it ran over his cracked lips before bending sharply, shaking.

Wiping his mouth with the back of a hand he rose and made his way towards the small casement that opened outwards onto the courtyard below. Imagining a future fellow slipping in one split from such an opening into the next world. Denying the nightmare of a spired keep tickling at his feet, he pushed the shutters properly apart and looked down on his employer's household. Ant-small and just as industrious, Dee's people went about their lowly lives while he, Ed, watched from on high.

But his sneer disappeared as Ed wondered whether the activity below would continue if – when – he turned away. He was not ready for the wholeness of the universe to be revealed, whatever he'd said to the Doctor when he inveigled his way in.

How far east were they now? A wave of some sickness swept through Ed as part of him wished he could return to the sleeping girls. One of these scenes must be a recurring dream, but they were each too familiar and yet too foreign for him to choose between. He had to wake, or send himself deeper into sleep, but had no idea how – he was not the doer; he was the one to whom things were done. The one *un*done. But even as he thought to return to dreams, Ed woke more fully into his post-swoon present. And found himself flat on his back before a scholar's joint-legged stool on the other side of the room. A long way from the window that he hadn't walked towards or looked down from.

Flames of recently tended candles climbed skywards, curling in the corners of the Mortlake attic roof. They hadn't left England yet then. Ed still had to persuade Dee to get their journey underway.

Groggily Di rolled over as Nat threw up. She scrambled to her feet, hearing snatches of mad talk retched between the poor girl's heaves. Nat's fingernails had left raised white welts on blotched red flesh. The crook of her ear was ripped as though she'd tried to tear off a mask.

'Nat!' With surprising strength the shorter girl resisted Di's attempt to stop her heading towards the kitchen. Di followed, throwing a look at Liz.

'Shhh, Nat. Easy, Nattie,' Di murmured, making her way slowly, as she would towards a sleepwalker.

SILENCE!

The command rang so loud Nat grabbed her throat as though to physically hold words in. Had the others heard it too? (Which others? Where was the Doctor when, for once, his unchanging mien would've been a relief? And why, instead, was there – here! – the very double of their Queen?) Again, the voice in her head advised silence and she obeyed. Not wanting to give herself away. Would hiding what was happening – what *was* happening? – give her time to win, or leave another Nat free to find an own way out? Not knowing, it seemed safest to refuse to admit that the voices were real.

This…

Was not! Nat stroked the island bench, fidgeted her hands beneath it.

What was true, was that the wood had finally overflowed its bounds: fronds had come in on their clothes; mud tramped through on their shoes. Wild dread grew in her. Angels were massing: from the treetops, in the flames, and inside her mind. Divine forms bridging the divide – watchers and messengers in the service of some, one or no god – pressed against them like creatures made of matter. Everywhere Nat looked they loomed over the trio, crowding the room with the many they were. The legion she now was.

'Did you doubt us, Edward Kelley?' Nat thought she heard, as Ed had half a millennium before. 'Did you demur? Dids't disbelieve?'

Yes! Nat wanted to yell, but had no voice, no place in this new world where all she could remember and hold onto – he reminded her – was the need for silence. She ducked her head, swearing beneath her breath that he'd never once believed, 'so leave us be!' It had been Dee.

The truth, if that was what it was, came tentatively: a sly confession. 'There were those who said we perjured our souls. Said *I* wrote the *Liber Loagaeth* – but how could

I have kept such maps in my head? Indeed,' Ed wheedled in her squirming brain, having waited lifetimes to explain, 'it would've been much easier if it *had* been my creation: I would happily have avoided those long days where *you* heavenlies pointed to positions that *I* dictated as coordinates so *Dee* could find the letters and write them down one by one by one.'

It took Di all of a minute – though that was a minute too long – to see what Nat held in her hand. By which time Nat had already taken the first thin precise slice at her own forearm. One and one and one: multiple crosshatched slashes. Until Di got to the blade just as Nat let it go, wrapping her arms around the other girl. Bloodying both their hands. 'What the, Fuck!'

'What the fuck?' The two girls sank to the floor in a corner of the kitchen. Di rocking them both as she wrapped Nat's wrist in a clean tea towel, telling everyone that everything would be okay. Not that anyone believed her now.

Liz put down the phone: 'Her parents are on their way.'

17 MARCH 2058

At every European poste restante in 2007 someone seemed to come back with a message from my mum. I often wished I'd written to her more – letters were never my strong suit. I'm trying, halfway into the next century, but in the first decade of the new millennium the occasional postcard home was the most I could manage. I shot off an odd email too, opening a Yahoo account for that first trip when I turned twenty – typing intentionally vague missives that weren't casual at all but carefully crafted. She, of all people, would've known that: the author of her own gothic log, an eighties book of hours.

Then again, maybe I *had* kept in touch; how else could she have known the route we took? Would Nat really have written letters – the same letter? How could I know if I never read them? – to every post office in every city on the off-chance? I wouldn't put it past her; she never bothered with that whole disappearing-into-the-background act around me.

It wasn't easy being her son, that's for sure. It isn't easy being anyone's; but an only one, to a single mum. All my friends were jealous – no curfew, no real rules: she gave me money for cab rides home and never waited up the way other mothers did. Sometimes I'd take advantage. Figuring if she couldn't work out how to act, why should I? Stealing her sleeping pills, convincing myself she wouldn't notice. Flaunting my flings, telling myself one of us should be getting some. Then feeling bad. *I* didn't think she was mad.

I'd make up for it by asking about Shakespearean England, pretending I was one of her Arts students hearing tales, for the first time, of that far-off age and place that was as opposite as you could get to her suburban upbringing. Our inner-Melbourne life.

Don't get me wrong, I was into it too: who wouldn't want to know about the glyphs Dr Dee's 'friend' Mr Kelley glimpsed in the crystal? Who could resist the strange symbols the Queen's own astronomer, Johannes Dee, and his offsider, the outsider Edward Kelley, had transcribed? The great grids of letters they'd concocted struck me as a pre-linguistic crossword: cryptic, yes, but complete. That was the idea, wasn't it? That those ancient emoticons contained the answers to every question men like them – like me! – might ask. An infinite Word Search, if you only knew what to look for. Oh yes, I could believe in an Enochian alphabet: a language of perfect oneness that revealed the wholeness of the universe. Then again, what did I know?

Only everything there was to! Growing up with the Renaissance as I had. And my own in-house expert. I was your clichéd neuroatypical word nerd who'd found himself in his mother's books, finding himself drawn to the teenage-hood of the Western world. Recognising alchemy as no metaphor. The base metal was – had always been – us: our civilisation, and our souls. We were the ones who could be transformed, through testing. Not into hard currency, but the gleaming gold of angelic antimatter.

I know. I sound like her. That's what I'd realised that gap year when, on a whim, I'd followed John Dee, the forefather of contemporary physics and quantum mechanics, onto the Continent. Nat, too, would've seen the evidence everywhere of the Doctor who'd lived in the shadows of the court she taught. Why was I surprised?

Like an old flame of Nat's, Dee popped up everywhere my first summer abroad: stargazer, navigator, imperialist, spy. Honestly, the man had had a hand in everything! A universal figure, if singularly unremembered. No Brits I met had ever heard of him. Which seemed a fitting finish for the diarist who wrote in code and hid his meaning behind pseudo-mathematical signs – always far more worried about being found out than lost for all time. Dee's quest might have been for mystic unity, but he'd never been great at sharing his epiphanies – with patrons, peers or common readers.

Could it be that I'd never told Nat how he haunted me because it's what I thought she wanted to hear, rather than what she most feared? Frankly, I'd had enough of the pair of them. My mother and the long-forgotten scholar I'd been reading about forever: astrologer, mathematician, secret alchemist, Queen's magician. I'd gone on that trip – bridging the divide between uni and whatever came next – in an effort to escape the past, not to delve deeper into it. But then I met Emily, who told me she was going to Trebon to bungee off an old ruin in Southern Bohemia.

It would be *hyper gothique*, she promised.

Did she know that one of Dee's sons had the town's name hidden in the middle of his? Theodorus Trebonianus Dee was born four hundred years before me, exactly. Did she know that Krakow, where Dee had transcribed the second set of coded texts – those with the all-important English translation – was near enough for an Aussie to think it close?

I told myself the trip was because of her – I told Em that, too – but I knew then that Nat was with me. I was channelling her – knowing full well that being around an expert in esoteric things was irresistible. The reason

I hadn't written wasn't because I didn't want to tell my mother about the clues leading me to Dee, but because I was so sure that she already knew.

Nat had done a job on me, all right – not that I ever thought she meant to, not that I really think it now. But it'd been like VCE all over again when I moved back for my final swot vac. Four hours for rest, two for food. Her brewing a pot of tea every morning, leaving it on the table so I could tell the time by its temperature. She never told me to get up earlier, just left the cold dark dregs to be read. She never *said* anything, but each act – my every reaction, I can see now – led me to then. To them: Dr Johannes Dee and Mr Edward Kelley, once called Talbot, who didn't appear in history books until he arrived at John Dee's door.

It was enough to make anyone grab the last seat on a cheap Contiki tour, pop a ten-quid E and go along with a girl he'd just met for the ride. Further on. Further from home. (Though actually, heading east from England meant I was starting to work my way back.) I figured drugs, at least, as well as drink, separated normal-enough me from my neurotic mother. How was I to know running would only speed me to our destiny?

First stop Germany: twenty hours to Prague.

MORTLAKE, 1582.

In the small scrying ball Edward Kelley spies a great glass house, unlike anything he's ever seen. It is early in their endeavours; he is still feeling his way. Sometimes his vision gains clarity as he gazes upon it – as though the crystal is the lens of a great man's spyglass projecting a vision from far away and Ed, homing in, is polishing the surface with his will. Other times what he sees emerges unbidden from the mist of a dreaming mind. His? Then, if he hones his sight, he starts to lose sense of this self. In that room. With the Doctor, John Dee. Spying, scrying, lying.

'Pillars of silver frame a black doorway – Bess's own colours. She is inviting us in,' he mutters, sensing his master tense at the liberty he takes in so calling their Queen. Some things – most women – were not to be nicknamed by the likes of him.

Light spills from impossibly large windows onto local marble polished to a European sheen. From the poured glass, panes held together with lead, Kelley glimpses a garden laid along symmetrical lines. Elsewhere fake panels conceal chimneys and stairs, but the effect of the whole is like light caught. Brightness brought in.

Oh the things he saw! The hints and glints he winked and blinked at. 'Courtiers pose like chess pieces awaiting an opening move,' he tries to describe it to Dee, ever at his shoulder. Wanting, both men know, to be the one. Wishing that he, too, could see. But John has not the power: the visions are Ed's alone. Was it a final queenside castling:

two steps towards the tower?

'What else?'

'Diamonds, gleaming on sloe backgrounds.' The whole tapestry-hung hall sparkles: gold rings adorn fingers and ears, brooches are tucked into folds of fabric, and everywhere there are pearls – small imperfect spheres, sewn or strung or set.

One trick of scrying, he is learning, is that he can chart his progress from above – from outside the crystal – at the same time as he makes his visionary way; so Ed knows the room he glides through makes up the cross-arm of a giant E. An audience is watching, falcon-eyed, as he makes his way towards a great stone fireplace. The only familiar-fashioned thing among the wondrous expanse of glass and light new oak. The court, he can tell, has been there some time by the smell of the throng: fabric and flesh waft stench and incense.

'Is she there?' asks Dee. The scritch of his goose quill splicing the silence as he writes, religiously, what Kelley reports.

Ed hesitates, how to say what he sees? How to capture the sense of being there? The *smell*? He wills himself towards the Queen and it's like making his way through water. Easy, and yet hard. He wades towards a murky mirror.

'Can you,' Dee asks again, 'see her?'

'I see —'

'What?' Dee is standing so close Ed can almost feel the other man's heat through the thick worked fabric of his clothes. Or could, if he weren't so absorbed by this secret pool he is leaning narcissistically over.

'I...*we* —'

'What, what do you see?'

Catching himself a beat before he falls, Ed curves protectively over the pearlescent sphere. (Who's to say what he does or doesn't?) He hides the vision within from the other man's eyes.

'Nary divine.' He hears the sharp intake of breath behind him, but doesn't share Dee's fear of heresy, not having his master's experience of the consequences – Ed has missed his ears far less than John regrets the months he was imprisoned. Kelley is well aware the world thinks they were lopped for forgery, cut for the crime of taking an identity that wasn't his God-given one. There are worse crimes than claiming an imitation to be the by-your-lady deal, which would be an act of defiance not so dissimilar to what they've embarked upon now, he thinks. Ed can hardly tell what really happened. He remembers fingering the side knife he'd lifted from another man's scabbard, thinking: 'This will do.' He doesn't know whether the creature he attacked was a person – was another person. He only knows that when he woke his poor head was held together by a bandage he would not now be without.

'Sh-h,' he says, returning to the scene he's spying on: the Princess, then. Though…when? 'Sh-h-he's…not yet a woman.' But the world he holds has already begun to cloud over as Ed's attention has wavered: where is the future castle of wood and light? Could it really be their Queen? Was anyone there at all? 'Her hair is loose and long. Her eyes are…' Any possible picture is obscured by his own gargantuan face, pocked and waxy as a moon.

'Closed.' Ed casts a sly look in the other's direction: Dee must know that Kelley, the latest in a line of scryers, can only see what's in his head to be seen, what is there to be reflected back. The Doctor is, after all, the pre-eminent scientist of their age. He'd petitioned for a mirror to be propelled into space at a speed exceeding light so people could see events from the distant past, and made his fame at Cambridge fooling audiences into believing that an actor flew on the back of a beetle. He must know the cunning cons of counterfeit cranks. And recognise the real wonder here – the original alchemical reaction – was this meeting of intellect and intuition. The frisson of their new friendship: he, Ed! Here, finally, with the royal astronomer and Queen's own tutor, who gives classes in navigation to captains of exploration, dreams of a British Armada and new Virginian empire. Who has a bonnie wife, a wealthy-enough life, and seeks angelic 'keys' to open doors best left locked when fellows like Kelley are around.

The Doctor taps his teeth with the forgotten feather, eyeing Ed steadily. 'Unbound hair means she's perfect, as a virgin; eyes shut signify…not blindness, but the importance of listening – our hearing what the spirits have to say.'

Offended, Ed stares back. Starts: 'She's…' not knowing that this time it's he who bites a breath, as an image clarifies, 'upon a…*stone*!'

'A throne, you say?' In an instant Dee decides: 'It is a mystery play, Mr Kelley. We must determine the message.' The Doctor pulls a sheet of vellum towards him, dipping his nib in an inkhorn of iron gall. 'An angel on an altar; that's a sign of some sacrifice.' He hesitates, looking at his recently arrived guest with something of an academe's eye, no doubt wondering who'll be asked to part with what, and hoping lodge and board are the coin with which he'll pay – they both know by now that the sweetest angel to speak to Kelley is the ten-shilling one. Probably hoping this new enterprise won't cost him more than what he's already committed to part with.

'Ask her to come to us, Kelley; tell her she is welcome in my home.'

But his new medium doesn't hear – Ed's ears are too full of other sounds: someone is calling his name, as someone has been calling for a while now. The sound crests towards him and pulls away. A tingling travels up his arms, causing his muscles to cramp and contract as though dragged down by a great weight. Ed feels the power of speech retract and flounders, drowning, drawn to a muffled cry that's snuck through a cosmic crack:

'*Kelly, Kell-eeeeeee…*'

Could everything that's made him *him* be stripped away? Was he to shed selves as easily as he'd abandoned his old name, as she will be asked to give up her innocence? Or – the moon looms in a faraway sky – has he never been unique at all: not any individual, let alone Ed?

Kelley stares deeper and deeper into the opaque-becoming-clear stone until he tumbles into she who will be their Queen – back when she lay waiting on a majestic bed a quart-century before. Small head, red on the pillow-bere, turned towards the door.

What an impossible act of retrospective possession! He fails to think as gasping, wordless for once, Ed falls onto a miniver-lined coverlet, beneath two ladies-in-waiting who stretch taut a Rennes sheet so the linen slices a body in two: cleaving torso from root. There is a rustle of fabric as petticoats are carefully, as respectfully as can be, pushed up. Past a young Queen's knees. Until her whole leg length is exposed to the chill of the room. Even the huge fire her maids have built up is not enough to keep the penetrating cold at bay.

Ed, become one with an earlier Bess, looks upon the ceiling as though seeing through it to the God-fixed firmament beyond. Sombre-robed men enter the room. Following their mistress's lead, her maids face fixedly forward as the chosen doctor steps up to the foot of Bess's bed and kneels with reverence. Before he can ask, Bess inches her limbs hip-width apart – parts her legs slingshot-like – to reveal the blazing triangle of tight gold curls.

While the women stare steadfastly ahead the doctor leans and looks into the most private part of the realm: between the cloth, betwixt the lips. Vagina Regina. Ed waits, bodiless, till Bess says, 'Enough!' Brusquely patting down her rucked-up dress as, obediently, the man steps back – gathering with his colleagues in the corner to confer while their sovereign swings her slim legs over the side of the canopied bed.

'Well, gentlemen?' The Princess Elizabeth raises a finely plucked brow as she pulls herself up to her full, not insignificant height. Daring the parliament of physicians to meet her father's daughter's eyes. She would not be the one humbled, but they.

And they were not the only ones. Edward Kelley, with a great effort, rips himself back – forward, to decades hence – into his own fleshly form above the scrying stone. Mending the rent in time and space. Twisting his face into its usual shape, righting robes, he wipes first one hand then the other until palms are once more sweat-free and heart steady. Wondering what he has conveyed.

He turns to Dee: 'Hopefully no one knows we have this…' he finds the Queen's words ready on his tongue – has she uttered them already, or would she soon? – 'unholy window into…*souls*.'

With exaggerated reverence, Ed places the sphere back on its cushion and, making a mock bow, re-finds his balance: 'I certainly wouldn't recommend you speak of this. Or breathe a word of it to *Her*.' He wags his tongue in the vulgar fashion he knows the other man finds gross but so neatly conveys his double meaning: he is thinking of both the Doctor's mistresses – the one his maid, Goodwife Jane; the other their master, God Bless Queen Bess.

LONDON, 1583.

Water laps at the wherry's bows and in the early morning stillness the oars lap back. No one says a word, leaving Edward Kelley to his thoughts and the melancholy hour. Crouching, concealed, in the aftmost part of John Dee's boat, he shivers, thinking of when Bess's sister had sent the Princess over the Thames to the White Tower of Caen stone. Of when she, in turn, as Queen, had sent Dee – those few months that were gone forever yet never gone, no matter how long she reigned or how old John grew.

Ed wondered if the others heard fate too, in that steady beat of wood on water: *to*-the *Tow*-er. To the Tower.

'You take your time, my good man,' Bess's voice comes surly with cold – she's strung as tight as any of her archers' bows.

'Accept our humble apologies!' The hour is early and mist only just beginning to lift as the smaller vessel ties up alongside.

'O Most Royal Prince – Princess —'

'I am King and Queen both, Dee. Queen *and* King.' But for how long? Was Ed the only one who heard the unasked question hanging in the silver not-yet-morning – or did his master, with the Doctor's fore- if not second-sight, know why Bess had made this secret assignation?

'Your Majesty,' Dee bends so low the smaller boat sways unsteadily. 'You are the perfect heart of the last Tudor rose – and such a rose, if I may say, Your Highness, so fragrant a flower and perfect a bloom.'

The Queen dips her head fractionally, accepting his flattery as no more than her due. Her beauty may be passing – ageing barely held at bay with masks of egg white and wigs of human hair – but her power lasts. Though not, perhaps, that of the Tudors. Bess lifts her chin, as though she's heard Ed's thoughts or caught Dee's gist. Will the dynasty's hundred-year rule really end with her? And, if so, is the future he's seen fixed or just how it now stands? Ah, the paradox of prophets! Bess smiles tightly under the packed ceruse, clearly knowing better than to ask what she doesn't want to know. Would that they were all so wise.

A whinny, carrying clear across the water, makes it seem an animal is right by the boat, about to gallop out of the gloom. Even a hardened horseman could've been forgiven for flinching. Not that Bess does. She, of all people, knows that Johannes Dee is more mathematician than magician. Like her father Harry the Great, she knows better than to waste her fear on the unknown. (Ed wonders what her mother might've taught her if Anne had lived: he knows a beauty mark came with the pox – their Queen is not as unscarred as they say. He suspects her dreams, too, are full of meaning.)

'Tell me, dithering Dee, sage of symbols and scientist of signs – what of this new star Nova that's made its home in our skies? And – more to the purpose – this comet that's come after: five years, almost to the day?'

'I know only what others know, Your Majesty. The Bohemian astrologer predicts new worlds will follow. The ancient sibyl Tiburtina said a star would rise to enlighten all the world – she foretold the heavenly spheres jostling one against another, fixed stars moving faster than the planets.'

'But what does it mean?' Bess fidgets, setting both boats

aquiver. 'I want answers, not more auguries that lead like ropes of sand or sea slime to the moon! I have little interest in your New World, Dee, and endless talk of ships and travel and the possibilities of per*fecte* exploration – I care for *this* world. Which includes the comet that's beset my court with fear and doubt.' Along with the many omens, likely ill, that Ed knows will follow after. 'You've heard of the earth beneath London quaking – as if England were an animal shrugging her skin?'

Dee nods, enthusiastic: 'Causing bells to ring out unprovoked – a pealing as for a royal procession!' His pause is unnecessary; he has her full attention. 'I tell you, m'lady, it's witness not of our imminent destruction but *your* ultimate elevation.' Ed imagines the trajectory of the celestial body: an invisible rainbow arching over both their boats. He bets Bess would've stared directly at the meteor while her fearful courtiers turned away.

'Our fulfilment of a destiny far greater than we ever imagined!' Dee speaks, inspired.

'I've imagined a lot, old man.' Has she even entertained Dee's dreams of a united empire: an unconquered virgin land? 'Some say the comet's closer than our nearest nightly neighbour – yet others measure it as far, far away.' Bess's naturally quick movements, at odds with the stately pace she adopts in public, cause the boats to jostle.

'We're lost in a universe infinitely larger than any of us supposed.'

Did Dee mean they were far smaller than they could ever know? The Queen sniffs; no time for popish debates about angels on a bodkin and whether dogs (or doggesses) have souls. She knows where – and what – the centre of the world is. *Her*. She is not like Ed, doubting everything.

'What of it, goodly Doctor? What of the flashings of fire

I've heard were seen over your own house?' She gestures north-west towards Dee's Mortlake estate.

'Grave signs, Your Majesty: great times. A comet forms in the west over the New World —'

'I've heard,' Bess interrupts, 'that it appeared in the seventh astrological house. That relating to marriage.' She waits, clearly wondering what to ask of this archimagus – she who's so adept at getting what she wants from men. But what did she want? And who is this man, Ed wonders; knowing Dee to be no common fortune teller providing answers at the Queen's command, just as she is no village virgin longing only to be lucky in love. True, she'd hired Dee to decide the date of her coronation, rather than arresting him for calculating horoscopes as her weak-minded half-sister had done – but that was back when she was young and Britannia new. What were they to each other now? Or who could they be? Ed's mind pulls and grinds. The pulse of the current beneath no longer soothes.

'The future, John,' Bess leans towards Dee, who observes the heavens through an eyeglass and – she must've heard – in a scrying glass. The whole court knows he dabbles in the dark arts more than her laws allow. The Doctor's name, after all, comes from the Welsh word for 'black'.

The Queen's slender shadow slides over the side to lie across the water between them: 'Tell me about the future.'

She gestures for her men to bring the boats closer yet, and hold them closer still, so she can whisper...what? They said she must marry; they always said that. They said she might not bear an heir; that, too, has been said before – though age hasn't always been the reason. Bess shifts with something firmer than resignation and straightens as the early light reveals Kelley skulking in the shadows.

Dee, too, turns towards Ed. Reaching for the papers to be passed over.

'Allow me to submit for your – and Walsingham's – approval, plans for the calendar reform. 'Tis a work of much significance and divine import. Indeed,' Dee stumbles in the face of Bess's lack of interest, 'an accurate calendar based on astronomical observations and mathematical principles is essential for the consideration of sacred prophesies. Without one 'twould be impossible to know when a millennial event – such as the fiery Trigon's arrival in our skies – were to occur.'

Bess accepts the parchment without so much as glancing at the Doctor's careful calculations, much to his evident distress. John has laboured long to determine where they are in time, and to patiently plot forward and back to find out where they've come from and where they might end up. As Dee tries to explain how a minute discrepancy was accumulating annually so three days might be lost every three hundred years – as though days were something to roll between the skirting and the wall, slipping down an unseen crack – she cuts him off, clearly convinced of a commonsense present tense: they are exiled from the past, the future is closed to them. What does it matter whether they adopt the Gregorian calendar or stick with the old style, add or subtract half a dozen days, if she not be their Virgin Queen?

Abruptly Bess turns to Kelley. 'And who is our new friend?'

'He's my right-hand man, Your Majesty. My trained apprentice and most loyal lackey, newly arrived among us. Heralded by the very signs you've been observing.' Dee bows before his one-time pupil, offering more information than he'd usually share: 'It's he who probes the shew-stone and communes with angels while I sit by and write what they import – through him.'

'So,' says Bess, 'he's privy to discussions such as these?'

'He's the vessel and my vassal,' the older man swears. 'He can hardly hear, m'lady: his ears are lopped. He's as good with secrets as a priest.'

'A priest?' she repeats.

'He means as good with secrecy as with sorcery,' Kelley speaks at last. 'And as comfortable in the company of angels as the presence of princes.' Ed holds her stare so he wonders if he's mad to be so bold. Has he seen her in the magic mirror?

Abruptly the Queen draws the meeting to a close. Kelley drops to one knee – following Dee's lead, only keeping his lawyer's cap on his head while the other man's, doffed, dandles in the small water that has collected in the bottom of their boat.

'Your companion pleases me, old conjurer – and talk of secrets pleases me still more. Bring him to court, Dee. I have need of *canny* men.' Her words ripple back as the vessels pull apart. 'Perhaps your New World venture is about to begin, dear Doctor. You'd do well to prepare your household – for I scry your future by my side!'

The lawyer–forger and philosopher–magician are left to follow after: first to Windsor and then – as the Queen has predicted and will soon instruct – on to the Continent, where she will charge the Doctor to negotiate navigation rights for her Company of Merchant Adventurers to New Lands. (Everyone knew the terrible Tsar's marriage proposal had only been him planning a possible escape route, and Bess would not be a means to an end. She will not be a *way*.)

It is as good a reason to go as any, Ed projects.

STRASBOURG, 1584.

Edward Kelley and John Dee are alone in their temporary quarters, far from home. The Irish rogue considers his Trinity-trained employer, at whose house he'd arrived so soon after Dee's previous prophet had vanished. Almost as though he'd known there was a post vacant. Almost as though he knew of Dee's attempts at angelic actions. And maybe he had, having the ways and means he did. Drying himself by a banked-up fire in the study, to which he'd gained access after saying he had a secret to sell the master – having first gained entrance to the kitchens by saying he'd lost his way (both of which were true enough) – Ed hadn't contradicted John when the Doctor confessed he thought he'd called his visitor up.

Had conjured Talbot from the thick charged air that hung about the great house and pressed in with the stranger when Ed's hammering had finally opened Mortlake's doors. Dee's own wife inviting him in.

How good it was to be unknown, Ed thinks: to have left the infamy of a forged identity behind not just a county but now a *country* ago. How far from home they already are! No tale of Talbot can have made it here. Still Ed's discontent twists and turns trying to find a target. The Doctor? Who had insisted on carting a great hillock of baggage across the Channel, afraid to leave his precious books and priceless instruments behind – as though they meant anything to anyone other than him. Or Her Highness, Bess, who'd started them on this journey? What did Ed care whether the Muscovy Company's charter was reinstated, or their fickle Queen got her north-east passage? (Forgetting, for the moment, that he's been the one edging them on: east, to the utter East!)

Ed remembers when Lord Łaski, leader of their current expedition, had made his progress down the Thames to meet them, clearly convinced he was a personage of some estimation. Clearly not needing to spare any expense. Dee had assumed their guest's invitation to Poland came from the Queen, her betrothed having briefly worn the crown there, and he let Łaski tarry after supper, staying till the summer sun went down. Settling in. Slipping between Kelley and Dee, until Ed had flung out of the room in a passion, mounting his mare and riding off, swearing he was leaving. And for good this time. Shouting that he cared not for the Doctor's stipend, which was a paltry thing. Nor for his own wife, whom he couldn't abide. Dee was welcome to the money and the women and could seek his own bloody visions henceforth alone. Ed whipped his mount, as if she were not already as scared as though the Devil rode her, and cut her flanks with Łaski's stolen spurs.

When he returned, the Doctor was full of a more proper appreciation. Promising all would be well. Welcoming his friend, who stepped softly up the stairs soon after the long midsummer twilight was over, and sat himself down where he was ever wont to sit. After Ed had finished off the wine and the silence between them had been exhausted, Kelley relented, saying that if John was so sure, so insistent, so absolutely convinced that they must go, then *he*, Ed, would find them a boat. And they – all together – would go on this *praeposterus* adventure. He'd said everything Dee might've against their trip, leaving the poor man no option. No, Ed stopped the Doctor with an imperious hand: leave it all to me. We will go despite my better advice.

And here they were, well on their way. Far from the men Ed owes and near to those he doesn't owe yet. Ah, the roving life of risky tricks and fickle sleights of hand. Ed denies any disquiet, the subtle sense that they are being directed by someone, some*thing*, other than him. He pays no mind to his superstitions. He's ready for this new territory they're already traversing: real *re*-invention. It's no scam: he can do it, discover the Philosopher's Stone that will unravel the very nature of things – make old men young again and precious metal so plentiful children would play at quoits with golden rings. If anyone could, it would be him. If anyone did, it would be Ed. If only they'd leave him alone to sift the red dust and sip the red —

'Nothing, I tell you, I see nothing!' Kelley snaps, though the Doctor hasn't said anything. Closing his eyes in frustration – or the semblance of it – which only seems to make the swirling colour clearer. After a brief interval and swift sideways glance at Dee he walks over to stare down at the crystal that sits in the centre of their hastily made travelling table. Trying to probe its obscure depths. Trying to look like he is probing what he suspects is simply a small glass ball: unusual, but not unnatural. Possibly mystical, but hardly magical. The benign sphere offers nothing other than a reflection of his own very far from fair face. Ed leans in closer and closer, until all he can see is his right eye much larger than life-size.

Each orb absorbs the other.

'It's no good,' Ed sniffs, disappointed that this tavern is the best their European patron can afford. 'No one is coming. I see nothing – nothing! – because there's nothing to see, Dee!' The bottom of Łaski's purse was surely in sight, which was why they must continue to Prague and make the acquaintance of the Bohemian King – the greatest art patron the world has ever seen! So Walsingham has whispered; as though Kelley needed encouragement to leave an England riddled with his not-always-small acts of artifice. And what Dee and Ed did was artful indeed.

'Come now, Mr Kelley, come, come. This is no time to give up,' Dee counsels. 'The waiting is just another test. We must stand steadfast or all will be for naught. Tomorrow or the next day we'll succeed.'

'You drive me to distraction,' Ed storms, more than bored. 'This emptiness is no test but proof there's nothing there – there's nothing to see because I. See. Nothing!' He shakes his head: his anger no act. 'Haven't you worked it out yet? How can such a *scholar* be so *simple*?' He roils his eyes.

'I am the *see*-er and an expert *con*-jurer – I, your so-called friend, *make them up*!' He snorts, heart racing with the thrill of self-exposure. Oh yes! Confess! 'Angels…out of air!' Enough of this game of blind man's buff, where each gropes arms outstretched looking for *it*. He was ready to betray whatever held them together, to sunder one from another.

But even as he does it – makes a show of throwing over their precious table – Kelley loses momentum. Wishing, as the emotional tide subsides, that he were elsewhere. In the tavern's crowded taproom. Mingling with men and maids who'd see right through his awful act, sense the danger in the Doctor's daydream, and know Dee instantly for the mark he is – men like Dee were, to such as Kelley, as honey to a bee: the Doctor had had other scryers before him and Ed is sure there'll be others after. Though none will be to John what Ed is, he would bet. As he would also bet that there is a buxom maid at the bar below who could be beguiled to linger beside a homey brew. There usually is; he still possesses a trick or two. And a coin he can magic out of nowhere when nothing but a gold conjuration will do.

Ed is disgusted at the pair of them, and the spell they've already started to wend in the warm, close room. Some science! It might as well be henbane, hemlock, mandrake and nightshade – just thinking those words seems to weave them about his head: cool as a compress, firm as a dressing. Binding him. Readying his senses to receive.

'Now, now, Mr Kelley,' soothes Dee, stroking his beard as he watches the younger man warily. 'You shouldn't entertain such doubts. Of course you're the one who sees; I know that, we all know that.'

The Doctor stifles a sigh, no doubt as tired of his medium's moods as Ed himself is. Might great heights not be his destiny after all? Kelley rubs his hands, washing himself of this dumb show. Preparing to go. Already planning on losing his self, not to other worlds but in the simple pleasure of a mug of sweet and heady mead – dew beading on a pewter tankard. He licks winter-cracked lips, tasting honey wine. Or better yet, sweet poppy syrup! He'd take soporific medicine over witching ointment every day. Dee's interminable abstinence has brought him to this pass.

Poor fool John, his scryer is a constant worry to him – like every medium ever known Ed sometimes applies himself and sometimes doesn't, is often uncomfortably honest, yet frequently a cheat. Oh he knows who he is. None wiser. Dee always rallies, no doubt reminding himself that such fickle temperaments are part of the mystic nature, but in his calmer moments Kelley wonders if his mind is truly sound. And in that odd calm moment tries not to hold the fear of being out of it, outside *his mind*, against his mentor – whom he knows he needs while wishing he didn't. The two of them are bound like brothers, though Ed can't see how and doesn't dare to ask the glass why. He hates the fact even as he exploits it in, lately, less than equal measure: telling gravediggers he's tried to bribe for a body that his name is Johannes Dee, so any ill will will be directed towards the Doctor. They are one, though not the same. Promising royals that he, Edward, is the ultimate alchemist, so all praise can come to him. Not that either the corpse of a dead virgin or praise of a live, royal one has found its way to him, yet. But he is a man of magnificent ambition.

Ed's roving mind moves on to Dee's wife, Jane: if he left the loft now he might have time to catch her in the courtyard. Carry something for her. Curry favour. Follow close behind that swinging farthingale – 'twasn't fair the Doctor got to copulate with a woman not half his age! Ed knew he did, and regularly too: he's read the other man's daily diary.

Odd how for all his shameless spying he's found no reference to the first Mistress Dee – who died after a brief year of marriage. Was't a story worth the knowing? You'd think the old miser – as tight with money as he was with words, and food, and time off for hard work (though you had to say he rode himself as hard as his man, not that Ed ever said it) – would've written something, anything, other than that the Queen had visited that day. John wrote enough about everything else: from his solitary hieroglyph to their search for a secret path between two places.

Scholarly mysteries held little meaning for a convincing fraud such as Ed, a nearly convicted felon. Ed's face flinches in a lopsided grin at the thought of the signature he'd forged on those promissory notes. It was his to crib:

his adopted daughter's bastard father owed him that much, more. Paying Ed's gambling debt was the least the cuckquean could do after saddling Kelley with a wife Ed only wanted less the more he knew her. No matter the terms of their original deal. Kelley has no doubt what *he* is all about: the trick – and quick financial fix – of transmutation. Alchemy, by any name; how poor Ned Talbot could be transformed, through tests, into soon not-so-poor Mr Kelley. Albeit saddled with the widow Joanna and her daughter Elizabeth Jane (whom he tutored in Latin – not that even he can imagine the future poet, Westonia, she will become).

Knuckling his nose, Ed moves across the room, mind – mad! – all but made up.

'Maybe,' the Doctor's apology knocks on blocked ears, 'maybe I *have* been driving us too hard. Heaven knows, I'm sorely overtired myself – four hours for sleep and two for food and rest is, perhaps...' Dee's words trail away. His mathematical mind might be returning to their forty-eight Enochian translation tables of over two thousand letters, revelling in the possible permutations and combinations – over a hundred thousand characters! But Kelley has already forgotten the coordinates he last conveyed: intent only on ending this interminable session and exiting the closed room. Eager to forgo fasting and, instead, feast: to use his silver tongue not for prayers of purification but to woo some nubile mistress to sit upon his lap.

And if she be comely as John's young wife, well, then he wanted to use it even more intimately. Ed's smile shows wolfish teeth. Dee didn't appreciate his good woman enough – Jane was more than just the Queen's ex-lady-in-waiting! A tongue pokes out, moistening Kelley's beard-hid lip.

The old scholar in his corner double-crosses lines riddled with secret triangles and strange formulations. Was't a code? Who cared! When the fustian doddy doesn't lift his head, Ed turns with the quick, light movements of one free to go. Only by chance throwing a last look at the cloudy-becoming-clear sphere. A glance, askance.

Oh! For something he sees makes Ed fall towards the table, grabbing the shew-stone in his fist and thrusting it up close to his scrunched-in, screwed-up face. Ye Gods, ho! A prick in the darkness. A hole (a key?) to another time and place. Sensing a scouting eye staring back at *him*, Ed thinks he feels his blood coagulate and collect.

'N? Did you say N?' Dee is asking, but Ed's as gone as he had meant to be.

A light. An angel in not-yet-human form: some faire messenger piercing the membrane between unconnected times. Kelley sways unsteadily, caught between one footfall and the next. There is no floor beneath his feet – no roadside hostelry or Europe even. Only a myrrh haze. In vain Ed tries to remember his training, to hold on to where he is by focusing on the flickering firelight here and Dee – *there*! – on his knob-kneed scholar's stool. But their rote-learnt prayers are lost; the words he's been taught gone. He is only what little is left after days of fasting and nights without sleep. He is nothing.

But '*Kel-ly*,' he thinks he hears, knowing better than to look around. He stumbles to the ground. That's earth beneath his knees! Presses hands to head as if to block out, or hold in, that disconnected cry: '*Kel-ley*.

'*We know it's you, coming through*.'

Ed peers into the precious crystal. Was it an angel there – as he'd made believe so many times? Or a red-haired sybil, gathering in the glass like wine clouding water?

The ball calls like a lodestone pulling iron. And who is he to resist? He bows low over: 'A hole!' Kelley cries in a breaking voice as time slams to a standstill.

Is that scratching sound Dee's quill chasing after Ed's words? Following where he has little wish to lead? (Both men remember – now the action is embarked upon – that neither wants these visions to come to them through Kelley. Ed would give anything not to bear them; John would do the same to be the one. In this they are united.)

'Did you doubt, Kelley? Didst demur, and disbelieve?' Was that the Doctor, guessing at questions? The flare, the flame, the not-yet-female flickers between shimmering states as Ed takes himself to task for his most recent – and so regular – blasphemy: disbelief.

'I don't know!' he tries to say, thinking of the infinite relay as strange angels pointed to coordinates that he read and the Doctor plotted. He had not the head for it. He has not the heart.

'Yes!' he cries. No.

'What is it, Mr Kelley? Who's there?' the Doctor begs. 'What do you…' he catches himself, '*think* you see?'

Someone was crying out, but whether it was Ed or a spirit in the glade – 'I don't know!' – Kelley couldn't say. Can only see his seraph caught in their crystal like a baby in a belly. Or was she trapped in a watery bubble? Hidden in a gouged-out gourde of wood…

'*Dee…*' he beseeches, unwrapping the tightly wound bandages that he is never without. Peeling away layer after layer of unclean cloth – ignoring the Doctor's distracted remonstrations – until the holes in his head are weepingly exposed. A foreign wind fingers where Ed's ears once were. The rustle of an evergreen winter whispers in. That familiar–unfamiliar forest, smelling of mint.

'Come,' he cajoles, kneeling before the miniature table – the pivot of their grimoire. Knowing he shouldn't, that she is God's messenger and not to be messed with, but he can't help…himself. (He remembers everything now. He denies nothing, now. He believes. Now.)

Come on *in*.

'There seems to be,' he mutters. 'She seems to see.' For she did, she seemed to *see* him. Their look of shocked surprise – across time, across place – the very same. So when they saw it in each other they experienced it again in themselves: an uncanny doubling. Not because *he* was some spiritual spouse who'd invited *her* in, but because in their obvious opposition they were the warp and weft of the whole woven world. The two of them dual poles: her sweet new grace, his sour old face.

'Tell her —'

'I know,' Ed snaps, not happy to be back. If she couldn't come to him then he would go to her. Wherever. Whenever. For in his thick-skinned hands, before his close-set eyes, he holds the shortest way. So Dee has said and said and said.

'Become…' Kelley commands, himself as much as her, '*one*.'

He is trying to remember what he is already forgetting. He is stuck and unstuck, spinning and spun; he is fast… becoming…un…

'Done!' Kelley cries, fainting to the floor. Falling hard from a stone eyrie that looms on their horizon – the one thing he's sure he saw; not that he'll tell Dee. Ed lets his mind drift. Believing – as anyone would – that what a scryer sees is not necessarily what will be.

$$\triangledown$$

His mouth open, Ed draws breath before snatching someone's hand back. An ancient on the cusp of death. Finger-hitting letter keys in an automatic action as though possessed. *Sh*-he is…what? He saw…*what*? There'd been fiery light and fey life but water like curtains, like veils, like skirts, like layers of skin had come between. Vernix and shroud. A fish out of. A duck taking to. In hot, in deep: dead in the – *water*.

He gulps, eyes thirsty but throat about drowned. Senses a coming clarity of moment. Rising up to spasm stroke some Skrying app and enter their world again – he almost can't connect. Then! She was: there. The thoughts that think him calm.

'I can't,' Ed whispers from where he lies forgetting on the floor. 'I can't see. Her!' He rubs his face with a hand, mashing the sunken skin beneath his brow with the base of a calloused palm – as though the visions of their virgin, become an ageing crone, came from there. He groans. There is no lid to lower over an inner eye. Kelley claws his way back.

Describing the feeling…Not of falling, for there'd been no fatal pull of a planet. Nor flying: he'd had no sense of the rush and push of wind. Sailing? He could almost see himself skimming across a glassy surface, skipping over blue–black depths like a thrown stone, tossed aloft by monstrous waves. Driven onwards to an unseen shore.

Returning to their rented room, wishing the other man would stop his constant scribble – the firk! – Ed steers their story seaward. Keeping up his rambling as long as Dee records it. Buying himself time to regather himself.

'A ship.' Ed's thoughts pull together: had he leapt from the rigging? Been plucked from the ocean with a hook so he was being dragged up while his clothing, heavy with salt water, pulled him back down? Had he stood drenched on a deck? Shielding his eyes from some sun until they reached the edge of a map and went over, suspended in oblivion before somersaulting into a waterfall of darkness. To land…

here.

Clearly not. But there is something about a ship that sounds right, that seems to fit, that suggests some truth his visions are guiding them towards.

'A passage!' Ed imagines an elegant vessel bound for the New World: a spy ship nosing in foreign waters, a warship sent to do the same. His lady, carved upon a prow pointed towards one new continent coming aground upon another – a siren singing sailor-him onto a wide white land.

Jane! Ed wills her hard up the stairs; he is done with travel and this whole racket. Tired of lies. He runs a rough hand over his head, groping for a covering cloth. Dee is so absorbed in what Kelley is sure he never saw that he misses the way Ed's eyes sting when the Doctor's wife brings in the last piney whiff of the Yule log that's been burning itself out in the great fireplace below. Along with a quilt, which she lays over their friend on the floor – so much more than a mere house guest now. Travelling together on this journey out and east, which will take them a long way into a dark Bohemian wood. Is she the only one suspecting there is no end to the men's quest?

Leaving, only to return a moment later with fresh bandages, Dee's pretty Janey avoids Ed's eye, as well as the stone's. She feels the fever transfer itself from his hot brow to her cool hand as he offers her a bracelet, coiled in an upturned palm. Not that her husband notices, covering a new page in spurting fits and slipped-up starts. The gold is cold, as though Kelley has brought it back from some nether realm and hasn't had it secured beneath his robe against just such an opportunity. Jane wonders how that is.

They said he could breathe the Devil into you with a kiss.

PRAGUE, 1585.

Here Kelley and Dee are, three years after first meeting, in the home of the Habsburgs and there, *there* he comes: the Roman Emperor, parting a sea of silken hose and sibilant whispers. Handsome men, flanked by flamboyant boys – human members of the menagerie of exotic animals that wander here – make way for the King of Hungary and Croatia (in his first incarnation, as Rudolph I), and Bohemia (as Rudolph II). Ed is well aware of the myriad titles the Archduke of Austria can claim: that's why they've come so far east to find him. But who could've known, when they sought a peer worth courting – one as eager for the shady side cast by its light as the sun of science itself – that they'd find a paragon after Kelley's own design?

Bright-eyed as a peacock Rudy preens, ready to receive their prostrations. Aflush with the Spanish humours that have his minions scampering: towards him and away.

Ed would never have recognised royalty in that fat hereditary lip if he'd come upon Rudy in the alchemist's alley below the castle. Dee has his uses, and knowledge of the peerage is one of them: another is his reputation – which seems only to grow the further from home they go. Is there nothing in which the Doctor has not had a hand? No scientific development, diplomatic intrigue or religious debate to which he is not privy? Not that it's vouchsafed them a living!

Ed's own fame is growing: almost as fast as his ambition, which shoots up beanstalk-like. His ego ever a plump and ready seed. The more a man changes – Rudy I to II; Talbot to Kelley – the less he's really altered.

Like Bess: surely she would never marry now. Rudy too had dangled himself as a matrimonial prize, but similarly avoided wedlock – if only Ed had done the same! Then he'd be free to pursue…whatever he liked. Whomsoever he wanted. These rulers knew what to do: flirt and forget. Tease, treatise and leave. Lovers were there for the taking. Or to take them, if that was their fancy – though Ed, try as he might (and he has, tried), could never actually see *see* Bess giving it up for her darling Robert Dudley. Too great a gift. Too grave a risk. She who was so fond of likening her body to England itself would know that any man mounting her would be doing the same to the throne. As well as, no doubt, planting his likeness upon in it – albeit in some future time, via that most ancient act of common copulation:

'Biological *transmutation*.'

Kelley isn't aware he's spoken till Dee hisses at him: 'This obsession with alchemy, Ed! As if it were the answer to everything.'

Ed must stay *stumm*; better he says naught until they hear an angel speak through him. He slips his left hand into a capacious pocket sewn for the purpose. Searching the stitching for copper crumbs – not that they're here to conduct the kind of experiment best undertaken in the Prince's private laboratory; crafty Rudy has no desire to share what he wants the pair of them to do down there.

The court hums with an expectant air. Courtiers hush.

The uncut gemstones of the naturalia exhibit in Prague Castle's new north wing join the crowd's collective stare. Rudy's cabinet of curiosities – an epic theatre of the world, propagandistically presenting him as ruler of all – is a fitting backdrop to Dee and Kelley's coming action. Ed is all admiration for what the King has accomplished: collected, catalogued. But even in this wonder-realm of objects (and the occasional fraud, he's sure), their orb is unique – Kelley had thought he might find its mate here. But no.

Beneath the custom-built chests he spies strongboxes. Behind the displays, beyond the open galleries, storehouses. This cabinet is a museum. The castle – with its churches, chapels and palaces – a city.

He brings his mind back to the present. Ed doesn't begrudge this request for a public performance; acts like his need an audience. Even if Dee pretends to take offence – such a fakir himself, Ed knows falsity when he sees it – the Doctor must know his magnum opus would provide little defence should they be called to court. 'Twere better they avoid a summoning by finding a benefactor who wanted what they could give: a glimpse of the Philosopher's Stone. A show! That would also prove how essential Dee and Ed would be in attaining the same.

Not that Ed would blame the Catholic Church for coming after them, if it did. He thought it would. How dare Dee suggest that neither man nor God was at the centre of their universe? The idea of infinitely expanding space keeps Ed awake at night – everything endlessly repeating was a Hell he couldn't bear to think on but couldn't stop returning to. Mirrored stars strung across sky after sky after sky. Some nights he has to drink or screw himself to sleep to get any rest at all.

Some nights, no thanks to Dee, Ed imagines a giant satellite orbiting the earth, relaying images from a world away. And who's to say it doesn't? Some mornings he is so drugged he cannot drag himself awake, and stumbles through the day.

Best to focus on what everyone was always really after: the richest *elixir vitae*. The liquid gold that could create life – not to mention secure them the protection that it increasingly looked like Dee and he might need, the Queen being so terribly tight, bent on refilling the royal coffers her father had wantonly plundered, rather than giving any out. Always, he came back to money. Ed rubs together his still-hidden forefinger and thumb as if seeking particles of the powerful powder and not simply avoiding the crystal that fills his secret pouch as completely as an eye sates a socket. Gold: a solid, inorganic mineral – though how else it might differ from their own precious stone was beyond his layman's mind. Their whole quest was, after all, about how much things might change and yet remain the same: Dee's ultimate unit of indivisibility.

From what Ed hears, Rudy, like Bess, also aspires to a unified empire. With himself, no doubt, as its revered head.

Making His Holiness wait no more, Ed lets the slippery sphere slide into his palm. He spins it out of his pocket, whirling it with a bold twirl so the nobility gawp and gasp at the master illusionist. No one other than the scryer ever seems disappointed by the smallness of the ball.

If Ed's thinking is reductive – if he sees the world in terms of having and having-not, as Dee's been known to accuse – it's only because life itself is so easily reduced, particularly when a man doesn't have two pennies, one to flip and the other to win back what was lost on the next toss. Privileged Dee has no idea: being at odds with Bess is nothing compared to the stony outcome – that Babelic building that towered like a finger crooked in warning – Ed foresees.

In the silence Ed readies himself. Concentrating on

controlling the crystal, not wanting to get lost in starveling trances that provide arcane answers from which they then have to work back from to find the right question. Not that he ever wants that, but especially not here and now, before this congregated crowd. What justice can there be if he's judged according to work that's hardly his? More than ever he wants to be in control.

Avoiding Rudy's look – Dee knew not what the King had privately asked of him! – Ed refocuses his talent on directing them all from the winding path that leads to a no-good wood. If their road overflowed with ruby-red gold there'd be no room for ought else: the fire of desire would diminish. The wide way would narrow before them, and the broad gate straighten. Ed hides his meaning from himself – blaming Rudy's lust and not his own, though both herd them where they should not go. He has told the Emperor so.

The power of a purse paves many a way. Ed considers the concept of currency the way the Doctor might a potential ingredient – testing its weight, estimating its virtue, trying to determine its hidden properties. It has solidity. It is quantifiable. Hanging tight to that thought, he dares to stare into the heart of the glass, holding a concrete question in the forefront of his mind: *How can we make more?*

Nothing has changed since the Romans, Ed thinks, enjoying the collective intake of air as, leaning forward, he breathes out over the surface of the sphere. Despite what might be said about the new age arriving – everyone waits with him for the mist to clear – history lives on in the signs for pounds, shillings and pence. Libra. Sestertius. Denarius: £. *s. d.* There is nothing new under the moon. Now is connected through the darkest times in one unending string to an ancient ongoing *then*.

'I cannot direct you, Ed,' Dee whispers, his words worming into Ed's head. 'I cannot protect you.' Is his hand raised in an attempt to halt what is coming? A finger, pointing heavenwards, stitching air to earth. Or does the gesture show he has no power to do aught more than record? A finger, upwards, points.

'You'll be believed, you know. That's your fate, I suspect. In the end someone will buy the stories you've been so desperate to sell.' Dee has firsthand experience of how convincing his once-employee can be. Even when he shouldn't, he can't help but believe.

But never mind destiny! Ed is burning up with what is never said: their one-sided lives. The unfairly allocated wives – *his* Jane, alone, on a conjugal bed, amoan. Bringing hands together in secret prayer, to silently separate dry lips. Dipping a finger in to open her sweet self. Using the other to rub softly forwards and gently back – first in slowish strokes and then smaller and smaller concentric circles around a swelling kernel. While he watched. When she came, he thought, beyond shame, it would be from within and without, as orgasm always was. That shortcut to enlightenment.

Ed watches. Wanting to see in the crystal what he always wants to see.

'*I* may be judged, but so will *you*!' The words are torn out of him by the power of his own eyeless tower and urgent need to seed. 'Our sins will be delivered on all our sons!'

Rudy starts back. Ed will remember that, later: how the father in the King heard a dread meaning in Kelley's words. At the time, though, he barely sees the scene of Rudy's mad progeny cutting his concubine to pieces and throwing her into a castle pond, too busy noticing anew his suddenly seeming sceptical compatriot. Comparing Dee to the frighted royal Roman, Ed realises, with the certainty that comes when we finally acknowledge what we already know, that his friend is no longer afraid of him – if he ever had been. The Doctor's eyes shine with an opposite emotion. Is it because he'd begun to believe his scryer when Kelley said he couldn't see? Or does Dee finally accept that Ed really *wearily* does? Either way, clearly he too now knows that Ed's episodes are not the God-given gift they sought.

Kelley brings the stone closer, until all he can see is his own curved lip. And presses it to his forehead, till it looks as though he is inside it and the sphere, large as a celestial star, fills the foreign room.

'I see!' Ed wills the crowd to lean in. Judging trees crown a secret circle. *Come on!*

'I, *She!*' he yells. Clenching his jaw against that future where rain is emptying out an ocean of sky. Against the overlaid vision of his own death-undefying leap.

The thing is – he tries not to think this too carefully, but he is also trying not to let his thoughts run away – the thing is, if you're not there when you fall into a fit then you don't really know how you do it. But he has to. Heavens knows he's done it often enough. Pretending both to bring it on and hold it at bay. Is it like this? He writhes inelegantly on the floor, dark robes curling and catching as the fabric polishes a pool at Rudy's feet. More like that?

'*Sine me*' – he Latinises the words to give them an otherworldly sparkle, the night sky of his eyelids studded with copperplate instructions to let go and leave be – '*nihil!*' His animal instincts are rearing up, but he grips lips as though he doesn't want to pass any advice on. And maybe he doesn't. Through half-moon eyes Ed sees Dee cock his head. Is the old man warning the King away? The patronising prick! Pulling reflectively on a whey-white beard.

Ed growls between gritted teeth. He quite likes everyone thinking him mad – he is, after all, aware that they *are* but parts in someone else's dream.

'We are but *bits*.' His low tone stands his own hairs up. All Ed knows – all Ed has ever known – is that everyone here, now, and those to come, are slaves to a mystery greater than any of them: the steady primal thrusting of an insistent growing will. Whether it was his or not is neither here nor there.

'And when the storm breaks, each man will react according to his nature, and every maid according to hers. The fearful will hide; the strong, fight; the bold stare into the utter eye of the tempest, needing neither courage nor knowledge. All will be the same, though none will remain unchanged.' He twists and turns.

'The eighty-seventh year,' he (who?) speaks the numbers, seeks the numbers, beseeches the numbers: eight and seven. Seven sins, seven wonders, seven days. The most magical prime combined with another – introduced by itself plus one. A tingle spreads up his arm to reeling head, loosening untight tongue.

'I, I, I,' Ed mutters, letting go the here and now – the there and then. His where and when. Giving in to the fit that's building. Why has he ever fought it? Come. In!

'I, I, I,' he repeats – seeing with his mind's eye three stick figures dancing 'cross Dee's page – as though there was such a singular thing as an I! *He* is the angelic horde. *He*, their sole angle.

With a clarity he's sure he will not lose, Ed suddenly sees that though their natures are not fixed each is more solid than any of them has supposed. More sure. And it is strength they'll need for the ordeal to come, which will be unlike anything any of them has ever known or anyone could imagine – certainly not a poor creature such as he.

Or Dee.

'I, I, I.' Ed spies an unanchored eye. He is at the door and John is the one to let him in, guide him through, welcome him home. He is, after all, isn't he: *she*? The one sure point in a spinning world: a fixed and constant…

'eye.'

Some one is watching someone watching. One looking, at one who looks: a perpetual *mise en abyme* that threatens to pull them all – all! – into the abyss. An impossible gravity well.

Until, succumbing to the lure of the stone like a criminal jumping from a keep towards a bottomless pool (a microscopic earth-circle of blue spied from on high), intending to but nevertheless still caught unawares by the sudden thrust of his own plummeting body, Ed leaps.

And Nat sees, with her mind's technically externalised eye, through the castle's circular window – vast as a globe, a planet, a pool, a pixel. Past winding stairs and bending stars. Before they both drop back to an earth a whirl away in rhymes.

Back in England, Bess is waiting with more patience than many would credit. Licking crumbs from the long fingers she's so proud of, she imagines herself free of the maiden garb she wears more as provocation than protection: part-exposed breasts and undone hair are gauntlets freely flung. She sees herself floating above the atmosphere, facing off her sister moon. No mirror need be magic to show Elizabeth she was still and always would be the fairest Virgin Queen.

Bess anticipates her old friend's return from a sojourn that is not beyond her reach – 'twas for a reason the gossips said her digits had been stretched by thumbkins! Not that she would've let her nursemaids. But her hands were surely born to hold this wholest world, and she to be Emperor: the ginger-haired Faerie Queene of everywhere and any-when.

'Come back soon, my milk-bearded man,' she whispers, biting into Dee's likeness – one of the first-ever figure-shaped sugar cakes, fashioned on her command – so Ed can almost taste it when her royal tongue sticks deliciously to the icing, crisp enough to crack.

When Rudolph recommends they take a break Kelley refuses – while wishing they would. This seeing nothing was hard work. But he had a sweat up now and starting again wouldn't make it any easier. Everyone was willing him. And hadn't he seen something?

Ed opens wide blind eyes, sensing a forest. He can hear Dee cracking his knuckles, ready for the wordy magic to begin – he hopes the Doctor's fingers cramp. Language might be the original enchantment, but the magician's portentous spelling seemed to mesmerise himself more than anyone else.

'I see…' Ed pushes on, pushes through. Pushes. In. 'The

Queen! I spy…her hive.'

Again, Rudy gives a start, so Ed knows he's on the money. He's heard the King can sit and stare for hours at all manner of paintings – from powerful romps to erotic rumps. And is in rapture when he finds an image that combines the two. Ed conjures a gallery: a working memory house. Filling it with the pictures of Bess he's seen, heard of, or read about in Dee's accumulating books.

'Her elegant hand rests atop a globe, covering a continent. The same pale palm holds an apple before three muses – *with*holds an apple – none of whom can compete with E— for beauty.' Complex ciphers he knows will appeal to a man like Rudy, who nods. Who wouldn't?

'Fireships threaten a fleet, driving it onto a rocky coast amid stormy seas.' So far, such a good carny show.

'A pelican,' Ed puzzles: why has he spied the sign of the red stone? 'Plucks at a milkless breast.'

He pauses, taking care how he describes the next: a scandalous cartoon with riding skirts hitched up to show bare flesh atop a horse's haunch. Rudy might appreciate the way the artist had worked the royal image but Ed has to watch his own licence – he has no desire to lose his tongue, should Bess ever hear tell.

Flitting through the rooms he's built, like the ghost he may as well be, Ed notices that in Regina's hand again and again is a book. Was it a symbol of piety? Or a particular text? Certainly the Queen has read Dee's *Hieroglyphica* – the two are united in their desire for the return of the one rule. But Ed wonders if it isn't a clue his inner eye means for him, alluding to another alchemical tract: the bound book he'd found at Northwick Hill – with the help of that madman John, who'd said he'd navigated his way back in time. Perhaps a polyglot here in Prague could translate the incomprehensible textings he'd left into a synthetic recipe of some sort?

'Ed,' Dee is murmuring, 'don't be convicted by your own success. Engendering faith in others comes at a cost.' But the advice of the man Ed used to admire is ousted by an iridescent image arising from the embers of his mind: a phoenix – the ultimate immortality. And their favoured sign for the Philosopher's Stone.

'Turning nothing into something, Dee! Death to life, dreams to reality, dross to gold.'

'This business with alchemy you obsess over – it's but the basest transformation of matter.'

'Turning *every*thing, Dee, into One Thing. You, of all people.'

Ed sighs, letting his old friend off the hook; *he* of all people knew what it was to pass on unwanted information. (For someone who could not scry, the Doctor's was a goodly premonition: Kelley, too, sees a dock, himself set for a defenestration from which there'd be no coming back – a window too high, a fall too far.)

Like Dee's faith in the mystic, which used to light up the room – buoying all the members of their little band along, including both their wives – the crystal was growing dim. Rather than filling the court it seemed to be absorbing the castle. The orb was surely becoming smaller and harder and more finite than it had been at the beginning of their story. As were the two men.

KRAKOW, 1586.

There are, of course, no stars. Just a blind sky above. No one to see what Dee and Kelley are about: just the sightless dead and them. Another year has passed. Are they any closer? Are the two men, in fact, further apart? Occasionally they glimpse the moon, but it appears watery – unable to penetrate the mid-lying clouds that promise a storm and unremitting rain. Another night and they would've found it hard to uncover the body without their feet being sucked into the soil. Another week and the corpse they're after would've begun to meld with its new home so no amount of care could've brought it up uninjured.

A month more of this rain and the earth will be running from the raised graveyard, exposing more inhabitants, from both inside and outside the consecrated wall. A midden belching bones – of the saved, and those still steeped in sin.

Dee finds the weather fitting. The long flat nebula suggests the Cloud of Unknowing supplication; it may be a sign that they *are* about to contact a soul One-ed with God. Dee had suspected that the threat of a storm was conjured by Kelley as a way to persuade his master that they couldn't wait to hire a helper but had to dig themselves. Ed was always forcing Dee's theory into reality (though for now the scholar's hands are still clean – he holds the lantern higher, aged arm aching). Dee tries to summon an angel, researching how and where and why Ed does it. Hating it, resisting it: doing it anyway. Dee considers contacting a departed spirit. He's read the old books, studied novel methods. Ed says let's. Do it. Any way. John suspects the other's hunger is not for knowledge, as he had first thought, but for experience. Experiments. Next Ed will be at him to hatch an homunculus. Ed wouldn't baulk at fermenting semen for forty days before adding horseshit to the retort. His lieutenant wouldn't baulk at much, Dee thinks, imagining a miniature man sloshing knee-deep towards them through this bone-churned gravesite. He shakes his head to clear the image: when one didn't believe, and one only wanted to, was that enough to bring something indescribable to pass? Sometimes he thought so. Sometimes he hopes not.

Here it comes! The first sign of rain interrupts Dee's reverie: a fat drop tapping the Doctor's shoulder. But though he looks to the heavens, no more follow; apparently it's a singular event, just enough to convince him of the coming downpour.

So it often was with Ed: predicting something he could not know that then comes true. Promising something not within his power that came to pass. When he first arrived at Mortlake – knocking on Dee's door in weather as wet and loamy as this, the kind of night when you might've expected a mired stranger to rattle up the housewife and beg entrance – John had suspected Edward was a spy. And maybe Talbot had been (who is Dee to blame a man for spying?), maybe Kelley is now, but they'd had such success – more than the Doctor had dared hope – that they quickly fell into their current close association. Like lovers, Ed once said, finding their lifelong helpmate.

So, John has come to see, it always is with Ed: Dee's doubts will never be disproven, new worries are always arising.

Glancing back from the eyeless sky to the ground at his feet, Dee imagines what a full flood might unearth: skeletons entwined to create new creatures – triple-headed, double-legged affairs swimming up from the underworld. Made of a union with neighbours from the next graveside or, even more monstrous, by coupling with ancestors from the plot below. The membrane that encloses our organs, and separates us from the world, having utterly given way.

Dee knows of man's composition – and decomposition – not only from Vesalius's pioneering work but his own personal dissections. Hands-on direct observation is the only reliable resource in all these areas where men like them were pushing back the shadows of ignorance and shedding the light of knowledge.

Hitching up the lantern, Dee turns it so the beam shines more brightly between the panes of horn. He's reminded of the land surveyor he was in a previous life; the wax tablet they travel with – the elaborately engraved *Sigillum Dei Aemeth*, the seal of God, surrounded by a ring of Enochian characters – is more than a little like an astrolabe, that elaborate inclinometer used by astronomers, navigators and astrologers. Dee pulls his cloak closer with a free hand: he's fooling himself. It isn't only the night that makes their work dark. Invoking angels is one thing, unearthing the dead quite another. His friend might seek divination in entrails and excrement but the Doctor has little appetite for it.

'Twere better Ed persuaded King Rudolph to plant coins he might dig up later – Dee wouldn't put it past him. That'd be a more reliable way to grow gold. Even when the spirits come they are never at Ed's call. They arrive when they want. They say what they will. There are no tame angels, answering only what is asked: everything is passed on in riddles and code. Filtered through a not-so-simple savant.

And no one can make any sense of it except Dee, who seeks not alchemy or some saleable elixir but the unifying principle that strings all life together: the smallest indivisible unit of which they are all made. (*Quantus*, he ponders: how many could they each contain? *Quantum*: how much might the discovery cost?) John burrows his beard in his civet-cat collar and shuffles his feet in the sludge, hoping it won't snow. Winter this close to the Baltics is so much harsher than London's meagre season. He tucks in his chin but still the cold gets in. No matter how rugged up he is the cold finds a crack, a gap, a way. Like doubt, Dee thinks, and disillusion. Like lust, he tries not to think, and base desire. His frozen ears ring as his numb nose runs.

Ed, meanwhile, is working up an honest sweat. Dee shivers, exhaling a great gust of air – always breathing out more than he seems to breathe in these days – and wonders whether he still believes or whether it's just that he can't afford not to. (What *can* they afford? Dee wonders, mind pulling against his will towards Ed's red powder.)

Somewhere along the way Dee has become a follower on the mission he used to lead – some way along alchemy has ousted augury. Now it's his protégée who hobknobs with European royalty, filling capacious pockets with new-shined gold and empty heads with angelic advice. The Doctor's exhalation freezes before his face and he could swear he hears it fall to his feet; once, no doubt, it would've seemed like fairy chimes, now it's the Devil whispering that some debt is due. Could this whole obscuring fog be made of the town's sad sighs? He adds another of his own. And its inhabitants doomed to lie here, buried beneath the thick press of each other's dread despair?

Dee hunches into his musky robe feeling like a man from an earlier age. An unenlightened, unEnglish *muž* from the period that separates the wisdom of the ancients from this new epoch of possibility ruled – mostly, he catches himself: ruled *mostly* – by empirical observations.

He lowers the light, peering into the plot of the newly passed maid they've picked, not because he believes the poor lass's despair – was it really the worst of the seven sins? – excludes her from God's grace. Though he does think it might make her more susceptible to their summoning. (Who wouldn't want to set the record straight? Name the father, the other half responsible for the condition she had to bear.) He thinks it took courage and not the Devil to act as she did, knowing she'd be tried posthumously and her family's goods forfeited to the crown. It's harsh punishment, but at least these ignorant villagers have buried her here. Better than carrying her corpse to a crossroads and flinging it naked into a pit for the crime of self-murder, as villagers far from the civilising lights of cities still often do.

Ed, Dee sees, has cast tools aside and is using his hands. He soon unearths a phalange. Followed quite quickly by four more and a palm. His and her nails are rimmed with dirt, fingers ringed.

The girl's tallow-white flesh reminds Dee of the effigy of Elizabeth that was dug up – was it seven years ago? – at Lincoln's Inn Fields, on the other side of the solid brick wall that barricaded the fourth inn of court, housed on Chancery Lane. Home to barristers from the Queen's own council. Dee'd kept that in mind when he cast his counter-spell to defeat the designs of any evilly disposed person. Or persons. As well as gently suggesting that Bess ease up on the sweetmeats if she would suffer less from the curse of black and aching teeth.

But what to do with the doll? How to unmake it in a way that did no harm? He could hardly melt it down! So Dee stowed it safely, and had it to this day. Pray Ed never find it. Never feel those features, rounded as though worn with rubbing. The elemental shape: small red head, widespread legs. (It'd been discovered waist-deep in the earth, soil like an ocean lapping at the loins. Looking for all the world as though it had grown there – a *woman*drake root. The mud that accentuated every crease only made its form more flesh-like.)

Twenty years after the Queen's accession, when Bishop Jewell had preached against sorcery, not knowing good Bess's reign would be as different from Bloody Mary's as men like Dee could hope for, that waxen image of Elizabeth had prompted a spate of persecution on a par with any of her predecessors'. Future folk will look back on this time of burgeoning understanding and see how supposed witches still suffer for common man's lack of knowledge about medicine and the natural world; even his Jane, who makes cures for most ailments as part of her housekeeping, could be called to account. Dee is doing what he can to dispel the ignorance: making mathematics accessible to everyone; inventing navigational aids that will benefit all at sea. Having already corrected the Julian calendar more accurately than any other – up goes the lamp! – despite his perfect work being turned down by the council of archbishops because it smacked of Popishness.

He sucks in a hiss. The girl's limbs are clear. Gingerly the Doctor helps roll her in the rugs they've brought and hoist her onto their handcart. Ed is panting and perspiring but seems not unhappy – more satisfied by this physical labour than he generally is with their study. Struggling with the awkwardness of their task, Dee mildly inquires again why they need the body when the girl can pass on knowledge unavailable to them precisely because she's no longer limited to the physical plane.

Ed snaps that *they* still are.

In strained silence the two men push uphill towards the tomb where the Polish people bury their dead when the ground is too cold to open easily. Dee gets the rushes from the cart, forcing the dried and grease-soaked grass into iron clips set high upon the walls before using the flame he's carefully tended to set the lights ablaze.

Kneeling in the centre of the chapel, Ed is drawing a large circle with a muddy middle finger. He goes slowly, shuffling back before the careful line. Licking his dirty tip to produce more mud-ink so he can complete the ring that will protect necromancer and assistant from any ill that might come of provoking the dead. Both men are aware how dangerous their work is – once a soul possesses a medium it can be reluctant to let go. The rituals demand meticulous execution and exact preparations: the choice of a proper place (*here*); the right time, between the hours of midnight and one in the morning (*now*); the use of specific incantations and accessories (*these*).

Dee joins Ed inside the circle, where they've already laid the girl.

'Hear that? No – *that!*'

Dee tilts his head but can only catch the sound of Ed picking at his fingernails. Talons to scratch any enchantress, believing if he draws her blood no seductress can harm him. Perhaps. Dee used not to doubt Ed's customs or the common superstitions: even the recently knighted Walter Raleigh – Bess's own 'water', who'd sailed a goodly stretch of the same to name Virginia after her – believed in witches.

Lately Kelley is bringing out this contrariness in him. They are stepping on each other's toes: into each other's shoes. Dee *had* wanted to commune with the dead (hadn't he?), so maybe his reluctance is just some new form of that old longing to be The One Who Sees.

As if on cue, the storm breaks. A downpouring upon their heads, gushing outside the door so it sounds as though they're within – not behind – a fall of water. Ed, Dee sees when he turns back, is prostrate by the girl's side, one arm flung over her as though he's about to unrobe and expose her. There he goes again, Dee thinks meanly, as winds howl around the building. He is glad, after all, not to be the one called. And prepares to wait with the bodies – one warm, one cold: both empty of their own souls. Tucking his gown inside their ring of three, he crouches down and begins to pray.

'I am the ghost – I am the writer. Of all!' Ed suddenly shouts, starting up. Dee searches for something with which to scratch upon the ground...but Ed's words are gibberish. Here they go, again. Perhaps he *has* driven Kelley to the brink of insanity with the long sessions he's been forcing on an almost daily basis. Jane is right: both men are bordering on mad.

On closer inspection he can see Ed's eyes are racing beneath the thin skin of his eyelids. Lashes flutter – an effect Dee has noted before. Is his friend floating back up to the surface or sinking deeper into dreams? This time sketchy Latin is offered, which Dee translates as: '*Dear to you is your wife, dearer to you is wisdom, dearest to you am I*,' but he is distracted from the message. Looking into his medium's cat-like slits it has occurred to him that the dead girl might not deserve their sympathy after all: for his friend's eyes are vacant. Void. And Dee is afraid of what is really here with him.

He whispers: 'Who's there?'

Wondering at the alto answer...

Hearing: 'Not.'

Ed enters the Queen's rooms again. Drawn down the same secret passageways, he trips up now-worn stairs, past windows whose cold old glass reflects the night sky piecemeal. If he were Dee he might've been able to work out when and where he was by studying the stars (was he travelling across the country, rather than through time? – not that that lessened his spying crime), but he is not.

Ed presses on, deeper into the world the crystal projects: another turn, another stair. Nearly there. This scrying time he seems to possess another man's body, be on another man's mission. Ed wonders if it's a lover's tryst. He finds himself weighing a woman's worth like that of a country a king might conquer and plunder – her wit; her wealth: she's lost the blush of youth and is fast losing the bloom of middle age. Still, the Queen has an energy the Duke's envoy had never expected. And then the name, d'Alençon, appears in Ed's mind's eye. That's who he was! De Simier, the French envoy to the English Queen and their Bess's last chance at love.

Tugging at a neat-trimmed beard (in the real world Ed's wiry whiskers twitch), de Simier pauses mid-stride, giving himself time to regain his courtly composure and control his divided mind before slipping into her innermost room – the royal chamber – to steal some token for his master. Dutifully playing his part in this courtship that might yet prove a masquerade. Ed cannot believe the scene he's stumbled upon.

Inside, it is silent and dark. De Simier had expected a gaggle of maids, giggling with faux surprise as they bustled him out. He'd expected a well-lit, crowded room – another public performance where he pressed the Duke of Anjou's suit. He stops inside the doorway, letting his eyes adjust. Her bed emerges from the darkness before him: curtains closed. Suspecting she is playing some game with them, Ed – in the French envoy – makes his way towards the Queen's own room-within-a-room. At every step expecting to hear her ladies' laughter, to see her fair face peeking out, poking fun at him. At every step ready to fall back in mock surprise and apologise for his gross impertinence – saying it was she who was driving him mad. Claiming it was love that made such a fool of men, and their manservants.

Whistling between his teeth in an attempt at nonchalance, de Simier stops short of the dais. The sound dying on dry lips. The darkness encourages dreams no man should ever dare: of mounting the steps, parting the drapes, climbing in. Limbs almost quaking, breath and body shaking, de Simier imagines lying inside her private sanctum as the scent of perfume wafts into his nostrils and beneath it – reverently, Ed closes his eyes and even sniffs the expectant air – could he smell *Her*?

The Master of the 'Robe turns at the rustle of angels' wings. In the far corner he glimpses a white apparition before a hidden door and stumbles where he stands – falls to the Queen's feet with something like relief as she, in turn, acts suitably surprised.

'My dear *Mon*-key,' she says, in a tone Ed's sure means more than mere amusement. Waving her ladies to leave the cushions and candles they carry and discreetly withdraw; 'Mon *pet*-ty Monkey,' she sings, offering an alabaster hand.

'That I may always be numbered among your beasts,' de Simier breathes, brushing her knuckles as lightly as he can. He steadies himself against his knee – foot atremble upon the floor – hoping his bent head invites her near. When she comes, Ed looks up and directly down the neck of her nightgown, open to the *nombril*. The translucent flesh between her virgin breasts reminds the envoy of the satin groin of the Duke's favourite hunting bitch: Ed, of the silky head of his own stirring prick.

'Your Majesty,' her visitor starts, 'I,' he stops, flirtatious phrases dissolving on his tongue. 'My predecessor had it right – you are the rarest creature Europe has seen for these five hundred years!'

Bess laughs then, and looks away, giving his eyes permission to linger.

'And what of the span to come? Will my singularity not last the same again?' She turns back, stopping his protestations with an imperious finger: 'Don't re-use other's flattery like minted coin, Monkey. Tell me...' she sighs. 'Speak of my husband-to-be.' Raising a brow not now buried beneath lead-white, her belladonna-bare eyes – wide – invite him to share the joke: 'In truth I was afraid paternosters would take the place of nuptials...'

'My lady!' de Simier admonishes, his indignation so close to genuine as makes no difference. Was her immortality not a fact? 'Truly, there's nothing old 'bout you but years.'

'Yet there are those years.' The Queen moves towards the fireplace vast enough to be a room unto itself, albeit a hell-hot one. 'Part of my trousseau – if not my treasure. Your master has not so many to match.' She sits herself down upon the piled cushions, tucking her gown around her.

'Now,' abruptly Bess abandons her girlish act. 'Now, now,' a playful slap, 'none of that. You're not some lovesick calf or lovelorn fool – that's why I like you so much.'

'Me?' He protests, flattered. Sitting as directed.

'Enough.' She chucks his close-cropped chin. 'Tell me what you're after in your master's lady's chamber. You know, Mon-*key*, not everything is mine to give.' The almost-old maiden tilts her head coyly – as though accusing him of aiming at her fortune rather than her person. Or does he have it wrong and she means *count*-ry matters? Oh, he thinks – and Ed, merged with him, agrees – he is not man enough to match her!

As he grabs her arm de Simier's voice thickens, almost as though he isn't acting. 'I came…' he swallows, 'for some remembrance, my lady – oh would that you were Our Lady!' Shaken at the mark he's raised on her royal flesh, he lets go the wrist he's dared to snare. 'Some sentimental thing that you won't miss. Some token his heart can fix on…'

'His *heart*?' The Queen who isn't yet his offers a mischievous chuckle that makes de Simier's slow smile return.

'Some trifle – infused with you – that like a potion will draw him 'cross the water.'

'Yes,' she nods, as though the idea is not her own: ' 'Tis time the groom came.' Bess raises slender hands above her head to unpin the nightcap nestled there and he sees how her forearms, exposed where the robe falls back, are the thin white of skimmed milk. 'It's not unlike a crown, and something like a sieve.'

'Now,' the princely Princess sighs, 'to bed with you,

Monkey – to bed, to bed. No!' she laughs delightedly when he raises an eyebrow after her own fashion, 'not my bed...' She shudders, 'Even I don't sleep there these days. If you had the dreams I did, you'd avoid it too.'

The ambassador stays silent – letting the pause between them swell, pregnant with potential – knowing when to woo with words and when without. Listening to the murmur of Bess's maids he dares to think – now he knows he is as good as in bed with the Queen – of all her ladies must know, of all they might've seen; after all, it was on their evidence that suitors such as his master knew Britannia was ripe for breeding, still monthly bleeding.

Ed, scrying through de Simier's eyes, homes his gaze in on the regal bed. Did the doctors examine her there, when they'd reconfirmed she could bear an heir? His loins seize at the thought of it. Her, waiting behind a curtain that would've masked the face of the realm and exposed the rest of her: making her any woman. Only a woman. All woman.

Bess continues her confession as though compelled: 'Sometimes I think I'm dreaming this kingdom – not its future, or its past; I mean dreaming England herself.' Her voice trails off.

Had the doctor – the Frenchman can't seem to stop himself – separated Regina's lean round legs? No doubt as shapely as her upper limbs. Parted supine thighs. Tipping slender feet towards the corners of her best featherbed to expose their kingdom's most precious and protected jewel. Nestled in its own shadowy crown.

'Some nights,' Bess murmurs, 'I am my father. And some my son. I am every Tudor and the very vine.'

De Simier snatches a breath, thinking of that secret

entrance where many ladies had let him – nay, begged him! – come. Glad of the nightcap on his lap as a spasm runs through him at the thought of all the times he's peeled back silken layers to plunge between. But he'd never knelt between a woman's hips and simply stared. Never peered like a spy with his eye to a pink chink.

Perhaps – Ed's imagination seems only inflamed by the air being sucked from the dreamt-of room – perhaps the doctor hadn't only looked but felt. With a finger. Could such an investigation take away the very virtue it was designed to determine? Was Bess still as she'd always been or had *he* (the man Ed dreams himself to be) been the very means of her deflowering?

De Simier draws a shaky breath, 'The vine, you say – you are?'

'The Rose! The red and white bloom of Britain. But – I fear – a beat away from withering on the tree.' Perhaps she should propagate like the flower on her coat of arms might, by artificially grafting a stem. 'But what of the seeds within me? My unborn children. Is it *my* immortal soul that I'm denying life?'

Spent, the pair stare into the flames.

'You say you see a child?' Dee transcribes. Muttering that he supposed they did say Bess could still beget. 'A son, coming?'

From the grey light Ed can't work out whether it's dusk or dawn. In the end it's the temperature that gives morning away: the chill is abating. It's a new day, and he is returned from the far reaches of a universe that can yet be held in a conman's hand. He sighs, drained, as after every episode.

Scratching at the parasites his headgear harbours, Ed wonders why his hands are sore – back when he was Talbot he'd cut away calluses to pass for a nobler man, but now it feels like the old blisters are back. Rolling onto his right side he tries to rise. Boldly calling on Jane for some wine. Kelley knows his luck won't last, but while it does he'll ride it hard. And it appears he has been: his whole body aches. What he wouldn't give for a drink! His temples are tight as a vice.

Looking around the room his vision is momentarily overlaid with some starker structure. Is it a sign they'll end up imprisoned for probing a world beyond the Queen's dominion? Ed will swear he sees neither the future nor her past – both of which would see them hanged – but a conjuration of consorts, who could be put to work for Britannia, searching out her New Green Land.

Belatedly he remembers that Dee and he have moved on to more persuadable patrons. Ah Rudy, whose love of collecting goes well beyond Art: a monarch who shares many of Kelley's passions, and has welcomed the pair as devotees of the occult, disciples of science and a charming new-come couple.

But Ed has led them on again, convinced now that it's at Trebon, where the High Burgrave's castle had been remodelled along Renaissance lines to include a cloud-scraping tower, that he and Dee will achieve their first alchemical transmutation. He has a new idea of how to manufacture a red tincture from the particles that the future angel – named for prophetic John – pointed him towards. Yes, it was in a dream. What of it? While he doesn't share the Doctor's magnanimous aims, Kelley too seeks the root heart of creation and has been working as tirelessly as Dee towards that end.

A son, the old man says? Could his visitor from the future be kin, as well as kind? Ed hauls himself upright, despite pains as sharp as when he last rose from the stocks. His hands, he notes, are black as a scholar's – he who couldn't craft a line without resharpening his nib. But it's not ink, Ed realises when he raises a finger to his lips to soothe the raw skin he's ripped. It's earth. Maybe his vision of a maid on stone is no message but some memory?

It was a business, this being a medium. It was a challenge, to be a blank page awaiting inscription. Fasting. Praying. Depriving all senses of sustenance. Fasting and praying more until his palsy pulsed. Oh Ed, poor fool you! Because he knows he is: a fool, and oh so pathetically poor. He should be out angling for carp in the Treasurer's vast pond, not fishing for verity in this bare border room.

He was being used: he and his red-hot white-hot lust.

At the mere thought of it Kelley can feel his desire swell: a potent vein running between he and Dee. A current coursing 'neath their every action. Eventually it was bound to erupt. It's beyond his control – Dee has taught him that. Ed is not playing, he is being played. He is a puny plaything in God's good game. Slowly the seer draws his dirty finger from his mouth. By cocke and cross whatever happens next will not be his fault.

'Do not make of it more than it is, Mr Kelley,' Dee tries to tell the younger man not to mind, but Ed suspects the other knows little more than Talbot ever did. He minds. Very much.

Dee might think a momentous decision lies before them with whatever latest instruction his so-far-faithful has passed on, but Ed believes the future is already set and the illusion that they are in any way free to exercise a God-given will is purely that: an illusion. As is the idea that he will not do anything he can to achieve his end – to fix the object of his attention – has not already done it a hundred times, in a thousand dreams and more than one life.

TREBON, 1587.

Pulling his woollen cloth-of-the-realm cap low to keep the light of the long northern eve out of his eyes, Dee takes a post-supper turn through the winding cobbled ways in the Southern Bohemian city of Trebon. He avoids those who doff their caps; his life is filled with too many people and not enough patronage. He never imagined he'd be reduced to this poverty when he left the Low Countries to lecture in Paris and, at twenty-three, had students crowding at the windows to listen. They'd offered him the post of King's Reader in Mathematics at the university there for a stipend of two hundred crowns – and Ivan the Fearful, Tsar of all the Russias, had promised him ten times that to be his adviser and court physician! Dee never imagined he'd be reduced to penury when he patriotically refused. His thoughts returned to England, so thither he went.

Neither had he thought *he'd* be the one spending thousands of pounds on hundreds of manuscripts – mathematical, astronomical and alchemical texts he's elaborately annotated and illustrated. No wonder he's so poor. The thought of his library soothes him. Thinking of the fifty pounds a year he pays Kelley has the opposite effect.

Dee winds his way towards the Gothic fortifications. The oddly late sun shimmers on the water of Trebon's famous fishponds, shivering his vision like ague. Or an angel appearing? Would these long days never end – eight of the clock and everyone still up! He hadn't been able to sit at table any longer, couldn't bear to rest opposite his closest friend, or be served by either wife, every presence in the house reminding him of Ed's latest request. Not Kelley's, Dee corrects his thoughts: despite the fact that it had come to them through Ed it was an angel's decree. Dee's mind keeps circling back. It's hard not to see this latest, surely impossible-to-act-upon instruction, as impure. He is at a loss – but it's not a sacrifice unless it comes at a cost.

Following the stony path that weaves through the city's shadows, the Doctor acknowledges himself unanchored for the first time in a long and not unsurprising life. He might see naught in the glass, but he knows as well as any that he's set to die John of all trades, not be remembered as a master of one. No Copernicus, he. Nor Tycho Brahe either, alone on his island working on a geocentric system – having proven (Dee had known it) there is no unchanging celestial realm: planets are not embedded in rotating spheres like jewels set in orbs.

But while Brahe was developing instruments to take ever more precise measurements, Dee was out here, walking foreign streets, a caller and conjurer. Companion to *what*? He knew not who Ed was, but had heard himself called Demonolator Dee.

Was he the master, Magus of Mortlake, or an obsessed fool? Would history know which? Witch! Dee steps cautiously over cracks, knowing he is too interested in too many things – the only unifying principle of a lifetime's work the cardinal rule of magical philosophy: that the world is a lyre, the overall structure determining its harmonies and dissonances, sympathies and antipathies. The infinite variety of marvellous music – including all puzzling perplexities – drawn from its individual strings.

Dee hides a rueful smile in his milk-white beard. He's not a boastful man, but neither does he countenance false modesty. A scientist, geographer, astronomer and – some suspect – secret agent for his Queen, he is interested only, *above all*, in knowledge. Empirical knowledge; imperial knowledge. Knowledge gleaned by the naked eye.

Experiential knowing.

Jane will not like it, of that he is sure. She's disliked Kelley from the start, when he first came to them as Ned Talbot, and none of their visitor's gifts have ever changed her tune. What if she has the right of it? Dee's mind spirals back to that sticking point. It's true Kelley's been praying loudly every day, saying he'll have no more dealing with the scrying glass if such cross-matches are the message he's asked to pass on, but Dee knows how obsessed his colleague is with the union of the red man of copper and the white woman of mercury. Kelley might be praying daily, but he's possessed by thoughts of generation. And the link from creation to procreation, getting to begetting, is as neat as any necklace loop.

Cross-hatching. The thought of what might come of exchanging Jane with Joanna is beyond him. Yet Dee does see how it is the literal realisation of everything he's been preaching – it'd just never occurred to him what his words might, practically, mean. The ultimate union. The one way two men might be conjoined.

Dee knows – knows! – singularity is real. Wholeness no mere speculation. All matter is of a unity: one hidden glyph, one perfect point that needs no path between.

And what if Jane did like it? Something in him loosens. Something in her aged husband comes away.

Dee might believe – and he does, he does believe! – that Ed sees things he doesn't, but the Doctor is also confident he has an understanding the other man lacks. What Kelley is proposing may end everything between them. As with alchemy, the separate ingredients won't be able to be reconstituted after. Kelley is an accidental adventurer, bringing back stories of otherworldly shores he longs to explore. Dee is the mapmaker, working a route from Delphic clues.

Neither of *them* is the virgin vessel that will be loaded up and cast off, both men know. Nor are they the fertile ground where *one* will put ashore.

Dee turns towards home – their temporary home: he'd never planned to stay away so long; it's three years on – hoping his wife might find a way of accepting what he's not sure he does yet. For better or worse they embarked upon this journey, and the path that brought them here is the only way out of their current impasse, even if it leads to a dead end rather than the new beginning they've come so far for.

When Dee broaches Ed's proposal, after he joins Jane in their bedchamber for the night, her reaction comes as a surprise. Like Lot's wife she seems pillared. Dee finds himself – momentarily – relieved. He's not sure he could've persuaded her: he's not sure he's convinced himself that it is right for each man to conjugate with the other's wife. Yet it seems they will do it anyway, so obedient are they. Could it be that inwardly she rages against his decision, but salts her anger down? And if so, is that because she thinks he doesn't care or because she knows he does?

All at once Dee sees the inevitability, realises Jane was there a breath ahead of him: there is no turning back. In the space between shutting the bedroom door and this open – closing – moment, there is suddenly nothing more to say. And if what's said remains unacted upon, then that would mean it *was* unholy. (Is that heart burn the stab of imminent or hint of eventual death? Could it be love, breaking open the ribs that hold him together? His Jane!)

Dee wishes there were a way to thank her for not asking him to make a case he cannot. Her silence reminds him how blessed he is to have such a capable consort who can run his household competently; an obedient third wife, raising his children wisely. A biddable young copesmate to host his stranger friends. The ancients knew such luck attracted the Gods' attention.

Kelley would say the same, as long as it were someone other than himself basking in fortune's sun.

Why, Dee ponders, did Ed find his own wife so unworthy? Many would disagree, but Kelley has confessed he had no natural inclination to marry and only did so because the spirits said to. Dee wonders, unworthily, if rumours of a nobleman paying Ed to stepfather someone else's bastards could be true. He should not think such things of poor put-upon Joanna; she's been a good companion to them all. It is Ed's nature never to value what he has, to strive constantly for what he has not. Or what he has not *yet*, Kelley would correct – Dee remembers when his colleague interrupted a session to ask an angel if she knew how to make gold. That had brought their evocation to an end!

It was soon after that Kelley conveyed a message – relayed in Greek, so he wouldn't know the warning he passed on – that Talbot was about to leave. Prompting Dee to pay his assistant more. But the price has kept on rising.

Dee puts a tentative arm around his wife's cold shoulders, steering them both towards the bed. They sit upon the edge: side by side. He is here, if she needs him.

(And what about him? He thinks fleetingly, who will comfort and console him for the price he's asked to pay?) She is there, if he wants her.

'How can he – we…' Jane murmurs, so low John barely hears.

He moves to stroke her hair, studies her profile: 'To participate in all things, one with another is a…a manifestation of our close community. It's not – just – about Love,' Dee struggles. 'It's about Law. Obedience and fidelity.' An unfortunate choice of words. He welcomes the silence, which shrouds them in a strange peace. Relief expands his breastbone, swelling his chest cavity: she can see there hasn't really been a choice. Just as she has no free will, neither does he. Which means nothing is Ed's fault either. Dee drops a hand to Janey's thigh.

'I can only see it as a sign we're ready. That we are – *spiritually* – prepared for what's to come.' And what is that? 'It's a way of binding us closer.'

He wonders how Mistress Kelley is taking the news.

'Jane,' Dee rubs an inky thumb on her lockram smock, not sure she can comprehend but convinced the angels' latest request means he's meant to share what he and Ed do with her – just as he'll share what she and he do with Ed, in turn. 'This is the culmination of our good work. We are all the same already: there isn't any difference, not between any of us. Not between any thing, one with another.'

The argument Dee is marshalling is not against his wife but his own doubts; for all his faith and reason he is no more reconciled to this than her. He doesn't need prescience to know there'll be no more sweet communion between their three: and what might come of such a union? The straight way is a sure path to one true thing:

'There's a magic in our basest union that mimics the most exalted conception – that Singular Moment from whence all matter sprang and that we carry within us still.'

Jane bows her head.

'To which we all return. In time.'

Perhaps – Dee exhales his effort, pushing away his dismay at the part his wife is asked to play – perhaps Ed has the right of it. Fate is rarely fair; they are lucky to have been chosen. Jane, he reminds himself, has never seen an angel – even though she's lived the past five years in accordance with their decrees. Sleeping, eating alone while he works night and day. Packing up everything and pilgrimaging. She's never even heard, as he has at least, the trumpets and the chimes! He thinks back to the strange knockings in the nights before Kelley's coming. The angels had been most eager to communicate.

Dee pulls his wife towards him, agreeing to draw up a document that will ensure no one tells of what's to happen – trust a woman to think of that. He pinches her shoulder, agreeing to let Ed know that Jane will go to his rooms once, and he must never come to her. Kissing his wife's closed eyes, Dee feels a burden lift like life leaving.

When the thin smile of moon can no longer be seen against the sky, Dee rises and records the date and time of their latest commixture. He writes that after a night of talking they reached their decision, that they discussed the matter in all details and then made love, referring to himself with the Greek letter delta: Δ. But omitting that at the very moment of climax he'd felt strangely separate – from her, and from himself. As though his spermatozoa were ejected into the hungry ether. And he and Jane abandoned on the shore like sea-scrubbed shells.

Dee shuffles his stool closer to the small round hole. The keyhole glows with candlelight from the room beyond. Pulses. Throbs. Quietly he scoots his stool so close to the whorl he can rest his wizened eye against the knot. Or where the knot was before he prized it out. It's as though he's on the inside, peering out from a hidden hollow in a dark wood. He bates his breath, not wanting them to know he's here. Not wanting them to know he is.

Here.

Kelley is standing in the middle of the room. He swills wine and flushes it around his mouth as he works his tongue like a tooth rag. Ed may be nervous but Dee's not sure whether that makes matters better or worse. He didn't think anything could make him feel worse, but now he's guessing nothing about this night will make him feel any better. Dee steadies the stool, fixes his eye to the hole, wishing the events he spies might unfold other than how he knows they must. Why punish himself with watching? He wants to bear witness; after all, this is his sacrifice too. He wants to feel every minute of the pain, every sting and dart. To own it, and be part of it.

If the angels are watching, he wants them to see him feeling. And if they're watching, he wants to be here with them too. He sucks his teeth briefly in unconscious imitation.

Kelley crosses the room, passing close by Dee's spy-hole. All Dee can see is the bed. Out of his range of sight the door opens and closes. He can't make out the words, only the low murmur of Ed's voice, offering refreshment perhaps? She'll have none. Again, a murmur, and again, a reply he can't make out. Dee is realising his pain – this torture – might extend beyond the coming act. What do they have to talk of? What have they ever talked about before? He cannot bear to think of the pair of them after.

The present extends into the future. The future expands into a once-perfect past.

Some small time passes. Not much, but to the Doctor it's an age. His back is sore before the couple moves towards the centre of his circle. His back already stiff when she puts down her glass and begins to undress. His wife! To watch what he's been privy to so many times, yet rarely really seen. To watch the habitual movements he's so used to not noticing. To watch what another man is more discreetly watching. Dee presses his head against the wall, forcing wide his beady eye. And feels an unsubtle stirring he didn't expect. He pushes his cheek against the ring of wood and presses his legs together.

Jane ignores Kelley's offer, having had her maid unlace her quilted damask before she came. She gestures that he should look to himself and finishes swiftly, piling high her whalebones with the unbroken ties, and slips quickly into bed. She pulls up the coverlet so not even the embroidered collar of her cambric chemise can be seen.

Ed slides in after.

John breathes the world in, behind the wall, having just seen the hard evidence of his rival's affection. His ache ratchets up a notch: this is giving, letting go the very core of base, ignoble self.

Dee cannot see his wife's face, only where the other man's hand grips the soft flesh of her upper arm. Only where the curve of her throat ends, cropped by the circle that frames his vision. But Dee can hear the other man's breathing. It seems so close he can hardly believe it is not his. He notes the movement of the bed as it – and they – strain. It all feels so familiar that he wonders, wildly, if he isn't watching himself. He wonders if it isn't him, there: hands gripping throat catching breath.

Spinning in a whirr of emotion, spilling into his hose.

Swimming in a pool of motion, swooning into his partner, Kelley looks up and catches his master's eye. Sees the bead of black staring out at him from the other side. His friend. And feels a wave of tenderness, a tide of loss. An ocean impossible to cross. Like a medium given over to a divine possession, Ed separates, and duplicates, so the two men share each other's desire and despair as it pulses through the air.

It's strange, thinks Jane, eyes fixed on the black-beamed roof above: it's strange how alike this room is to the one she shares with her husband on the other side of the stairs. Same size, same shape, though here the window's on the wrong wall. She turns her head to follow her eyes, and looks towards the bright expanse of sky. She shifts towards the middle of the bed.

It's strange, Jane thinks, to lie naked with a man. To lie, like Eve, under a naked man. No nightgown fabric bunched between – she hadn't expected that. Their breasts and bellies joined just as much as their private parts. She shifts beneath him, slides her fists beneath her hips.

How strange *copulation* is, she thinks, in the end. How basic and brute and simple. And how similar it seems with, for the first time in her life, another man. It's strange. And even stranger that at the end of this dark tunnel there might be a baby. That's the way this works; she knows that even if they don't. Theodorus Trebonianus Dee. A boy wholly rooted in this world and not the in-between place from which these two quarrelsome men might imagine they've conjured him. That nowhere place that she knows

– with a cramp of unwanted intuition as Kelley clambers off – her husband will try to get him to spy on.

Strange. But that is the way these stories go: the present giving way to the future. The past, gone.

9 JUNE 2058

I'll try to explain. I'm writing to you, John, from Nat's old house, the North Carlton terrace where I grew up. I'm sitting at an old school desk in my mother's study – your grandmother's room – tucked up under the eaves. It used to be open, airy, now the attic is dark with leaf shadow. There's an underwater atmosphere. The city's Reforestation Act has been effective, with unforeseen consequences: the greenification has drastically lowered temperatures. Not even Melbourne's famous northerly – the hot, dry wind that set off asthma and allergies and a tickling anticipation – can find a way in.

The house beats around me, alive: animistic. Its light and warmth modulated to my needs. You must've programmed it to respond to my presence, guessing I'd come – unless it thinks she's back. Now you're hooking her up to your mainframe, getting ready to upload Nat's cipher into the cloud; crowning her skull in a cap of cups as she prepares to leave her body. Soon, for good. Her mobile intelligence already loosing itself from moorings I'm not yet ready for her to lose. I need to know where I came from before I can let my mother go. Our selves are entangled – through her, I am one with what came before; through you, my son, I live on.

I will Nat back to that night, such a long time ago. It's three-score years and ten since a trio of girls summoned a spirit and Nat heard Elizabethan Ed – in her mind, at least. And mine. I know myself as the son of that cross-matching, rather than the unacknowledged offspring of a teenage one-night stand. Some ghostly reincarnation. A fantastic projection.

I was born into a dark wood where the straight way was pretty clearly lost; Nat and I had to carve a new path out. Which we did. Leaving a trail leading back to a midnight pool. I was fertile soil for dream-planted clues, and sowed my own conspiracies, to reap when grown. It was almost as though I were programmed to seek some pre-experienced state where everything was One. Find some fitting philosophy. What do I mean? I was born to join disconnected dots, sketch the trajectory of Dee and Kelley's brief partnership. Inevitably downplaying the everyday, in-between moments of Nat's and my time together – the real life that happened while my tale was on the way to somewhere else – focusing instead on my mother's unique experience, which was, I was sure, what made us both so singular. Missing the point entirely: that we were universal.

Family history – all histories, actually – are the stories we choose to tell ourselves, as well as the stories we're told. One point of view doesn't cut it; you have to marry other peoples' perspectives. *You* have to, too.

Along with these letters from me you'll find your grandmother's old diary, and my own – speculative – research. I've tried projecting myself back to 1587, now I need to propel myself forward. In the words of Dr Dee, we must bring something to perfection. To some conclusion. I'm not so sure any more that I can lay my Elizabethan obsession at Nat's door: maybe I was the precocious, home-schooled child who asked 'What' and 'Whether' – drawing us deeper into Kelley's dark mystery. I feel such an affinity for Dee: who wouldn't risk everything for life's *elixir vitae*? Spoken like the old man I finally am. You're probably already primed to sympathise with the Doctor's quest: his 'almanac' has been accessible for a century now. But even with these interlinked texts of hers, mine and his, don't expect to get a complete picture. Life, I've learnt, isn't like that. Ed, after all, left no record – there's only a second-hand script of what Dee's right-hand man might've said.

Long before our story starts, in 1579, John Dee had a dream where the words *sine me nihil potestis facere* were tattooed on his right arm: 'without me you can do nothing'. (He was standing naked before the hooded gaze of the Queen's principal secretary and chief spymaster Sir Francis Walsingham – but that's another story. Or maybe it isn't, if everything connects.)

The thing is, *this* is all you have: me. My words are the ink connecting you to me, her to there. From my conception, in 1987, to Kelley's procreation, in 1587.

The thing is, I suppose, how little the world changes even when the way we understand it seems to be reinvented so radically.

But I mustn't get sidetracked trying to insert myself into a fantastic future where all Dee dreamt has come to pass and *you can do everything*, including delay our Nat's inevitable death. I want to tell you of your own beginning, John: John Jnr. Little John. So I called you because of something unchildlike I saw in your face when you were hauled forth, howling, into the breathing world. And regarded me like another who'd been here before.

At first I'd thought the keening was my own. Then I thought – and this was worse – that it was her. Oh Em! Mothers ripped apart to birth our giant brains; only now, thanks to modern obstetrics, surviving deliveries such as yours.

Emily said afterwards she heard your otherworldly cry before you were born. Said she heard it before they'd finished cutting you out. The very thought of that – the serrating that she'd been sure was the surgeon's knife but found out later was his fingers prizing her uterus apart – making her shake again. Then, when they dragged you from where you were wedged up under her ribs, her whole body was lifted off the table in a tug of war she didn't want to win.

The surgeon climbed onto her chest, kneeling like an incubus to pull you up and out and into the light. The room roaring around us.

Later, I tried to be glad that she hadn't seen what I had, but at the time I just wished they hadn't asked me to come behind the plastic sheet that sliced her, belly from head. What could I do, anyway? It was nothing, that tie which bound you to your mother – but who was I to cut it?

Time sped up. Heart rates too. A theatre was opened and they wheeled Em off, leaving me holding: you. The whole world weeping. (If only I'd known it was going to be all right – for both of you; for us all – but as far I knew *we* were the ones death was reviewing. I held you as if you were a sacrifice and I supplicating some heavenly father.)

I don't know how long I stood there wishing that you would open your eyes and look. See me. But I realised then, with the unforgiving knife of too-late insight, that I had never loved as I'd been loved.

Please, *son*.

There we were then, here we are, our perfect unit of three. Thanks to that team of doctors who knew what I didn't: how close birth is to the other side – how fine the membrane that separates those apparently opposing but really mystically connected states.

I suppose I rocked you, if you could call it that: I'm surprised you were able to breathe I held on so tight, swung us so roughly – swaying from side to side on a boat of life, unbalanced. Rougher and longer than I would've thought I should. Until your desperate squalling ceased. The animal in both of us finally subsiding: convinced – for the moment – that we were not freefalling limbs flinching into space but gripped by gravity. Safe in our father's arms.

00:03:00

It's 2087, the year a digital deviation will be accessed from outside the mainframe. That's how this story starts; that's where it really begins – when an icon containing infinite space, maintaining ultimate time, is tapped by a once-was-girl who never knew what possessed her.

Not that it was meant for Nat. Her grandson John built the app not to search for his father's origins but to seek out his namesake Dee's ideas for a projected-time machine. He planned to work from the Doctor's notes to program a spacecraft's code. All he had to do was identify a gravitational anomaly in the four space-time dimensions, and he thought he could. Oh and harness it, which would be trickier. And then, the tricksiest move of all, return! And use Dee's clues to set a fantastical action – which would, by then, have already transported him – into mechanical motion.

He was living at the crest of science and fiction, where mirrors and screens project truths human brains can barely grasp. Inhabiting borderlands where real and virtual converge, angels and flesh merge for the briefest time – the dive-roll of an imploding universe, caught! Contracting back.

He could hardly be blamed for his father Jo's conception, or grandmother Nat's self-deception, even if authoring an anomaly might seem an unsurprising outcome, and potentially predictable, in so far as anything to do with time travel was. Contradictions, after all – doesn't he know it – abound. But who was anyone to point a finger? (Unless *Jo* had trialled his son's Skrying app a moon ago, in a parallel universe, and spied this future. Could *he* have been that tempo-spatially untied agent scouting out mutual histories? The haunting that damn near drove Nat crazy? In which case…well, this John could hardly be blamed for such a world and mind-bending improbability.)

He closes his eyes.

'Clinical death,' Nat fears she hears, 'is the cessation of blood circulation and breathing. After three minutes the brain cannot recover.' But she's not sure – words are blurred by the breathing machines that whisper her age as they in- and exhale: one one-hundred, two one-hundred… one hundred and seventeen. Older than she'd have ever thought possible, if she'd ever thought about it. Older than should be possible, she thinks. A hundred years ago people knew when they were done. Five hundred years before, their lives were often over before their time.

Beneath the disinfectant, beneath the perfect, scented flowers, Nat can smell death on her breath. And beneath that, the damp green of a waiting forest. Tendrils toey to tuck her in.

Sensing her grandson's lowering lids, Nat finds herself finally free to leave – and begins to rise above them both. Drawn to the wall of pseudo-windows that shows the city as it once was. Nat remembers when the skirted spire – taller than Dr Dee's giant maypole – had shone like that for real. A latticed lighthouse drawing moths, which in turn lured birds, so lost seagulls were a common sight on the southern night skyline. Circling the gold triangle that's now towered over by apartment blocks that crowd around.

She is floating towards that water which flows to an infinite ocean: dreaming of sailing to Dee's speculated

Terra Australis; of rowing on an Old World river; of swimming through incalculable space. Ah! The River Styx. But then, Nat's passage slows. Suddenly she remembers how very much she once wanted answers. Was this a last time to find them? Soon she might know everything but be nothing.

Three minutes. It takes a housefly's wings three milliseconds to beat: three hundred, for the human eye to blink. Light travels 300,000 kilometres in a second – she has, Nat thinks, time to go far.

A minute: from the Latin, meaning first small part. (So she imagines someone from a long way away saying.) A second: named for the second, smaller part. The Poles had a word for the smallest third – she might be counting on that. Nat puts a cold foot on the floor and slips from the bed, a mere body bag of bones. Glides past curtains as though they're not. Light billows as she wills herself towards the bank of screens that monitor her nearly nonness, thinking one might be a window that truly opens out. There is still that, isn't there? Outside? An emerald forest waiting to absorb all: roots thirsty to soak up matter and release bodies, such as hers, back into the atmosphere – effervescent as forest air.

When she finds herself before the flat polished mirrorscreens – and it is like she finds herself, like she's returning, even as her last minutes tick away. As if she isn't hastening towards death but has been other for an age and is about to be utterly again. Nat makes herself turn back. She feels so connected to him in that chair – son of her son – that she could almost believe it is her sleeping there, chin neatly tucked into rising-and-falling chest, and John (which, she wonders, of the three Johns she's known in this lifetime would that be?) out here, launching a final unfinished string of code that will program a satellite of precision-cut crystal with a: click.

The physicists' man-made planet – but woman-named, since the word Nova has come to John from Good Queen Bess, via Nat (the arch thought of which makes Nat think she still is: *thinking*! and might live on too, in his thoughts) – is a hecto-ball. A hundred-eyed crystal with which to play 'I Spy'. What magic science has become! The dying woman taps an icon with her bony finger, aligning herself to a blackhole opening. Rotors move in slow motion as planes align. He couldn't have done it if he'd tried. Dark obsidian discs turn and cast their brilliant light onto a world that once was. One diametrically opposite in space and time. She sees that, now.

If the perfect, polished supra-lenses of the John who'll see in the twenty-second century had been other-directed, would Nat have ever found another self? Was she elsewhere – every-when! – too? The almost-ghost-woman savours the question. Looking forward – in due course, she has every time and all space at her disposal (via his time machine, or her coming transmutation) – to hearing the Doctor–Philosopher expound on that: were Dee and she opposites, at either ends of an imagined earth, or are they both the same?

Nat is all ears.

Only hearing now – the first dying minute ending, no heartbeat or pulse of blood distracts. Nat doesn't know she hasn't left the bed. That John is picking back up an iPen, the better to transcribe the phrases that fall from his grandmother's lips as she – like Ed, when he went out of his head and into another's – fits.

I close my eyes; lower my hands to the desk. What desk? This desk. Hard, though not as hard as I can be; old, but not as old as I should feel. A school desk from last century, blonde wood with secret cuts, some coloured in. I remember this. I run my finger along a groove as I push back the wooden chair I'm sitting on and stand, seeing it all afresh: the messy bedroom, the messier bed. Where am I and when is now?

(Who are we, again? Still Nat. An earlier version of my own familiar self.)

Piles of papers and towers of books crowd around; am I the lonely girl trawling through tomes from the library in her last year of school, or the Renaissance lecturer of a decade later – who's learnt her subject from the inside out? The room is as untidy as a teenage den but it's the first house I ever owned: a crumbling North Carlton terrace. I'd thought I was so different then from who I'd been, from who I was going to be. So bloody sure I took a different path out of that wood than the one I'd walked in on. But now I wonder how far you have to walk into a goddamn forest before you're heading out the other side.

Wearier than that - me knows, I leave the notebook where it is – open pages weighted with a worn set square – and stumble towards the bed. Falling onto it, I barely feel the body I'm back in connect with the crumpled linen. Barely feeling. I'm done, as if I were one of the Fox sisters who's been channelling some spirit – who's been possessed, against her will, and to her infinite surprise, since she knows herself to be an utter fraud.

So thinking, I inch out of that world and toe towards the realm of sleep. Twitching as I succumb to the exhaustion of an interstellar traveller. *Don't, don't, don't…*I whisper, wanting to stay: *there's work to be done!* But the sun is so soothing on the back of my neck, the air so soft. I don't remember flesh feeling like this; I can't not give in to the tiredness – I have a lifetime to catch up on.

Sighing like the old woman I – for a brief relieving moment – am not, caught on the very cusp of slumber, I wonder: if teenage Nat wasn't lost that long-ago May, would *I* still be found?

Did it, the thought drifts up as I slip down, truly happen? What happened anyway, really? Then I was too young to understand and now, quite suddenly it seems, I am beyond old. All I clearly remember is the three of us encircling that rock – that bloody rock! That bloody cold and unrelenting rock: Di on one side and Lizzie, the other. Their arms around each other's shoulders as my head lolled forward towards the centre stone. As though the three of us have never unlinked hands and that scene is a stage still set.

Or could it be that I was never really part of it at all, but always somehow outside it? Only ever a watcher. Like I was – am! – some spirit, ears straining for the spell that will call *me* into being.

From the watery underworld of sleep ink-stained fingers tweak. I hear someone – who might be me – cry out in a quiet room: 'Don't!

Come.' A voice is calling and I am falling towards it, tumbling from the middle of Nat's life into another past: and from there, through Kelley's darkening days, towards his traitorous dreams of a long-limbed rosy Queen.

I knew I should fight it – I've come back to face facts – but I also knew that the dying woman I still was, too, wasn't about to pass up on the chance to relive the release of real sleep. My head already rests on my arms, ducking half-forgotten memories, resisting half-remembered fragments. Was that the smell of damp earth? Surely not a sheen of wet rock? My teenage past tries to rear up, to trip me from the reality I've crafted so carefully over the in-between baby- and then schoolboy-busy years.

It must be 2010, the year Jo took off to Europe – where I'd not yet been. That was when I became lost in dreams of Elizabethan queens. Strange visions of courts and curios, characters I'd met through my research coming to life at night. All because I was alone, and my son had asked the obvious question: who had his father been? Back in the beginning I'd buried myself in history because of what had happened – turning Ed's world into my specialty, myself into an expert – but after Jo left it wasn't me who sought out Bess but Dee's world that drew me in. I was caught as an ouroboros: the tail-devouring snake neatly summing up my self-reflexive, seemingly cyclic existence.

I recognised the way my mind dragged and snagged: 2010, then.

The wheel of life turns again and again. In every beginning, a sign of its end; in every ending the seeds of a new beginning. As an acorn is filled to the brim with not-yet and once-was tree, so I am *her* and she will, in time, be me. How my heart had started, that year, at the picture Jo sent of bungeeing from the keep of an ancient Bohemian castle. What did he know? Could he possibly be blessed – or cursed – with some direct connection? What if he were to see the seal of God and be able to read its wax inscription? My mind snags.

What if, indeed? I was not, and would not be, John Dee!

Here I was, then, forty years on; not yet back in 1987. I needed to travel further, but there was no way this body wasn't giving in to the spell of forgetfulness that unconsciousness offered. Who would've thought dying would be so exhausting that you'd long for the sleep you'd be deprived of until the utter end? I'd had my fill of thin and unsatisfying naps, drifting across the surface of a pool that promised a deeper and more satisfying immersion. I was staying put. I was sinking down.

From outside my old room come the sounds of a new day – the metal-on-metal of early trams rounding an empty corner; the harsh scold of a noisy miner bird. Further away a mower starts up at the cemetery south of my first grown-up home – but it was impossible to resist: another minute? Another hour? Another lifetime of not being me.

Of not being Nat.

Of not *being*.

When I wake, it's mid-morning. Late. The blue sky shimmers with sun and my old upstairs bedroom is filled with light. It seems less cluttered now, more composed. Still full of the flotsam and jetsam of an odd academic's life, but the unstable tables of books and leaning stacks of papers look more like they've been put there by me and less like they're what's holding me here.

I roll onto my back and stretch, first one side and then the other. Even the stiffness feels good.

Early morning in Melbourne and already it was another sweltering day. Wasn't this when summers had started coming later, lingering longer – or had they always been like that? I remember how the back of my knees used to stick to the blue vinyl bus seat on the way home from school; the back of my dress was always wet with sweat in those first months of term. And then the contrast when we arrived at Lizzie's new house and the temperature dropped by noticeable degrees. Walking from the last station to her home on the hill as we left the local shops behind and traipsed single file along the edge of the cool green forest that smelt so wet and enticing, seemed so cool and inviting.

Singing some shit song – though the other girls' voices never carried back and I always wondered if I weren't really singing it alone: '*Bess, I hear you calling, but I can't phone home right now...*'

Not that I'd been there for much of first term.

Abruptly I swing strong legs over the side of the bed and cross the room to hitch up the window, propping it open with an old ruler to let in the northerly that's been pushing against the glass. This time I would make myself take the advice they'd offered half my life: write it, to right it. Jo deserved that, given everything I could never give him. This way he, *here* in 2010, would get the full recorded story – aero and Instagram: words from now, pictures from then. The memories of a quarter of a century after the event combined with Skrying-app flashbacks filmed a century hence. This time I'd believe; at least I'll try. And I am: trying to control the wilful, wayward mind that seems so much stronger and bolder than anything that could possibly be mine.

I direct myself, insofar as I can – from this no-place between being and keying – but I don't know how to get to that night when those final-year friends crossed some line that I, at least, never really came back from. There are bugs aplenty in the app John's built; I'm not as in control of this adventure as I ought to be.

It'd been the last month of autumn, I remind myself, when even the most tenacious deciduous leaves were beginning to let go. I meditate on the seasons turning: winter wafting from the wings. Me trying to settle back in after my unexpected stint away: everyone had acted as though I was the same, which had just made me more sure I wasn't – only Di and Lizzie had looked me in the eye to see if I was still me. Not that any of us knew the answer to that one: maybe I was as much Nat as I had ever been. More, for sure, than I am now. (Or should that be, *was then*? Travelling through time is confusing my never-that-stable sense of self – am I me-*now* in 2087 or me-*then* in 2010? I settle for one continuous but contradictory Nat: this forty-year-old at that desk, trying to remember, with the help of John's spy device, the night Jo began.)

I wonder, closer to that side of the millennial divide, if my once-best friends ever experience something similar: a sense that who they are now is not the real them. That who we really were was who we were then, when we saw ourselves reflected in each other's shining eyes. Then, we'd thought life was before us. Now, I know it's all behind me.

I sigh before the warm wind the window lets in, hoping I was once part of something grand. Something bigger than the three of us. Running middle-aged fingers through hair that's thicker than I remember – as though clearing my face will do the same for my mind. This-me might try to accept what I've been told, to get better for good – that writing is an exercise in exorcism – but other-me suspects that, by the time I actually believe that, I'll already be well. The whole strategy smacks of Liz; like when she'd said we could fly if we only believed. Really, truly believed.

And what if she was right? I yank ponytail tight. Was it so long ago that I was that naïve-wise girl? It seems like yesterday that three friends ducked beneath dripping leaves and I fell further and further behind, horrified that what we'd hoped for might actually happen.

Clearly, at forty, my thoughts are as mad as when I was sent away. Was it possible that I'd never wanted to be well? Anything and everything was possible, but could I be reverting to some pseudo-psychosis, decades on – do I really think I'm possessed by some future self?! – because I didn't know who I'd be without it?

Time keeps looping back.

Time kept trooping on.

Returning my attention to the second-hand desk and pinned-open notepad, I rub at the crease age is cleaving between my brows. No doubt my short-term memory is clouded by sleep, or the lack of it – another stupidly wakeful night. Another morning where I've risen more exhausted than when I went to bed. Another night in a long line of nights that ties this new year to that decades-old one. I rub my eyes; I did have a recollection of sitting here scribbling away. Scratch-scratch: a tightly held biro moving, almost automatically, over pages. What had I been doing? My memory is faint as a dream…

The dream! I pick up a pen, intent on capturing another night's fantasy before it fades any further – before I get distracted by the strange mathematical symbols peopling facing pages. (I've been trawling the web since Jo left, searching for answers in scientific journals, seeking consolation in arcane contemplations. Home alone for pretty much the first time in my whole life, I've been buffing up on space and time to see if I can't come up with an answer to what actually happened that night. And why.) What about my recent reading into singularity? When matter has infinite density and infinitesimal value? As it did in the Big Bang beginning. I imagine, if only for a second, that I'm caught inside my own space-time distortion – and have been for the decades since the

Dandenong Ranges, when there was one and one and one more girl.

Trying to shake the latest snippet of science I've seized out of any context – maybe I'm the one free while everyone else is trapped, bound by unstoppable, indisputable, gravitational forces. And which would I rather be: the one caught, or the only one not? I pinch my nose tight enough to leave the indentation of old-fashioned eyeglasses. If modern astronomy and quantum mechanics offer no explanations…well, evidence of Dr Dee was all over the esoteric sites my late-night investigations had stumbled across. Maybe he was onto something, after all.

A word disappears in a diminishing triangle:

ABRACADABRA

ABRACADABR

ABRACADAB

ABRACADA

ABRACAD

ABRACA

ABRAC

ABRA

ABR

AB

A

– so the spell, 'Create, I say', can be read from the apex back up the right-hand side. Is finding the ancient Aramaic inscription a happy enough coincidence to be called serendipity, or is it another word I'm looking for? I resist a shiver at the sign of the three-cornered polygon. When I stumble upon such geometric shapes, scribbled in the margins of the pages riddled with the dreams I'm trying to decipher, I feel a panic not far off fear. Like a dyslexic faced with unreadable sentences, unspellable words – or your average maths-phobic teenager dreading some coming exam, I sense a test: impossible, unpassable. Impenetrable.

If I died *now*, and Jo read these words, overlapping as though paper is a luxury, or the writer blind to what's already been recorded, what would he make of who his mum has been? Surely other mothers – left bereft in an empty nest – don't do this: wonder if their reflections are centenarian selves trapped in two dimensions? An older iteration, projecting herself back to direct some fantastic action.

I flip to a new page, having nearly convinced myself my night-time world holds the clues Jo's after, if only I could map them. Or at least points a way, if only I can navigate it. I am not yet ready to descend into that fecund forest.

'*I dreamt it again last night,*' I write, fingers waking as they pace out the page – holding this present to ransom so in his future he can mine my past. '*That dream within a dream within…*' I wriggle my feet on the bottom rung, lean elbows on knees as I try to seize on specifics that must – surely? – lead somewhere. I tap the pen against my teeth and launch into the ghost writing that might seem like procrastination but isn't, I am nearly certain now. I can almost believe the night of Jo's conception is the dream, and this nightly court I'm trying to capture some half-remembered life.

'*I felt…*'

The divide between worlds dissolves. All I need do is relax my constant effort to keep the veil down…I let go my desperate hold and waking life gives way to Elizabethan dreams.

'*…her ghost breath on my lips. But at the very point*

where we must've merged, the dream dissolved. Only to be bereft all over again. '*I was alone...*' Only to be... '*Or, was I finally and forever never to be alone again?*'

I pinch a breath laced with dread and something more. Letting myself remember...Liz. Eating a frozen Sara Lee cheesecake with one teaspoon: thinking with each icy bite how no boy would ever know her better. Later, shivering under her yellow blanket – my body temperature brought low by pre-binge starving – the taste of fake lemon burnt the back of my throat.

'*Waking on the wet woodland floor, back in that fucking forest.*' Suddenly I am zooming towards the hungover, coming-down morning. I pull myself up short: as I had – I remember! I was a Queen, in a bed, on a stone – last night. It was only after that, after I'd woken again in the woods, that I'd been able to wake myself for real to find it was sheets – not roots and leaves – that my hands were twisting into ropes.

But realising I was in my own Carlton home had brought little relief: I'd been gripped with the conviction that I hadn't escaped. A dreadful feeling that *now* was still *then* and time hadn't moved on one fraction of a second. I – some essential part of me – was there. In a circle, beneath a tree: *that* teenage threesome was my reality and *this* forty-something life the crazy made-up dream.

I'd tossed and turned through the rest of the night, first stretching my mouth to release the cramp in my jaw that came from grinding my teeth, before forcing my breathing to slow as I reminded myself they were only dreams I was remembering. It was all – only – a dream: if awash with seeming, and alive with meaning.

I may have lain awake a while longer, looking at the strangely leaf-shaped shadows on the far wall of my room,

but eventually I drifted into a fitful early morning doze...
Sleep, I can only suppose, finally easing my frown and
releasing my still-clenched fists. Certainly sealing my eyes
as firmly as needle and thread were ever used to blind a
bird – so I now wrote, slipping neatly into the words of
Kelley's world.

Was this regal dream the same as the one before, and
that no doubt to come? Or were the versions of virgins
all subtly different? Bess might not be the world's most
famous virgin – she wasn't even the first Britain made
Queen – but there was clearly a connection: she, too,
had had to present her sealed state before disbelieving
medicos. When I finally submitted to an ultrasound, I'd
wondered whether it would show my hymen still intact –
if they'd been looking for evidence of destruction, rather
than confirmation of creation. Was it a doctor's out-breath
I'd felt whisper across my sweat-soaked skin? Or the warm
sigh of a summer night, creeping in? In my bed and in the
dream I'd sensed the future could already be read if there
was only a seer to see: in the whorls rendered on metre-
thick walls, the curls of eucalyptus leaves tapping against a
Belgrave bathroom window.

If I follow faithfully, I think, these dreams should lead
to what I've spent the past quarter of a century repressing:
John's cross-matching and my Jo's hatching. If I can
document every detail – demented or otherwise, dreamt or
remembered – Jo should be able to spy any secrets within
the scenes. (He was born a code-breaker: had birthed an
expert coder son.) Or so I'd justify it if anyone asked – not
that they would; back then they'd always encouraged it.
Back when I was so lost I couldn't see the forest for its
multiplying trees.

(Doubt fingers in: what if telling him is the worst thing

I can do, unintentionally damning Jo too? That Jo *was*, was so much more important than who his father had been. Or how he'd been conceived.)

I pause, pen in air – 'they' never seemed to suspect that the act (of writing and remembering and dreamy *Dee* dreaming) might've been the 'in' the chimera was after. That's what I've been afraid of over the intervening years: what if the search for meaning leads to madness, to more madness? Back to madness. I will not let myself get lost again – I block out the freakishly familiar voice in my head – I will not lose, not this time or any other. I will not be. Lost.

No one knows better how obsessed I can be with coincidence, how persuaded by coexistence – I've been searching forever for signs of synchronicity, even when I wasn't aware that's what I was doing. I am so desperate for answers, I'm afraid I might just make them up. The idea of arbitrary accident is anathema to me. Still, any teenager – whether Gen X, Y or Ω – knows that, while meaning might seem the opposite of an empty vortex, the quest for the first can lead directly to the last. I must step carefully on this dangerous path. Not let the puzzle drive me insane before any answer has the chance.

For now, I reassure myself as the January sun shines down, the exercise is purely purgative: the memories well up; the writing will draw them out. Making sense of it is up to someone else. I do not need to lose myself in dreams. Quite the opposite: I need to wake myself up. I will myself to stop analysing – a habit that's its own futile search for truth. To stop. I have only to gather my thoughts, garner my past, concentrate on pushing the balled point of this pen along. Regardless of what it all means, this is what I do. Where I have ended up, after all this time: writing, like the good Doctor himself. It doesn't really matter whether it's for my son, in the end. Jo has just – again – started me on a journey: this time backwards towards the beginning of us rather than onwards into the healing minutiae of the everyday life that came next.

I am ready now, and just waiting for him to *come*.

(There isn't any chance, is there, that I'm afraid of what I might *not* find in the stories from English history – or is it only one story? – that I revisit on certain nights, when conditions are right, like stepping onto the stage of another, alternative life? My Elizabethan project couldn't be more escapist than dangerous, could it? The dreaming is certainly starting to seem more real than my waking Jo-less days. Could the writing act be a way of building up an antipodean life: putting myself at the centre of a mystical world? Just one more example of my messed-up reaction to the emptiness of existence – since Jo's taken off and I've found myself so strangely aimless and unnaturally aged. As left out as I'd always thought I was before he was born. Clearly I've been spending too much time alone!)

Fidgeting in the warming morning, I remind myself how mutable reality – and relationships – can be. What could I possibly write that would free Jo from the weightlessness of not knowing without saddling him with the burden of what I thought I did (didn't I?)? That wanting – being wanted – isn't everything.

Maybe it wasn't up to me. Maybe everything had already been passed on. After all, every generation is the culmination of evolution up to the moment of its conception: a newborn's molecular matter the product of worlds that've formed again and again. Back then, when I was seventeen – and even before that, way back when – my dark yin already contained his perfect seed. All I knew for sure was that once upon a turbulent time three friends swore to love each other forever: it seemed so certain they always would that to vow it had seemed silly. And then, one night…Though in my heart of hearts I suspect events were set in motion long before that tableau in time: the tightly locked triangle where you might think things started.

And then. One night.

Something, surely, had *made* Fate's pendulum slow between one swing and the next. Finally coming to rest over our teenage heads. I let the twenty-first century pen drop, crack knuckles distractedly as I imagine it from a Google Earth's eye perspective. Imagine if that technology could be programmed to show not just the Street View of months before, or satellite perspective of a year past, but decades ago. That ever-present, never-ending night when who I was became who I'd be, who I've been ever since.

'Who I am,' I whisper, trying to rein my thinking in.

The planets, I conclude, however improbably, however implausibly, however not-possibly, may as well have been aligned. Who am I to say otherwise? Certainly no expert on everything that can or can't have happened, which could or couldn't ever be; I, of all people, know that. There are truths that are stranger than anything I can imagine: I've been privy to things I would never have believed, things I'm not sure I do credit, even now. Things I'm not sure I don't. Things no one should be asked to – and usually, no one is. Certainly some aspects seem weird and wild, and any explanation is bound to sound outright crazy.

The pull of the past proves planetary strong. Can three friends coming together throw moons out of orbit and constellations off their course?

'*The year of the Slippery When Wet Tour,*' I imagine

writing, and can almost see the text appearing, read a date emerging. Is it foresight? Hindsight? Hard-wrought insight? When is now and where am I?

1987 was when our circle was the closest it would ever be to complete. Not that we knew it then. I pick up the pen again, ready for the real work to begin: writing the world to recognise it, in myself. To recognise myself in it. How to convey the absolute high? Life, peaking. Doubt, however temporarily, retreating. Lizzie's voice rippling, ripping back:

'We'll fake it TO WHE-RE?!'

Ed brings his gaze to the man opposite. No longer interested in the blue earth glimpsed beyond the curved pane of glass. Clouds are clearing; he is on the cusp of understanding something. Might there be no actual line between inside and out? Is the distance between him and Dee not real, when he has spent their whole friendship thinking it is the one true thing? That Dee had this and Ed did not; that Dee was this and Kelley the other.

In that imagined city at the world's end, as far away as he could see and still – he believed – be on the same small ball, the streets were unnaturally straight and preternaturally clean. People, ears blocked with white buds or otherwise bound, pushed past in waves, transfixed by small screens held in their hands. He peers over shoulders, leaning in, feeling as much a part of them – as much apart from them – as she does. Ed shakes his head, which is, here, hers: there is a buzzing.

'Bees,' he whispers, beneath his breath (inside her brain): *bzz bzz.* It was a positive portent when not much else was.

The men were, finally, at an end. Death beckoned. There was no one else he could be, nowhere else he could flee to.

The Doctor taps his nose with the quill in a gesture Ed has come to hate. At other times he's been sure it is a secret sign to an angel in Kelley's own head: tap – the quill waves wand-like in the non-light – tap.

Like a drunkard waking, shaking, Kelley gulps at the cold damp that goes by the name of air and drinks till he is full. He is filled to the absolute hilt with the fetid prison. No longer an arrow seeking its destiny, no longer an arc in sight of its mark, his story has nowhere left to go. His sentence stops. Ends with Ed extending his hand into the no-man's-land between him and his imaginary friend, knowing only that he is not and never was alone.

He is Bess, again. In a crystalline dream, Kelley finds himself back in the body of their Queen. When Ed straightens his shoulders he sees the sarcenet, pulled through the slashed brocade, flashing the scarlet only royalty is allowed to wear – according to her sumptuary laws. She is not the young maid he has been before, nor the middle-aged maiden. She is old now, older than perhaps she is yet in the real world where he spends his waking days.

She is daydreaming. Remembering her darling Robert Dudley. And what could have been when, as a new Queen, she'd ridden out with him before her people were astir. Kicking her heels into her horse's flanks so her handsome Master of the Horse had had to race to keep up. That was back when he'd been 'her eyes', and wasn't yet the fifty-year-old traitor married to a she-wolf Lord Leicester would become! The pair had put more and more distance between themselves and her lagging staff as their imaginations had leapt ahead of horses' hooves.

Aged heart thumping in Ed's breast, Bess can almost hear again the drumming.

Until she'd reminded herself – and it had been a sobering thought – of her Uncle Seymour, who'd lost his head while she'd kept hers. He had been her first love. Ed's interest quickens, and the Queen's thoughts turn further that way.

In the end she'd been more mistress of that situation than either she or her foster-father had supposed; more master of most scenes – even those that revolved around her dear Rob – she'd come to learn. Fourteen in years, Bess might have been, when Thomas Seymour had had her under his wing, inside his house, atop his bed – though only ever romping above the sheets, never rousing beneath – and only recently ready to bear a child, but so much older in soul and not remotely ready to be bidden or beholden.

Nor likely ever ready for that, old Bess now knows, her mind washing from that first flush of young love back to the later fevered Rob-run years. Via a de Simier detour. Oh the wanton wanting! That flickering flame of feeling that begets the urgent fire of desire. A time…two times… thrice when Bess had wanted someone, some*thing*, so badly that she thought she would've given anything, whether it was hers to give or not. His head. Her self. And once upon a time the crown? (Of a sudden, she thinks of Dr Dee and what he might have known; how much his star charts might have shown. She wondered whether her mother Anne had ever been the mistress of witchcraft old Henry had claimed, and if so whether she would've condoned her daughter's secret mission to claim strange new lands or warned her daughter well away.)

No matter: the woman who bore Bess was long dead, as were too many of the Queen's old friends. Politicking was a deadly game, and ageing a fatal one.

But oh ye glorious Gods, Thomas had been a handsome forty! In Bess's mind's eye Ed spies the virile Lord's beauty, preserved forever as the Queen had seen it when she was a slim slip of a thing. She'd realised – riding out with Rob, her hair unravelled like a red roan mane – that her companions might never age as well: not if she spoilt him the way she had a mind to now the crown was hers.

It still gave her pleasure to think on Tom's charms now the diadem was heavy on her wig's gauze wings. Please remember, Ed begs.

That time her guardian had come into his ward's room in the early morning, wearing only his nightgown. They'd rolled playfully until her own attire had tied limbs tight. The time he'd pulled her over his knee as if to paddle – as though she were a child and he her father. Bess remembers when her stepmother–aunt Catherine (now Tom's but formerly the old King's wife) had joined in the horseplay. Tickling, until Bess wriggled and giggled between them. Oh she remembered that all right! And now Ed, too, would forever.

Lusty old Tom had known what he was doing – there was no doubt about that – and what he'd had to hold back from doing to tame her and inflame her and make her want him the way he'd wanted her to. And, oh God, oh yes! She had. Good Princess Bess had never once cried foul. She'd fought a little, but just for fun – to make the master of the house show his strength, the better to relish in her own rare weakness. When he finally released her, she'd lain limp beneath the pair of them with sharply shining eyes. Looking from t'other to one.

Catherine and she had worked together to overthrow the virile baron. What a pair of dummerers! Straddling Tom, Henry's widow and his bastard daughter had gripped husband–uncle between their thighs as he roared and writhed in a great display of trying to throw them off. Which only made them cling more fiercely, riding him hysterically, shrieking all the more when some fall of fabric exposed a pale shoulder or peeping roundly knee. Or when some softness of theirs rubbed against a hardness in him. Bess had thought – not that she'd thought at all, really, she who was s'posed to be so very smart – that it must've been well if his lady was privy to their games. But it wasn't. It was not well at all.

It was hard to believe she was ever such a doxy. When she considered their action, she realised that, not only did their threesome not make it right, it made everything that much more wrong.

Which was when Bess had realised that she was the one pushing them on. She the one praying he wouldn't hold back. Another morning and she might have lifted his gown. Or *hers*. Another minute. (Another minute! But Ed cannot control what he sees and the dream is already ebbing.) With every breath the three of them were being willed over an edge from which there was no coming back: that was the fact of it. Bess had started out teasing him, but along the way had helped Tom build a blaze in her that would not easily be denied. They were generating an infernal heat that had no outlet, sparking an unnatural flame that needed no fuel and never faltered. Romping nowhere but to hell.

Luckily – wise Bess catches herself: it had hardly been luck! – propitiously, when Seymour's story had come out, she'd known to hold her peace, stubbornly staring down her interrogators, daring them to read guilt in her schoolgirl face. She knew better than to speak against her stepmother's second husband, realising a pointing finger would've only proved personal stain, but promised herself that she would never again be so at the mercy, not of a man but her own want.

The vision of Seymour wanes and Ed senses again Robert hard on the young Queen's heels. How Bess had treasured those stolen mornings – her excitement passing to her high-strung horse so she'd had to work hard to get them both back in hand. Only slowing her riding with a subtle touch to the reins – so the beast beneath barely felt the bit – at the thought of poor Seymour. So she no longer thrilled at how easy it was for her, and the dashing Lord Dudley – who was following all unknowing where Tom'd tried to lead – to escape their chaperones.

Was this the same dilemma that Bess's mother Anne had failed to navigate with her own Thomas, the handsome poet Wyatt? Charting a fraught course between wanting and being wanted, between who she was becoming and who she'd really been? Was her only daughter leading Rob, whom she thought of as another ourself, towards the same fate? Not yet lovers – maybe neither Boleyn woman would ever have that – still, the new Queen knew she had to think sharp to cut a path through the web of her own amorets.

An image springs strongly to the fore of Ed's mind as Bess's 'membering ends up where it always does: on that walking path that he finds is no puzzle at all. The unicursal labyrinth at her uncle and aunt's house where she'd run, heart pumping – thrilling at her own fear, fearful of her own thrill – between low hedges of green that spiralled in only one direction.

When they caught her up, Catherine had seized her

stepdaughter in a close embrace. Holding Bess still as her husband sliced at the young girl's dress. At first he'd slashed wildly, rending fabric and risking flesh, but when there was no sound other than three sets of ragged breaths, the slits became more specific. Practised and precise. They all knew they were getting somewhere.

It was then – in that dead end – that Bess had realised she was the only one who could put a stop to what they'd started. Born knowing what to do, she did it. Picking up torn skirts and shaking them so dark cut ribbons floated to the ground, Bess accepted the hard-won truth: she no longer cared for the crown or her virginity or the fact that Thomas was not the man she'd have him be. She cared only for who she was. Caring only, finally, for who she *would* be.

Running back the way they'd come, Bess knew the pair would follow fast. Into the house. Through a wing. Down stairs to where walls narrowed like the future closing in. Silk shreds drifting in her wake.

Turning in time to meet his lips with the open rosebud of her mouth, as she bid love goodbye with the first and last kiss from her own traitorous lips, Bess let flesh meld for an instant to Tom's hardening core – feeling, physically, his cry sink from gasp to groan. Reaching up round arms to weave her fingers into his hair so he couldn't get away before her aunt–mother, her uncle–father's wife, caught them. Not that he tried to – thinking, no doubt, of the tupping he must've been sure was as good as his. Or maybe of marrying her and usurping his brother, their Lord Protector. No thought of who saw.

Or, perhaps – like Ed – no longer thinking at all.

My forehead scraping across the desk as I turn my head wakes me up. Again. When? Still then.

I come to, to a dark room and the childish feeling of feet kicking free. The bloodless numbness of a hand beneath my cheek – which turns out to be mine. Returned to that time, half my life away, like a stroke victim waking: silent, watchful, needing to relearn the simplest things. A foot kicks against the desk leg in a snatch of unconscious code.

Clumsily, I push myself up from the chair and away from the table so paper slips to the floor: falling asleep writing again – the never-ending words that bound us all about! Those Ed once spoke, that Dee wrote, and now I too note. Lifting my hair from my sticky neck, I walk to the window where smoke hangs like a warning. Has it travelled in from the north-west, where the houses give way to sunburnt grass? Or the eastern perimeter, where they're hemmed in by iridescent trees? Or were, back when we hung out there.

Where I've come from, when the first century of the new millennium is nearing its end, the green isn't so neatly contained. Banned burning has given the ancient giants a chance to send their descendants down: inching, one seed at a time, towards Melbourne town. Turning the abandoned outer-burbs back into the forest they once were – cracking open rarely used roads. Stretching their ancient network of roots, sending off new shoots.

I make my way to the bathroom between mine and the other now-empty bedroom. Water to cool my skin and soak my dreams off in. Sleepily I turn my hand under the uncapped tap so diamonds and pearls splash into my palm. A royal ransom? A watery illusion. Elizabethan allusions abound – my mind hoards Kelley's history the way a crazy person collects what everyone else knows is rubbish, and maybe I do too: stacking it ceiling-high until it crowds me out of my own brain.

I try to tell myself I should head into the city and pay a visit to the State Library's old microfiche archive; there'd be a million stories of odd goings-on at the foot of those godforsaken hills, which lure at the end of the Burwood Highway like a gateway to more than the ranges beyond. Though I'd take the EastLink to get there in 2010 – not that we ever drove. We rode the Belgrave train, knowing we were getting near Liz's place when that wet peaty smell filled the carriage, even if we missed the signs for the stops before: Upwey, once called Mast Gully for how ships used its wood, and then the tiny timber town of Tecoma.

Stepping out of my crumpled clothes and into the bath, I can't help but sigh as I lower myself and slowly – slow-*ly* – lie back in the tub. High temperature dropping and, for the moment, agitation easing.

It'd been cold then, the night of the séance – I don't just remember it, I feel it too; the way the cold crept into my bones until I'd thought I was made of stone. Until I was sure I'd never be warm again. And maybe I haven't. Is that why I've loved the summers getting hotter and hotter: the now-normal days of blistering temperatures topping forty degrees? Because my blood turned sluggish that night. Because my marble limbs never entirely warmed again. Looking down at my body in the bath – laid out like a corpse, or a maiden on her marriage bed – I'm sure I can still feel that end-of-autumn chill.

(I am at risk of forgetting that a darker, colder ocean is by the minute bearing elder-me away. I have almost forgotten the oldest me, who is by the minute becoming more spirit than flesh, as I channel myself back and back and back.)

I close my eyes and lower my head into the water until only my face remains in the room. By May, winter had already come to the woods east of Melbourne: branches bowed before the coming cold. The forest floor was so soft it retreated beneath our feet. Decades later and suburbs away I can still smell the moss-moist earth. And, as though drifting above, see three friends making their cautious way down the overgrown path that led from the remote house into the forest proper.

One, two, three girls leave the dark garden and vanish into the overhanging gloom.

I exhale deeply, breathing everything out. Inhale exaggeratedly. Pinch my nose closed and sink beneath the surface, not wanting to get distracted from what had or hadn't happened once upon a teenage time.

Below, all is quiet. The only sound the steady thrum, thrum of my heartbeat. That's what it is, isn't it? Not a baroque drum. Not a heel strumming an invitation to a prancing dance. I let a minuscule breath seep out. Tiny bubbles escape parted lips to rest on my skin like miniature worlds. The white bathroom on the other side of the watery divide is very far away. The tiled walls vague: receding into lightness like an over-bright overcast day.

I hold out until I think I might burst, the water absorbing any tears the way it did another night. A night I'm not about to revisit. Am…

NOT.

Furiously scratching fingers through hair until my scalp sings, I rush my remembering further back instead: an earlier instance of night-swimming, when I'd almost drowned in a backyard pool and, staring up at a distant sky, had wondered whether I'd even wanted to make my way back into the fray.

Year Twelve loomed and though I hated school I didn't know what else to do. Didn't want to go; didn't know how to get out of it.

There were my bathers – abandoned on the concrete next to a heap of other clothes: someone had said only skinny-dippers were allowed. At first I'd thrilled at the new sensation – water everywhere – feeling so almost thin, so unusually light. No Speedos or T-shirt. My puppy fat no longer weighed me down: if anything, it was buoying me up. But then I'd felt beyond free. Bodiless. The only girl knickerless, I'd realised as I swam mermaidly between scissoring legs. Ashamed to emerge. Unable to find a corner to cling to, paddling this way and then that as fear rose with my frantic hands. Finally I'd floated, gasping, towards the deep end, out of my depth. Breath in my ears louder than the music. A small girl lost beneath cold old stars.

The water had been not malevolent exactly, just uncaring. Slapping me casually as it'd moved me – incidentally, but relentlessly – towards the darkest pocket of the overcrowded pool. It was only when I'd stopped scrabbling for the other side and let myself lie back, tucking chin towards chest and flexing feet so toes tipped up, that my panic had subsided. Naked beneath the outside lights I closed my eyes so I couldn't see anyone else's. The water in my ears blocking out screams of laughter as I floated in my own limbo. Would I ever reach the distant tiles?

I never noticed when I spun face down, or wondered why I was taking in first one and then another lungful of chlorinated water. It only registered that I was eyeing not the sky but the bottom of a packed pool when my shoulder was grabbed by some longhaired stoner, who hauled me out. Dragging me to an edge and draping me over it so my nose and mouth ran as I retched water. He breathed smoke into my face in a friendly enough fashion as I lay beached on the concrete. Wet feet slapping into the distance when he went off to find my friends.

'You fool,' Di said fondly, roughing me with a towel while Lizzie rattled on about how you didn't do it like that. What was it that I hadn't done, I wondered as she wrapped her arms around me, neat scars reminding me that I was with them and had no reason to be sad – my life wasn't that bad.

When I'd sicked up the last of the pool water and blown my nose a final time I struggled back into my clothes. Drained. Only now, rearing out of the bath, did I remember the pinpricks of light I was sure I'd seen shining through from another world. I was never really suicidal, whatever they said: just so self-conscious, or unconscious – so *something*, that growing up nearly did me in.

No matter how much we changed over the years – how much weight I lost once I started worrying about other things, like looking after little him – the way I thought of myself back then had stuck: the chubby one. The shyest of our three. Who then had the others been? Typecast by our classmates, we'd revelled in calling ourselves freaks.

Stepping out of the bath before the water gurgles away, I reach for a towel I don't need in the heat – wrapping it around the angles age will further reveal – forgetting for a moment that the house is empty. What was it about normalcy that we'd so despised? Now it seems some kind of weird wishful thinking. Like the last night of all our old lives – or was it just mine? – which was, after all, only an answer to that eternal teenage craving for the party to end all parties. The rapture, the rupture: whatever. Bring it on, we'd cried, calling all angels, never thinking of what we might lose. Or what we could gain.

I rub my skin roughly, telling myself that maybe a certain oddness was all we'd had in common in the end. An awkward edge, if we'd even had that. It was so damn easy to doubt everything.

I hang the towel distractedly on the rack before padding back to my room. Which has that golden glow that means it's going to be a scorcher. Not smoke then, but a heat haze that hadn't yet burnt off. I pull on underwear, loose linen pants and a lightweight cotton top, hoping distraction, and perhaps direction, can come from the library where I've always felt at home.

It would do me good to step into that cone of calm. It always did. Every time I ever arrived the silence of the State Library came as a physical surprise, the famous dome seeming to absorb the words whispered within. Sure, there'd be the background murmur of muted voices, but the bluestone blocked out the sounds of the modern city. Inside, it could be 1887. I picture the reading room rising above Melbourne at the turn of last century, proud to think it was one of the world's first free libraries – where rich and poor alike could learn, through other people's words, of the wondrous wider world. Every book, every magazine, every pamphlet ever published in Victoria was housed there. Every map! Where to start?

Such a wealth of knowledge reminds me of the largest library ever amassed in England, by Dee: 1587 – though by then his books would've already been recirculating.

And the smell! Just the thought of the cool atrium is enough to transport me back to Year Twelve. Catching the train in from the suburbs to study; it stopped at Flinders Street on weekends so I had to get out and walk up to what had been Museum Station. Not that I remembered getting that much done, but the voice in my head that was running me ragged had seemed to calm. As though the building offered some protection, though whether it was sanctuary for him or me I couldn't have said. Stonehenge – I'm not sure how I know or if I'm right – was once called bluestone too, though those dolerites weren't local but transported by an ancient glacier or prehistoric hands.

Inside, the temperature drops. Fine hairs rise on bare arms. The automatic doors open and close as visitors file past, making their purposeful ways while I lose myself in the vaulted ceiling above. That's the plan, anyway. (Now it occurs to me what a great place the library would've been to hide out in when the bushfires burnt up the horizon. There it would've been still, and quiet, even when outside the end of days raged.)

Tidying the notes strewn over every surface, I hurry up. I don't want to get distracted – again. The answers I'm after lie in the act of writing, not reading, of that I'm sure: these notes are meant for Jo. But still, I stop, disturbed to see how my handwriting alternates between two distinct styles: in some places letters have been pressed into the paper so hard they've broken through the page. In others large loops slide right off the lines. It's almost as though two people have had hold of the pen.

Like that crazy duet that once jousted in my head: youth and age this time, rather than male and female. I bundle up the books, slipping stray pieces of paper between random pages, not wanting to feel too keenly the low point of that winter when I'd roamed the school alone, pulling down the sleeves of my jumper so I could poke thumbs through the cuffs to make holes. Shrugging my shoulders in their getting-bigger blazer. I'd tried to hide inside my uniform – from everyone, Di and Lizzie too, having finally accepted that those BFFs were just like all the rest.

Refusing to feel any sorrier for my then-self than I already did, I toss my head, keys into bag, and head out the door. I will not let this morning get away. The past mustn't be allowed to hijack what looks like becoming a brilliant day – I feel anticipation in the air. It seems an age since I've felt anything at all.

Hanging on to the here and now by a taut spun thread I tuck the last loose sheet into my pocket, but not before three letters leap off the page. One syllable. Forcing me, for the first time in a long time, to directly address the presence that I'd once been so convinced possessed me.

Ned.

Ed.

Kelley, a name I recognise almost as well as my own. *Kell—* ringing out from the stone, seeping up from the ground *—ey*. Keying me towards the fraught months that followed our autumn adventure: this time-trip is a wormhole I can't control! John's shortest-cut hasn't connected me to the space-time coordinates I've journeyed so far for. I want the perfect vanishing point, not the empty term before or dark time that came after when I nearly lost everything I was and wasn't yet.

I'd passed the rest of that year like a shadow aping movements made by someone offstage. Now jerky... was that when I'd been overcome? Or when I won? Now smooth. In the end I left my English exam before time was up because I'd suddenly thought of some mathematical equation I was sure I should be studying. Though maths had been that morning, I'd realised after I left the hall. Not that anyone seemed to think it was weird when I ducked out the door. I did, by then, always need to wee.

Honestly, it was a fucking wonder I passed Year Twelve at all. Purely on the back of the hard work I'd put in the previous year, when I lost the plot swotting like the nerd I wouldn't be for much longer. It was as though I saw the next year coming and the months of studying before weren't what pushed me over but, when I was falling, what pulled me through.

At first I'd tried to use food to smother my manic thoughts, pushing down the tricky teasing, filling the anxious vortex with other feelings – of fullness and fat. But the more I ate the hungrier I seemed to get. And then I got this idea that there was a cold cruel elf nestled evilly at my core. So I decided to starve him out instead. I would diet, so he could die. I layered up, to hide my fat dropping away. And took the fact that my period stopped as a sign I was on my anorexic way, accepting without question when my vomiting escalated until I had to detour via bins between classes. The sudden purges left me briefly elated: shaking, but hyper-alive. Believing I was doing it to *him*. Not he to me. No idea that there might be another, more natural explanation.

I took to missing the bus and staying late at school so I could head home later, avoiding the others girls. I liked the quiet that swelled to fill the locker room as their footsteps faded. I purged the little that was left into the long metal trough as I tried not to lose what remained of my mind, wondering if cutting my skin might make corruption seep out with my blood.

Cupping – the word arises, uninvited. I fidget as I wait for the tram, remembering how Lizzie's splinter-thin cuts had looked more like slices to let salt into meat than an outlet via which something festering might drain away. Bloodletting to balance a black humour? (Am I remembering or pre-empting a bub thumb on shiny pages, slipping?)

I'd looked older as soon as the weight came off, almost androgynous, except for the taut skin around belly and breasts. I pulled up scrunched socks over shins sharp enough to cut the wind. Closed my blazer till lapels overlapped. Who knew where I might've been by year end except that by then I was under another spell and the rapid weight loss had stopped. We were stabilising.

How much had the others known? I'd been different ever since I'd come back – grades had never mattered much again – but at first, at the start of that year, I'd wanted to fit in. And I had, for a bit. Or I'd thought I had. Or I'd been sure I would, soon. But then, after that May night nothing was the same again, the previous paranoia taking on a whole new aspect. I became convinced I hadn't been initiated into a peer-perfect clique but sacrificed as some kind of sick joke. Honestly, I hadn't known who to blame – Lizzie, myself or another force entirely. It wasn't about being one of three any more; that moment had passed so fast it was as though it'd never been. I was just trying to stay whole, as one.

I scuttled between classes, clenched fists by my side, almost falling on the bricks as I tried to cross the quadrangle with rigid hands and torso tight as if it were laced. Braced. Bending so as not to be broken – the stoop of a primal thing, scooting beneath a cloud of wings. Having to remind myself how the left–right rhythm went, which arm swung forward with which striding foot, all the while hunched over to protect myself from my own buzzing imagination.

Oh we'd've been relieved if we could've believed we were making it up!

My forty-something brain sticks on thoughts of then, without the distance the future usually feels for the past:

how had I ever made it back in one piece? These hands, too, gripped by the side of a grown-up but not-yet-grown-old body, I remember how my head had hummed with Ed's confessions. He swore we could call up flying fiends, summon storms – or so he'd have had me believe. Making me glance askance at other girls – judging, questioning, critiquing: them and me – until I lost the ability to do even the simplest thing.

Like look someone in the eye. Or avoid doing that. Were you supposed to look directly at them coming towards you? Then when did you look away? Was I – suddenly, or had I always been – making eye contact too early? Had I ever known, instinctively, the answers to such questions? What if *they* were mad? Look? Look away! I couldn't bear to think my churned-up thoughts, even to myself…which only went to show how bad at simply *being* I must've always been. The more I thought about it, the more apparent it became how mad I obviously already was. He wasn't to blame; he was just the latest form of my mania.

But also: my new friend. He was the only one who understood, the only soul as out of time as me – unless he was worse and making me more like him with his picking and poking.

I sigh, a finite breath expelled. I have to get out of here. I see my ride approaching with relief.

Or maybe everyone else wondered the same, and it was actually a sign of how normal I was that I was perplexed. I lost myself in teen angst – until an arm threw my almost-natural rhythm and I had to pull the pace back, skirting cracks. God, if only Di had been there to take my mind off things. Lizzie would've known how to catch me from those sickening sinking spins. But. They were not.

I sigh again, pathetically spelling an infinite breath.

Things had begun to change – thank God – when I'd realised that there would be, and already was, *you*. Jo. Which was well before we were actually two. It was when I'd become so desperate that I'd finally risked drawing attention to my state – which had clued me to the fact that I had one, and was in one. Raising my hand in class to ask if I could, please, see the nurse.

On my way to the sick bay I'd become confused, circling the grass we weren't allowed to walk on as my breath grew short. Behind me, in high-up red-brick rooms, I'd sensed the others still studying as I floundered among waist-high agapanthus that waved lopped heads on wooden spikes. Only to find the door locked when I arrived and knocked.

By the time I'd made it back I had to lie down with knees bent and feet up on a chair. Tears polishing the sides of my face as the small of my back ached under your not-yet-real weight. I will never forget the smell of that schoolroom carpet as I hyperventilated, waiting for the chaos to clarify, the morning sickness to subside. Eventually accepting that – by whatever circuitous route and imperfect art – I was pregnant. With child. Knocked up.

Done.

I look around the empty change room, wondering what time, what place it is. Have I finally travelled further back, or am I still on some city tram; before a flat black screen; lost in a last-ditch dream?

I shuffle my feet in their scuffed T-bars, registering my shape beneath late-eighties-large clothes. I feel neither normal nor particularly not. Was I different just because I (now, knew, I) was up the duff? I shrug, almost feeling the 'whatever' I'd been pretending, and discard the latest mixtape Liz had wedged into my bag. No longer interested in her over-the-top odes – *locked down, a slave to his story.* Once upon a rhyme I'd have given anything for her to woo me; now I could've snorted at our old game: twisting cock-rock quotes into selfie-conscious codes.

Then: the pounding in my brain, the gasping of heart and sickly sweet taste in my cheeks. I race across the room to just make the toilet in time, wiping tears from my eyes with coarse squares of paper. I shut the lid and sit down to think. A minute later I'm up again, but there's nothing left. When I've stopped dry-retching I leave the stall and scrub and scrub and scrub my hands. Who'd have thought that would be it? The moment when I free myself from a past that never was. Commit to a future that's already happened.

At first, like any ascetic, Ed had thrived on my famished high. But as I held out, held more tightly on, my confidence had grown. I would turn his table, make the man *my* conjuration.

I almost felt sorry for him: I'd always been a stubborn thing, the slyest of our three. Even when I went to bed fully clothed, wrapped in rope with a pocket of chocolate and torch tight in my hand, it hadn't been because I'd really thought we were going to another world like the ouija board had said, but because I would *not* be caught out as the ring-in I was.

I lock the thought away: a secret pearl made from the grit of his rub. A tiny hardness I will harbour within. I know – insofar as there is any 'I' to know any thing – that I am both before and after him. Having always been, I am in all likelihood the one possessing Ed. Whether he would or no.

And he was, I realise – straightening infinitesimally then, I think, on my bed four-score years hence where I will never straighten again – already

gone

.

00:02:00

The book of Nat's life flutters its pages before her dying eyes – from the future–present 2087 end-date, to her unplanned pregnancy, via chapters crafted around an obsession with Elizabethan England that nearly undid her in 2010. But she has to travel further to find a more malleable Nat. She needs to come upon lost best friends at that time when the straight path through a strange wood first diverged, if she wants to change the way everything after went: alter the past, her then-future, to make their present.

Two minutes. She is running out of time to GoogleMaps back to where three girls thought nothing would ever come between them – and on to four hundred years before, when two men prayed the same.

Tendrils snake towards an underwater light. I flinch the thought away. Bees buzz. I physically flick: it's time for wine. A white so cold I can barely taste it – I am not as grown-up as I seem. I will fill my glass unfashionably to the brim. Make a TV dinner, since Jo isn't here. Where is he, then? Too young yet to be off by himself…this must be when he went on his first-ever camp.

I move to the head of the stairs, wondering what nine-year-old boys play at when they're away. Jo's world is so much a part of mine I can't imagine him out of it.

He seems a normal enough kid, despite having me for a mother. And no father. Which is not to say I can't see the fantasies that consume him; building palaces around the room, books for bricks and a chessboard for the tiled court. My china figurine for Queen. Isn't that a sign of how well I've done, how far we've come? That he acts it all out rather than keeping it in? I never expected to have a kid who'd play kick-to-kick with other boys' dads, but I also never thought he'd hold on quite so tight. Then again, I'm hardly letting him go.

Halfway down the stairs a square of white on the doormat catches my eye. From where I stand – if I dip my head and squint to see – it actually looks more like an equal-sided quadrilateral than a right-angled rhombus. So someone into such things might think; I screw my eyes so the paper kite dances in the evening light. The diamond seems to spin in homage to the Greek word it's coined from. I press my palm against head; errant facts I never knew are bouncing around my brain: the area of a rhombus is fucking K! The winged letter practically causes pain.

K—.

In the dim downstairs the envelope shines. The mail slit above it is shut, but framed by the extended daylight-savings dusk. Next month is the last of the Julian calendar and the first of the Gregorian, of a sudden I remember: Thursday 4 October 1582 was followed by Friday 15. Though not in England, despite Dee's best efforts, but on the Continent as night followed day nearly a dozen dates went astray.

That was the year Dr Johannes Dee met and took in his helpmate Mr Edward Kelley. I hesitate, my hand on the banister: who took in whom? I have a sudden image of

Kelley stowing those stray hours in a dirty sack. Hiding them in the hold of some dodgy boat, skulking across the channel with a secret stash of European time, squirrelled against the day.

As quickly as the picture surfaces it sinks away.

Unwincing – where is that wine? I give myself a shake. Turning on lights and Triple J so the stop–start of Nirvana chases ghosts away. Could grunge be any less like the music we'd been into? From teased to greasy hair, the gender-bending metal we'd loved so much, which had triggered such satanic panic, merging with punk to make the underground sound that's morphed into this chart-topping heart-stopping pound: *Come, AS you are, AS you were…*

When I turn back, there the card still is. Of course I recognise the crest. I suppose the university has passed on my address – it's hardly surprising someone in admin acquiesced to a request. It couldn't have been Jo? I know he'd want me to go; I guess it's a reunion for the class of '87 before I've even opened the envelope. It seems inevitable.

I tell myself it's not that odd, that ten years is something for everyone to celebrate – it's harder to believe it hasn't been hundreds more – but the sense of déjà vu is so strong it's like I've been here before. I haven't, have I? Received a loaded invitation after an extended time away. Had I dreamt I was Dee, preparing his return to court, wondering whether Bess had aged – more or less than him? He must've thought Sir Walsingham's plans were as sure a route as any to the Queen, which would've been one reason he'd gone.

And why he came back: to dance attendance upon their sovereign. How could I not think of Liz! The leader of our Year Twelve clique, who'd bossed us other two, assuming our adulation as her due – which it had been, most of the time. Had I really loved her more than life itself? What a stupid thing to think! More than my own, perhaps, or the life I knew then. Was it love, though? The way I'd longed to slip inside Liz's skin and be *that girl*: the one we all loved best. Who, in the end, got the guy.

It is not odd, I tell myself again. Time cannot be a curled leaf, one point touching another precisely so everyone slips willy-nilly – in their minds and memories at least – from here to there, but never into the arching years between. (And if it was, if such a sci-fi explanation were true and everyone, in fact, did, that'd just confirm my own worst fears: that we are all stuck, viciously circling. I think, and it might even be the truth, that I'd rather be the odd one out, neurotically obsessed with something I've repressed while the world around me – and everyone else in it – remains relatively sane.)

' 'kay,' I mutter out loud, thinking time was more like a fiddlehead of fern frond. In my case, anyway: spiralling around a central circle that didn't actually exist yet would still prove the ultimate end point once all was uncurled.

'Okay,' I repeat, slower, as though someone is waiting to see what I will do. And someone is: I'm sure I sense the girl I used to be – or is it the woman I'll become? – watching present-tense me twist and turn, wriggle and squirm. Should I go, to show I've come good? Not go, to prove I've always been okay?

Pouring that wine, pinning the card to the fridge – its stiff parchment reminding me of regal documents another woman similarly put off addressing, once upon a far-off time – I wonder how it would feel, going back to the old school. I've driven past the grounds a few times over the years, seen new buildings going up, noted when it went co-ed. Not that I'd ever have sent Jo there, even if my folks had footed the bill. My parents, and my friends' too, had spent every cent they had on fees so there was never any money left for that all-important first tan of summer or last ski trip of the season. The off-the-shoulder bright-white tee, designer-ripped jeans and naturally perfect perm – not to mention the class excursion to France: Liz and I had never even told our folks about that one. Not that money was the only thing that'd made us different, but it might've been the easiest to see.

I like to think we'd chosen not to know what we had to do in order to fit in, or at least chose not to do it, but maybe Lizzie had never noticed.

I'd had to point out that T-shirts should be worn untucked, except for an optional scrunch at the front. Liz had moved, as though to comply, but then stopped. It would've been so easy to rearrange her top, roll down a sock! I would've done it in a shot. It'd never occurred to me not to. Not that Lizzie was showing off, she was just being herself. Her true self. Showing us other two that what went on outside our threesome mattered less and less. What mattered was what was between us. And that mattered so much more. My intense self-scrutiny amped up as I began to understand that there was an unspoken anti-uniform, under the unwritten uniform.

Now I'm a mother myself – albeit years younger than any others I've met – I have more sympathy for those tennis mums who'd idled their BMWs in the circular drive, waiting for their precious 'mini-me's to emerge. I wouldn't be surprised to find the lacquered nails and toned arms hid secrets worse than chewed quicks and loose flab. Who picks their kids up anyway? At nearly thirty-something, I imagine days given shape by the school runs that topped and tailed them while my misfit friends and I took the bus. Our parents were barely part of our lives – we'd hardly known what was going on in our own empty homes, let alone each other's. Which was the whole point. Friends were the new family and our gang of three was all-powerful. Though not, in the end, as strong as triangles are supposed to be.

That night, after a bowl of cornflakes for tea, I dream of walking up the long curved drive. The red spires of the original building rising out of the rubble of what I remembered. On my right, in its own bricked circle, the tree we'd sat under every lunchtime of our high-school lives. Its gnarled branches growing around the dinky tin, long rusted in, where Liz and I had hidden our daily notes. Small, scrawled fortune-cookie codes. Love letters from detention, where we were always doing time apart for whispering together in class.

'A cunning virgin waiting in a curtained room,' did one of us write? 'For her doom,' had another answered? Racing when the bell rang to add our couplet to the endless ode we wove between us. Folding and refolding the paper until it was too thick to fold again.

Before I reach the main hall with its walls of floor-to-ceiling glass from another era, set in old oak almost as hard as metal, I wake up. For the moment I don't know where I am. Was that my bedroom door? An eye at a keyhole, peeping. A waiting stool beside a warming wall – I squirm. The coming reunion has me in a fluster. I've been trying not to think about it, have even waved the invitation over the bin, but something keeps telling me I should put in a show, and back on to the fridge it goes.

Awake in the dark, the sense of the old–new school and fast pace of my heart remind me of when we'd broken in after hours: 'We're on a plane!' Lizzie had whispered, pointing to the exit lights as we ran through empty rooms. Along long corridors and down dark stairs that spiralled in a smooth space curve. A helix. I shiver at the un-me word. I'd been struck by the smell – dry chalk dust and wet whiteboard markers, mouldy cheese sandwiches and old bananas. Overlaid with antiseptic. It wasn't that the school had smelt so different; it was that it had smelt the same when everything else was changed. The tide of sound – the shrieks of hundreds of hormonal girls – sucked out. Waves of silence rolling in.

My fear is laced with excitement. My confidence that I won't go being effaced by a growing conviction that I will. Excitement, braced with fear. Maybe the invite – stamped with the school logo dead centre like a hex – is traced in invisible ink and if I lit a joint the smoke would reveal a secret message directing me towards a more fantastic meeting.

It seemed like the séance all over again: a set time and place. I'm mature enough to smile, insecure enough for it to soon slip. I've never had another puff. The rift that had been opened – between us, within myself – wasn't so easily closed: that gap, prised a crack, had soon yawned wide. When we came out the other side of that May weekend, and it was time to walk through the school gates on Monday morning, I hadn't been able to get off the bus. And yet, here I was. Psyching myself to return to that faraway forest where my story got so lost.

It was a bloody mystery, worth not mulling over if I can. I roll out of bed to get a glass of water. Knowing one reason I'm so wary is that it isn't some May date we're heading towards this time – which is only significant at a stretch (when I remember Dee's midsummer festivities:

resurrecting the Celtic tradition of a towering maypole 150 feet tall) – but the last day of October. I don't want to believe all the superstitious things I think, but everyone knows that once upon an ancient time the 31st was when the old year ended and next began. Spirits – hallowed or not – hovered: ghosts of futures past, angels of pasts present. The last hurrah of the Old World's summer, when the dead were remembered and the future could be summoned.

The absolute flipside of the start of spring. It makes sense that the membrane between worlds thins in more than one place: if there's a front door, why wouldn't there be a back one? And if the latter opens so easily, what would happen if we hammered on the main entrance? (I wonder if Lizzie'd known about such things: had she wanted us to be wandering in the woods when fairies were known to ride? If anyone was all over that it would've been Liz, our font of all fantastic lore.)

I catch myself in the bathroom mirror. If I were looking in at Halloween it might've been the face of my future companion staring out. The thought makes me snort, pulls me up short – did divination always have to be about love? *If you love me, pop and fly; if you hate me, burn and die.* What time had I ever had for that? Neither suitors nor hazelnuts being in abundance. Scraping together enough tutoring to repay the mortgage my parents had guaranteed. Looking after my son who, admittedly, seemed so much more mature and less in need of looking after than I had ever been.

There's nothing for it but to crawl back into bed. Pull the doona up over my head. If we were to Freudianly re-enact that formative scene, who would I call up: which John? The Doctor, or that stranger I never really figured for Jo's father? Though I was wise enough to know it didn't matter who you dialled; the operator would choose who to put through.

As night ticks towards morning I remember how one Halloween we'd huddled over the Yellow Pages – the landline like a planchette between us – dialling number after number, looking for a likely lad. Lizzie had said we should peel an apple all around and fling the paring on the ground to see the first letter of our sweetheart's name.

'E, for E-*liz*-abeth!' she'd laughed at our tightly turned attempt, which I know now had been E for Ed.

'D, is for Di!' she'd hooted at the next loop, pre-empting the way our token would be pushed and pulled between those two letters, come winter: E. D.

D-e-e.

At last I remember, hurtling through the cosmos – summoned and sent – that *I'd* been the one who'd thought we should call an outlaw: 'Wank, so he can slide into our cunts on wet fingers and travel up fertile streams to merge with us inside our heads.' Had I had anyone in mind?

The others had looked impressed. Liz, laughing hysterically before I had a chance to backtrack: 'Where's the fun in that?'

And realise, as the past reaches out to suck me in with its relentless gravitational pull, that I do – after all, after everything – want to see them again. I have never stopped wanting that, even though everything I did after was to be free of them: and there, and then. I would have given anything, I would…so I almost think, caution catching me just in time: I would not give him. I will never give over Jo.

So. I am not going to go to our class reunion because I want to reassure myself how boringly normal our lives are – my own included, these nineties days – but to remind myself that time really has rolled on. None of us will be who we were. And what we had – or almost had, or tried so hard to have – was long gone; I know that. There is never any going back. Only the possibility, the absolute necessity, of pressing on. I will go because it might mean something if I hadn't.

'I'll check on you when I get in.' I kiss the top of Jo's head, muss his hair the way mothers do. He's not the little kid he was and pulls back to stare at me.

'You won.' I shrug, we both know this is not the kind of thing I normally do. I avoid his questions about that time and those girls. But here I am: as ready as I will ever be. Eager, in fact, to see that final scene from three points of view – hoping triangulation might help me see true.

I pull at my modest black dress, thinking how opposite it is to those bridalesque gowns Liz had made us try on in bogan boutiques – dramatic satin affairs with ruched leg-of-mutton sleeves. Planning what she'd wear to a school dance I never got to go to. Nervously, I pat. I'm over blaming them; that's the difference between these mostly sane years and the mad maelstrom of our micro-family's first few. It'd taken a while to convince myself that it couldn't all be Lizzie or John's fault, not everything. Maybe not anything – even if it'd fucking felt like it. I pick at the black. In the end, though, I'd succeeded.

It would be nice if they were nice. Not necessarily nice to me even, just nice people. It'd be nice to know that the friends I'd had had been worth having. That we had been friends, and if I were knocking on the door of heaven and St Peter said, 'Who'll vouch for this lost soul?' they'd put up their hands. That my memory of Who We Were – and who I'd been – was *right*.

Calling goodbye to the babysitter I pick up my bag. Give my son the high five he's after. Tucking mouse-brown hair behind an ear I smile at the hall mirror, welcoming the lines I've worked so hard to earn. Turning to go, I watch myself disappear: no butt to speak of and flat post-baby boobs. In some ways – not just weight-wise – I am more girlish than I ever was.

Putting on a spare 500 grams throughout the pregnancy, I'd emerged from hospital lighter in more ways than just weight. As my fat had faded so had the solid outlines of our old world: I was reborn into a silver shining-brightly day. Kissing the new moon of Jo's head, I'd inhaled him and fallen in love as only someone who hasn't can. Sensing then that he would be the one to keep me safe, and not the other way around.

Double-checking the front door with an automatic tug, I head to the tram stop, suspecting the others aren't so caught between not wanting to be early and afraid of being late. Aren't trying so hard to time their arrival perfectly.

A teenager unable to find my friends, I duck through the crowd. It isn't just being back here – the school hall so familiar, if festooned with balloons, desks ill-concealed beneath pristine linen. A mother and lecturer I might be, but I still feel like a child much of the time. Back then it'd been the opposite: I'd felt like an old woman already – some storytelling crone. Will I never be the age I am?

Choosing to stop thinking. Choosing not to think about not thinking; NOT seriously thinking, I dodge familiar-ish faces, age blurring features into an out-of-focus class photograph. An unregistered Greek chorus whose names I'd recognise – if spoken Christian first and maiden last

– as the background to my super-vivid technicolor close-ups of Di and Liz.

'They just chose sepia, you know. I mean when they invented photography it could've been any colour – black and blue, red. Whatever. They *chose* sepia.' I scan the crowd. So strange to hear that voice out loud.

No sign of Liz; I arrive at the bar. A row of tables stacked with wineglasses, buckets of bubbles at the ready behind. It was all so daggy: the eskies of ice plastered with scratched stickers bearing the school coat of arms. It didn't fit my memories of money and class and privilege. What else could I have got wrong? Next thing you knew, there'd be no bitches!

'There was this guy right, in England, who had a blister that was actually, no joke, *this* big. When they popped it they found a fish. Not like a fish fish, but a fish all the same – some early mutant swimmer.' It was Liz all right; now I could see her pale hand in the air. The connection between her words and my thoughts was, as always, freaky.

I couldn't really hear her, but I got the gushing gist: my old friend was a second heart that beat outside this body. Her mania made me calm, as though anxiety were an infection and, in spreading, had passed from me. I didn't remember that, though: I don't remember Liz ever being nervous at all.

'I was so sick, I mean soooooo sick. We were sick *as*. Flu is one thing, and bird another, and then there's swine, but this just took the cake – I thought there was no way we'd make it. But then, here we are – a hundred kilos lighter,' Liz strokes her belly – did that mean anything? Shakes her head, as if in answer; as though we are still umbilically connected. 'I couldn't touch a drop...'

'Sick as a *dog*, huh?' I interrupt, an in-joke only I enjoy

– riffing off thoughts only I have had.

The two of them turn and, squealing, pull me into a scrum. Squeezing shoulders hard with their hands so fingers gouge flesh. They push each other back to get a better look, prompting me to see the box-cut diamond on Di's tanned hand. Framed by square nails and a fancy oversized watch worthy of one of the trendites we'd never had any time for. How much else hadn't I seen?

I've spent the years picking holes in Lizzie's lies, ready to catch her out if I ever got the chance: 'Come on,' I nod, 'tell us more!' but it's no fun giving someone enough rope if they too happily hang themselves. I tip back my glass and slip off for a top-up. I have to take the edge off this. It's like I'm here, and at the same time I'm not. It's like we're all back there – could it be that I am not the only dyschronic one, and our whole class is lost in time? A ghosts' ball in an old school hall.

'Here we are then!'

That was better.

'Here we are.' Three glasses chink. The partners of the other two, I discover, are deep in conversation – as though the guys who don't know each other have more in common than the three of us, who do. Or did. Now it's obvious how well Di fits in with the rest of our year I wonder if the others have caught up in the interim. Quizzically, I look to Liz.

It turns out Di hasn't just stayed in touch with girls I never knew she knew, but has even married the brother of one them. Kristine? Kirsten? Who'd ironed her hair till the split ends frizzed with static; overdyed it black, so greenish streaks ran down her blazer when it rained. She'd gone on to become a catwalk model and had always, apparently, been a family friend. Well, what did I know?

We clink glasses again. It wasn't that awkward; it wasn't, really. What did I expect? Lizzie was still electric, her strawberry hair dulled to a burnished blonde. And, it turned out, less in love. Or maybe she just enjoyed a more open relationship, reminding us – with a raised eyebrow – that her mother had run off with another woman. Remember! I didn't. Clearly too wrapped up in my own world then: so self-absorbed I wasn't even sure it'd registered that Liz's mum had left.

Which was just what I needed to be reminded of to soften towards them. I was the one who'd been crap! Lizzie's man looks over with that mixture of care and concern I used to feel – but don't, right now, feel – as Liz leans in, and plants an open-mouthed kiss on me. Smack. Bang.

'Remember,' I blurt out, 'the tennis centre?' I hadn't meant to be the one to start, but everyone around us is playing 'remember when' and I'm feeling so forgiving – towards the pair and, by association, my juvenile self. What else were we here for, after all, except to remember?

'The David Lee Roth gig?' Pimply boys had pushed towards us yelling, 'make way, make way, lady with a pram!' which seemed so witty I didn't notice – busy dragging on my own new T-shirt and awkwardly threading the old one out through a sleeve – that Liz was sitting pretty, babs out in the city. Flaunting her new buds between taking one top off and putting another on.

I wished I'd thought how the story went before I'd started it.

'Hullo, boys!' Lizzie laughs hysterically, making the men look over. Attracting stares from nearby girls: were we having more fun? Oh fuck, now I remember. Oh fuck yes, I remember now – tears come without a sound as something hungry in me is fed again.

'What about Poison, at the Metro?'

I am laughing. I am crying: 'The Met! Dollar pots and watered wine. Us waiting in that back alleyway – singing "*I want traction all right!*" like some naff a cappella trio.' C.C. had kissed the window, asking where we were staying as the white stretch limo pulled away. It was all so clichéd. 'And we were like: "*I don't think so*"!'

'No, Nat, *we* were like: I don't think so.'

Perhaps. Perhaps. The laughter settles. It's disconcerting the way I seem to have acted the opposite of how I felt. How odd. To have appeared, to have *been*, not how I'd thought I was. Or is it just how I remember it now? Things that happened to other people as having happened to me; things I'd done as having been done by other people. Who had sat before the tennis court with proudly bared breasts? Oh we were one and the same, all right.

'What about…' Liz nudges, like she's been waiting. 'What about our book?'

'Mills & Bon!' Di shrieks behind her sparkling hand – a gesture that draws as much attention as it hides. Is she showing us off as a couple of kooks? I wave the thought away, leaning towards Lizzie as I remember those rock-star locks and rugged good looks we'd stuck all over the cover of our precious book. And bedrooms: walls plastered with life-size cutouts of Jon and Richie – not that we'd rubbed up against them, much. We'd practice-kissed the paper until the coating had come away, leaving wet pocks where pictures of lips had been, but our teenage lust had been all about courtship: wooing, and unrequited lurrrrrrve.

As those stories had shown. Or would, if that old journal were ever found. How could I have forgotten that excruciating choose-your-own-romance Liz and I had overshared? It makes me wonder whether the information overload of today's electronic mail might hide my students' embarrassing exposés. Or seem to, so online communication – already proliferating; e-letters passing in the ether, myriad messages missed – gives everyone a chance to let it all out, leaving nothing to fester and ferment. No desire repressed or rejection unexpressed. If we were teenagers today Lizzie and I would've done the same.

We'd hardly been reticent – quite the opposite in fact: our friendship had demanded nothing except that nothing be out of bounds. Every feeling had to be echoed, every emotion amplified. Once upon an eighties time I'd shared every thought I'd had before I'd properly held it.

Maybe instant messaging would be the medium of the future – if the internet survived Y2K and we weren't all back out living in the hills, picking bugs from the undersides of bark. Working out where the sun was and which way the rain ran by how moss grew on trees.

(The smell of green is reaching out towards ancient Nat, frozen in her last repose. Cool is rising from within, passing through the surface of her skin to chill the room where Little John is waiting. Her scrivener, he hovers his iPen, sensing she is speeding towards a rendezvous with Father Time, who twiddles his milk-white beard as queens come of age, grow old, and are reborn phoenix-like from their own pyres, amethyst wings burning in a glorious act of self-sacrifice and self-preservation.)

'That day you left your locker open —'

'*I* left it!'

'And our book did the rounds faster than the lie that we'd been lesbians.' I look sharply at Liz. Our classmates had added their own scenarios in a flirtatious game of textual erotica while juniors graffitied the precious clippings with a cornucopia of cocks. Di's eyes shine.

When had the fantasising begun? Had we been that much older than the bastard Elizabeth, when she'd nearly lost her life playing grown-up games? Our titillating tales had grown like a weed well watered – each of us writing a chapter then handing it back on a cliffhanger, daring our friend to take it further.

A suspicion sneaks in that, if I asked, it'd turn out Lizzie hadn't been the one to start it. That it'd been me: lying on a folded blanket on the floor – the other two squeezed into her wrought-iron bed above. Eyes closed the better to imagine ourselves slim, with big hair, wide eyes and casually breeze-blown clothes. Who's to say which of us had been speaking? And yet, I have a feeling now that they'd be right: and everything had come from me.

'*Once upon a twilight time,*' our stories always started: '*three hitchhiking girls sought shelter in an old house at the end of a train line as a great storm broke. Thunder crackled overhead and lightning split the sky before they could make the creaking porch. Panting, they pushed past the broken door and ran into the abandoned homestead. Huddling together in their wet clothes, white lace skirts dripping puddles around pixie boots as a wind shook the building – rough enough to blow them all to Oz.*

'*Upstairs, though the girls didn't know it yet, three other runaways were already asleep in unmade beds. Three beautiful young men. And the girls were about to slip on up and slide right in beside them.*'

It was always raining, so our clothes clung revealingly and we could slip and slide against each other – and the boys too, when they appeared. Which they often did on horseback, when filming a music video nearby; or sometimes running and out of breath, when they'd been mistaken for criminals or ne'er-do-wells from the wrong side of town. Warm jackets were then wrapped around us, and we were lifted and carried to trailers or tents or houses or the nearby protective covering of sometimes evergreen and sometimes deciduous trees. Where clothes were, eventually, at least partially, peeled away.

Which was how the tales had ended, no one knowing where to take them from there. None of us having any idea what came next – well, sex, but we weren't interested in that. We were after the long drawn-out play before.

'Another drink?' I come back from miles away, pretending to wipe sweat from my brow and springing Lizzie doing the same thing at the same time. 'Jinx!' Together we make our way to the drinks table, waving Di away when other girls call out to her: who knew?

'So, how're things?' I ask carefully.

Does Liz see Ed flashing towards our meeting faster than light beaming between showers? She is focusing on her breathing, slowing it down – feigned disinterest always was the best way to keep him at bay. Stop the self-consciousness, I'd advise; he thrives on that. I imagine a future female pitying my now-present then-past person. Imagine, hard: a future, un-so-conscious self. Leaving no room for him in me. Or her, I hope.

'Good.' Nodding. 'You?'

Where was that drink? Both girls think.

'I'm kind of surprised to see you here.'

He is not far off. Liz's feeling might be drawing him in. She should pretend she can't: feel.

'I just thought…you know?'

I only have to get a whiff of the insanity I was lucky enough to shake to re-appreciate how I – just – got away.

But I am so well now I am ready to risk it. And dive right in, sensing time pressing: 'What the fuck happened – then, Liz?'

She has only to raise an eyebrow in that inimitable way for me to nearly come undone. Could my friend possibly know everything I'd been through? Possibly be feeling it now? Was Ed already needling in? I'd save her from that, if I could; I would save both of us, if I can.

'I've been thinking,' I start. Stop. I have though, oh I have.

'Never a good idea!' Liz's half-laugh is an unplayed card between us.

'I mean, thinking differently,' but mid-apology I'm not sure whether I mean thinking my own thoughts: or – I catch a breath as she catches hers and we're suddenly slipping sideways into the alternative realities of each other's lives. We are *all* points of view. (Which reminds me of the son of our son who is not sleeping in his chair but watching my no-longer-rising-and-falling chest. Counting down the last minute. Watching closely to spy me leave.)

'*Welcome to the rumble / we got one unnamed*,' Guns 'N Roses screams through the stereo, targeting my heart like an assassin in an Elizabethan daydream. Everyone here is covering their ears except Lizzie and me. We are laughing, we are looking at each other and need no words. We should be running down empty corridors, guided by old exit signs. Giggling in the dark. Leaving these stiffs for dead. But I'm frozen in place, holding a glass to my lips, lost in the liquid within.

'Here I come,' Ed whispers, 'ready or fucking not. Here I bloody come!'

An ocean of me rushes out as a tsunami of him rushes in.

Staring into the reflective surface of a small still pool with unblinking eyes, Ed sees, from high up, a room reflected very far away. An event Nat never went to, or hasn't been at yet. He launches himself into that dream scene, and out the other side; backwards, towards the younger man he'd been when he first looked – in 1582 – and was hooked by the Doctor's lure. Forward, to when he will leap from a parapet in 1587, gasping: 'Here! Come! I!'

(Unless Nat – drifting out death's door, passing through the rooms of her own life and opening windows into world history – was making even this epiphany up?)

Unable to believe what he sees – himself in a tower, or her holding court – Ed caresses the cold surface of the stone: as though to unsee what he is scarce able to believe. The face in the convex lens distorts, the smudge of his print warping thoughts. He feels, more than wonder at the angel's presence, more than awe or fear at how like Elizabeth the girl before them looks, relief. Relief that he has not failed, that he even seems to have succeeded. Relief that this could work, that she might choose him for her channel just as God had chosen them. He *will* be the messenger – never mind what the message is.

Who would've thought that what he'd said he could do would prove true! Who would've thought? Not him: he was a doer, ever chasing an action, only asking after what he had done and why. Often not even asking.

Confidence rebuilding, Ed sets novice reverence aside to ask what everyone is always after. His future self has nothing to lose but the universal need to know...

'What happened?' I prompt.

'Nothing.' Liz leans towards me, brushing long-untouched skin with sticky lips. How dare she.

'Nothing?'

'We didn't *do* anything.' She shrugs like it's no big deal. Like this is not news when it is everything to me: but is it true? Answers elude, as though what's factual is yet not actual.

'He was done, Nat; he'd come. We never *knew* each other, in the biblical sense.'

I'm unconvinced – though I wouldn't put acting orgasm past our Liz – but that wasn't what I'd meant. I wanted to know: 'What happened *next*?'

Avoiding the fearful face in the bottom of my up-tipped glass, not recognising it as mine, I look at Liz and see – copper hair, burning mercury, magenta powder; bright and shiny gold! Ed's orb would burst a bloodshot vein, a hairline crack snake across its glossy surface at my poor-little-rich-girl vision of a ruby Red Queen. Tough times at teenage high, that's how I like to look back on then – belittling my grandiose emotions. The way she used to make me feel. D&M, that's what we used to say: deep *and* meaningful. Which was how I used to knock the Ed in my head off his keel, push him back to his shore: by believing that there was a world outside, and it was real and actually mattered. Even if there isn't, and it didn't – doesn't still.

'I guess, I wish…' I'm saying, concentrating on the vessel in her hand, the fluid it holds: has Lizzie seen, in the interim years, the face that haunted me then? The one I still sometimes ken? I drop my drink so the sound of its shattering cuts across the party. He is there. 'That we never had! Oh Liz, not any of it – swinging, or swapping: crossing.

'Not even,' it was true, 'with you.'

But I'm here, too.

I sigh Ed out for the last time, wondering now what happens next. But it's Liz's turn not to hear, transfixed by a ragged-edged prism of glass and freakishly familiar face staring up. At her.

Even before he came round, Talbot's sweating sickness had gone a fair way to convince Dee of his new guest's sincerity. That, and the fact that Kelley didn't know where or when he was when he returned: shaking, like one in the throes of a fit or fatal ague, clinging to the good wife of the house as though he didn't know Jane was not his. Telling his master that Dee would not be him for all the world. Ed – as he now wanted to be called, not liking how someone had a handle on old Ned – said he'd glimpsed a fearful future five hundred years hence. An infernally hot down-under land an astronomical distance away.

What could the Doctor do but bow his head? Pulling parchment, nib and knife obediently towards him.

'Death flips us backwards through the play script of our lives,' said newly named Ed, 'so we end as we began: stripped of the self – the selves – we layer up like onion skin, lay down like layers of rock.'

When Dee pressed, more prosaically: 'But who was N—? Where is this hall with walls of glass, and who the uncrowned Queen?' Ned hissed the word 'reunion', which came out: 'union', but spoke no word about how desire, stirred, beset. Confident, dangerously confident, that he could manage that; he was onto a good thing here.

Tongue working at his teeth, Ed's worried brow unfurrows under the soothing ministrations of his host's fine fair wife.

A wanderer in her own mind, death ending the work dementia had started, stripping away time and self, turning eking minutes into one unending moment of convergence – Nat becomes Ed becoming Nat becoming Ned. Between the two–three–one sum of them they hold the whole world, knotting the line of time tight. Unasked-for love pulling space itself into a pin*prick* of unrequite.

'I want to know,' Nat, as Ed, had overheard Bess buzzing in the Doctor's ear, 'what happens *next*. Go – so you can hurry home. Come to me by the most direct route, Dee.' Not on a Renaissance ship then, but in secret, coded notes. Permission, even, to enter the Queen's dreams. This was a hundred years before men took on board dogs with open wounds, thinking they might use the poor creatures' pain to communicate with those left behind – who held the knife that had caused the cut. But Dee knew all about sympathetic magic. Time had always been the connecting construct needed for true navigation.

How to chart it, though? How to mark it? Maybe it couldn't be understood, only moved through: ridden as best one could, like a broiling ocean. Any explanation was, after all, only an approximation, as the Philosopher's Stone was no concrete thing to set in a ring but an alchemical substance: an *elixir vitae* – some formula, symbol or metaphor! So Nat's grandson thinks, as the silver plates of his 2087 machine project forward pictures from further and further back: 1997, 1987, 1587. Project back echoes from a future shore. Nat, turning from the berth where a ghost of self rests under a tented hospital sheet, returning to the screen, types. *Skry*pes. Intent on seeing for herself, if only with her mind's eye, as Kelley once did, what happens. Next.

Resisting, this time, the call of sleep; recognising its pull as not unslated tiredness but death – just as once upon a morning-after she was about to realise that it wasn't really lethargy that'd made her hurry bedwards.

I'd been so desperate to reach the sanctuary of my own room and shut a door upon that day. No idea then that I wouldn't be able to sleep properly again for a good while to come – first because of the residual chemicals ripping up my bloodstream, then because of the manic form my madness took: I never felt depressed, whatever their diagnosis, just anxious beyond all reason. I'd been so desperate that all my energy was focused on getting me there, not on what I would do once I was.

First, I had a shower, standing under the water until it had run from stinging hot to slamming cold. The towel against my skin so rough I'd half expected flesh to bleed. My vagina aching as though he were still inside me – or was I throbbing with unsatisfied want? How could such opposite states feel at all the same? I was a mess. Limbs tingling, fingertips turned numb; my waterlogged hair hung heavy as I struggled to know how to go on: to bed? Don't go to bed. Stay up.

That Saturday I was simply glad to have made it back alive, listening aghast to my own groans as I turned my body on its side. Trying to settle into a normal sleeping position. Was this it? Did it usually feel like this? That was the start of my darkest winter: get up? Don't get up. Go back to bed.

I burrowed in, trying to tune out the thoughts that circled my head. Bed. My eyes, not weeping. Sleep. The aching where his ears had been. Dream! My limbs twitched involuntarily. Lying, poisoned, on my side, I waited out the hours until compulsive cogs began to slow. Time will pass, I told myself, not knowing if it was true, but hoping I could make it so. Time will. Pass, I promised my spiralling selves.

And yet, not now – right now time was not passing. I may as well have stayed at Liz's house. Or outside, hidden in the empty heart of a hollow tree. Not sleeping; dreaming I was sleeping. Dreaming I was not sleeping – napping on an English throne. There, in my childhood home, the night before 6 May: vividly planning the party to come. A custom-made adventure for one. Counting down from midnight to morning, when shoulder-to-shoulder on the top step my friends will watch me go.

Right hand on the rail, Liz raises her left in an awkward wave. Sliding on sunglasses and putting a *shhh*-ing finger to her lips. Turning the gesture into a carelessly blown kiss as though I was already gone. How did it come to this? In the passenger seat of our family car I imagine being in bed remembering being in the car: time not passing, but having passed. My friend's face framed in halo-bright hair.

(Could it be – the echo of Ed that dying Nat has called up stares through the tinted glass. Could it really be…? To have come so far and found someone so the same: God, she was the very likeness! He sat the body he was in back into the fleshy seat, reminding his host's lungs to pump and heart to beat. Could *she* – Bess – too, be a traveller between worlds? For so he now recognised himself.

Of course their Queen would rule the time-space waves! She was the centre of their universe, Dee had that right. Ned was but a satellite.

He remembers, as if it were a recent morning, when he'd last seen the Queen: materialising out of the mist at that pre-Bohemia meeting, pretty as any princess from an unfair tale. Presenting the pair of men with a picture they would not forget: the Thames, flat as the sheets of a bed prepped for birth or death. Her voice, lapping at them. Who was he to resist?)

In a sudden surge of action, as the car reverses down the drive, I reach for the handle – press my other palm to the window, fingers splayed against the glass. But before I can open the door my father has accelerated. Not intentionally, surely. Small stones fly out from under the heavy sedan as he takes off down the road we'd walked arm-in-arm along to Johnno's party – hadn't we? Was it really only hours before?

'You're all right, Nat?' he asks the rear-vision mirror as we head towards the highway that will take us back to town. Awkwardly reaching his hand between the front seats to squeeze my knee: 'You're right?' No idea that *I* am not all there, that some aspect of who I've been was gone forever, I know now.

Unable to shake my aching head, I pick at the bandage beneath my sleeve. Belly churning – in my head 'Silence!' buzzed – and swallow hard, vowing to keep my peace. For now, at least. There was no rush. Nothing would come of pushing, or so I had to believe because right now there was nothing I could do: except be. Accept that I had him for company – and our repeating thoughts, which were one and the same thing, really: them, and him. And me. And it looked set to be that way for some time to come.

Maybe, a candle of fear flickers in my ribcage, maybe this one is the other world – the pool, a path between. Could we be trapped in Dee's shew-stone? Caught in a sphere spinning so fast – scenes are blurring beyond the glass. I close my eyes as a rip of nausea rises.

'I'm sorry,' I say weakly a moment later, straddling a puddle of spew by the side of the road, wishing there was more. *Would that he could expel everything and then some!* Thinks hungover and head-sore Ed, a thin string of spittle dribbling from his chin. I concentrate on my crawling skin, the sick slack of sunken belly, until I'm back. 'Sorry, Dad.' I spit again, wiping my mouth with the back of a hand. Feeling, actually, a little better. The physical act brings my attention to the precise points of ache and pain that join my body into a coherent-enough whole – bruised bones here, chaffed thighs there, aching neck above and sensitive snatch below. Even the acid afterburn is worth it.

Back in the car I close my eyes, falling quickly into sleep. Barely waking when we make it home so my father has to half-carry me in. As if I were a child, still, or he my friend. He turns on the shower and leaves me to it as I mumble my thanks and stumble in. Kneeling on the tiles so the warm water pummels my back. Pulling myself up to wash and dry myself, and turn my fragile body over to bed.

Which when I'd found that sleep wasn't the sanctuary I sought, but rather a doorway into the strangest dreams. Weird images churned in the whitewash of my mind and rose to the choppy top, covering over the clue-crumbs my virgin-self had dropped on the way out of a fairytale forest. In case I'd ever wanted to go back: I wanted to! But kept eyes shut and limbs in simulated repose, biding my time; ignored the new self planted within – not yet ready to welcome anyone *home*.

00:01:00

Nat's future is changed as surely as if a comet's discoloured mane had scarred her sky. Not that she sees a Queen on water, now – hand hidden in an ocean of brocade. Nor the friend whose half-wave from a doorstep long-eroded barely stirred the air. She is hastening towards the forest that stretches out swollen arms, straining against man-made boundaries. (A changed climate makes growing green no metaphor, just as new technologies prove possession temporally possible. The imagined has 'come possible.) Down through the century, Nat feels the pull of that night flexing its checked might, warping years into hours into one last minute…

I hesitate, in 2010. Mind briefly backtracking to the reunion I had not planned to go to. But to which I then went. Not that I think about that for long, because already – in this new version of that next decade – I am set to confront the union that came before. I am peering so far backwards through time, scanning the images in my mind, that it's like I'm seeing into a possible, probable future. Or spying so far ahead that my gaze has circled the world and come upon me from behind. Either way, I'm fast approaching that night that is catching up to who we – Liz and me – were.

Who we are.

'Who we *will be*,' I write decisively – pressing so hard my pen pierces holes in the page – as though the ending is mine alone to script. I could cry at the thought of finally letting myself be: for a fleeting present moment, a fleeing moment past. That night. Our three. I am not just stumbling between tenses; I'm tumbling between worlds. Oh Jo! (Or John? My audience of two merges in my mind into one: you.) The true story is not as either of us have written it: the act of remembering is itself a time-travelling trap – like spying, via an inbuilt mental app; like scrying via this iSpy-device – it snaps me back. To relive then: again.

So thinking, so knowing, I reach behind me to grab a throw off the bed that I'm leaning against. Ward off the evening chill that of a sudden I feel. I don't remember waking up, let alone napping; I can't remember grabbing the notebook that lies in my lap. But here I seem to be, sleeping sporadically, writing obsessively. Jo may have taken our routine with him when he headed overseas, but not my sanity. No thanks – I don't think – to the journey he started me on. Whose grand tour would this year turn out to be? I dig my toes into the shaggy pile of wiry rug, ready at last, ready now, ready any minute to return us all to that magic night.

The night to end all nights. The night that never, ever, ends.

And so. I re-read the words I've scribbled and scrawled through these pages. There's me, here, but there's a whole lot of you – and others – too. It's weird, what I re-read has so little to do with what I'd thought I was transcribing: Dee and Ed, Di and Liz, circle a mearstone of my making. I shrug, bemused, that it has come to this. It's what the doctors were always doing: Ed's, on his scholar's stool, reporting on a speculated future; mine, in his psychologist's chair, recording a contested past. Now it's my turn to try to find some greater design in our strange tale. By reading back, and writing on. To understand what happened in the wider scheme of things: the wilder scheme. And, secretly, I'm lured by what I might learn, drawn by the answers I dream of turning up. As well as being, really, scared.

(I can't help but wonder if my words might prove the spell that unravels reality itself. How much does that sound like Dee? I may have lived a different life, in another world, but the fact remains: reality is debatable.)

Still, there's no point getting ahead of myself; right now I'm where I need to be: in the clearing moment where three girls become two, and then one, who's coming undone. Our tightly locked ménage-à-fucking-trois: that's where this story starts, and seems set to end. A trinary – the image lingers, suggesting some kind of chemical composition: three elements, three variables, three parts.

'*Nary a one among us had any idea where our crossed paths would lead or what our passions could conceive.*' I chew a strand of hair, considering what I've written. The words don't even sound like me. Is the formal language a writerly trick – a wordy magic worthy of Dee himself: a way of warming my hands, flexing fingers before some meaningful tract to follow? I crack my knuckles theatrically and begin. Again.

'*1587: the year Catholic Mary was executed for trying to topple her sister from the throne. In far-off Bohemia two English alchemists were coming to conjure for Rudolph's court.*'

Not that! I hope this is the right thing to do: burrow into a dark work that springs from a black wood. What if my mad attempt to recreate the minutes that went before, the seconds that signalled one world's ending and heralded in a new, was only an attempt to comprehend the event that came after and shaped me into who I am and was and would forever be? A single, sane-ish mum: best friend to my dear beloved son. Or what if breathing life back into my '87 virgin self isn't purgative at all but draws author–reader deeper in? These inky inscriptions couldn't be his, could they? A last great enchantment, spelled by myself!

I might be sceptical, but I can think of nothing else to do. (And someone – some part of me – is making me do it.) I reassure myself that I'm writing in the hope my son – some descended self my DNA has become – can comprehend what until now I haven't. Why me? Why him? Ignoring what's been and gone, not letting myself think too much about what's to come, has got me nowhere. Or, rather, has got me where I am: trapped in a constantly passing present and never passed past. Writing it out should help make sense of it, in time. Because Time does that, has already: helped me make my own fantastic sense of things. It's funny how we know not what we know, but what we need to believe.

I take solace in the novel idea that everything might not be about me, in the end; if it ever was at the beginning. What a reprieve that would be.

Knotting the white wool with my toes, remembering how I used to backcomb Liz's hair – teasing the rose-gold until it was spun the other way, to hay – I welcome the night that's almost upon us now. In under a minute, less than a second, barely a Polish *tercja*, I'll be right where I am and at the same time somewhere else entirely: a darkened cellar beneath an empty house at the end of a remote cul-de-sac. Across a long lawn from the forest that might seem a neatly contained square of green on any map but is already augmenting. I imagine it as clearly as if I were there and am still, hovering a beat above the three. As vividly as if I saw it all before me in a magic mirror: that filmic forest and gothic house. As if I had a slipstream device that could join those dots. As if, if I could – or when some future-self does – they'd make a perfect arc.

From here – 2087? 2010? – to there: 1987. Where Liz is calling us to '*Come on!*' As she will again, later, when she leads your father and me back into the forest: past the watching pool. Towards the waiting stone.

As she had when we saw each other again a decade later, a dozen years ago, at our old school. Telling me – in that way she had, so I never knew whether to believe her – that the treat neighbours had originally knocked for at Halloween were spirits of the alcoholic kind. So we owed it to history to each sneak a bottle of vin de '97 from the crates behind the bar. Which was what we'd done: me rising to the dare as I ever had. Whose dare? Who cared! Stealing them, we ran down empty corridors as if we were still teens, but instead of narrowing claustrophobically, the hallway had opened out into a light and airy new wing: an award-winning architectural design. That was more like it. Some things did change.

Loving her, loving seeing her again, but intent on not losing the self I'd fought so hard to find, I told Liz how sick I'd been. How I might've died if it hadn't been for what had happened; though, weirdly, that was also what had almost killed me.

For once Lizzie was silent. And I kept talking, telling her about the shrink who'd been Doctor–Father–best friend to me. Maybe I was saying it for her sake too: the drugs had helped a heap. She said it seemed only fitting that they'd had a part to play in making me whole again, since they'd broken me so wide open. Oh I had missed her! My other self, who'd known me better than I ever had. Had known who I could be – and, now I wondered, might've seen who I had been. I confessed everything, about the doctor's trusty sidekick Prozac – which I called The Pro, as in, 'Send in The Pro', 'Blame it on The Pro'. Though there hadn't been much need for blame once he'd tweaked the dosage and I'd stopped clinging to an illusion that, he'd almost managed to convince me, was already gone. If it had ever been.

I told her how I'd surprised everyone with how quickly I'd come good. Beginning with easing up on myself, which was made easier with the new consciousness hatching within – loving a bub was a subtle segue to accepting myself as a good-enough mum.

Ending now, a couple of decades later, with this weird-arse memento mori – a crafted diary of one unbelievable night, our very own homegrown Slippery When Wet Tour. I recap my millennium pen. Having read it, finished it, reached the end. Hugging my knees in the mirror that hangs on the back of my bedroom door, the image echoes my conviction that I am – and have always been – more than one. Which was where we'd started – on the second or third or maybe it was even the fourth visit to the old doc's office, when I'd begun to open up to my new shrink. Not telling him about that night, which I was so sure had changed everything, but about the end of primary school, when the three of us had first met. Thinking that was the safest bet; no idea how much I probably gave away with everything I said. I surprised myself with how much I talked once I'd popped his blue-and-white antis and had someone to listen who – I was almost completely positive – existed outside of me. Like Liz finally, *finally*, was a decade on.

'The Pro knows,' I nod to the mirror another decade along, remembering how every night I'd gargled toothpaste and spat before – mostly – downing my prescription. Only once or twice time had frozen, fractured around that moment: when I held a pill in the palm of my hand and considered what magic might lie within the meds. A capsule far smaller than Dee's famous crystal, on display half a globe away.

One gulp and gone. I move on – as you probably will too, once you've crossed that wonder off your gap-year list.

'We met at the end of Grade Six,' I told my shrink, taking us back to the time before Liz. A time before sickness. It had been a pre-teen party for our junior school, when the old girls got to welcome those coming in from outside. Had it been my first after-dark do? Other than a sleepover, where we might've set an alarm for midnight but had only woken briefly to wolf down chocolate and prove a point before hopping back into bed. I got ready with Di, who'd asked her mum to drop us at the corner before.

Double denim, that's what we wore; I scrunched down bright-pink floppy socks, remembering how the lolly shade had offset acid-wash even in the dark. Peering into the driver's rear-vision mirror to pick two small pieces of hair and twist them until they encircled my head like a crown. Which might've suggested how young we were, though I was wearing my first bra – but that was probably more fat than breast.

It was our last outing as little-ish girls, trying to appear older than we were. From the tipping point of middle age I can see how we weren't just stepping prissily into tweendom. Real life was reeling us in as fast as anyone could want – or, later, might've wished it hadn't. We needn't have spent such energy dressing up; we couldn't have held back the future if we'd tried. Only in the effort to be mature were we marked as not.

Later, we'd graduate from adolescence even faster: over the course of one night, and all its flow-on fucked-up effects.

It'd been clear to me, talking at the end of '87, how everything that would shape our senior year was fated in that first meeting. So I still think in 2010; in '97 I'd said as much to Liz: how Di and I had been waiting for her our whole lives long. Not that we'd been looking – or known how deeply we were longing – until she'd arrived. She'd been the answer to a question we hadn't known to ask. I never knew how empty my life was before, or could be after, until she filled it.

Our Liz: that skinny, strawberry blonde in cropped bubblegum jeans and cut-down sneakers who'd won a scholarship from a state school on the edge of town, a good hour away. About as far as you could get and still be in Melbourne. She was all, 'I'm not from here and don't fit in, but could if I wanted to.' That brittle air of needing to prove herself, combined with proving herself by refusing to give in to that need, created an aura of otherness that made her seem so different *and* somehow the same.

'I painted these runners myself – I used a stencil, that's why they look so perfect, but I cut them down and bought these fabric paints that dry super-professional. See?' But when we leant down to take a closer look, Liz pulled her foot away. 'It's hard to get the lines this good. I mean, I'm not sure I could get it so neat again.'

Soon she had a circle of girls around her, laughing at insane stories of absent parents, an open house and running off into the nearby forest. Was she for real? No one believed half the stuff that came out her mouth as the disco ball cast fluorescent flecks over the day-glo punch. No one believed most of it anyway, but that didn't make it any less fun. Maybe more so: she was crazy, man!

If, that night, Di and I had been happy to hang on the edge of Liz's entourage, we were even happier the following year, when our new class queen lost her crown. Once the other girls saw her every day, they quickly tired of her inability to tire: she was too much. Toooooo much! Adoration shifted, as it did among teenage girls, but Di and I never forgot how the coming of Lizzie had changed everything: shown our snobbish school up as the conservative ladies' college it was. And our loyalty was rewarded. Liz shared her tattered copy of *Puberty Blues*, dog-eared and bath-stained, with its cryptic Vaseline scene; showed us *The Blue Lagoon*, knowing how to tweak the tracking when the tape stuck so we wouldn't miss our first seaweedy full-frontal.

She dragged us to *Witness* at the Belgrave Cinema, so we all heard Harrison Ford say, 'If we'd made love last night, I'd have to stay. Or you'd have to leave.'

In the darkened school a decade later I would've liked to ask Liz how the hell she'd discovered such things. Were there kids at the train station who'd talked about *The Vampire Lestat*? That pocket-sized bible of how to be three, complete with a historic version of Jon le Bon in velvet pants and to-die-for ruffs. It seemed unlikely: the ferny gullies might be shrines to the sublime, but Belgrave had always been a bogan outpost. Popping the top of the other champagne bottle, I suspected the real question was why Di and I had never uncovered anything new. We toasted in companionable silence: how could it feel so much like nothing had happened, then or after? Nothing at all.

Maybe I was as much like the rest of our class as I could see now Di had always been. Maybe the woman beside me was the only person I would ever know who wasn't – thinking that in 2010 sends me back where I began: she was nothing like me; I was the one who'd always wanted to be her. My crazy ensuing years were just a goddamn copycat act. She was Queen Regina, showing me how far I had to go. Teaching me to use a tampon, shave my legs, wag school and phone in sick. Smoke cigarettes without inhaling, and then with. Teaching me everything until that May night – and even then: everything I'd ever learnt until Jo came along.

I'd almost forgotten you. (I have forgotten John: listening, scribbling, just like his Elizabethan namesake.) Scraping hair back behind ears I uncap my pen, ready to write again – appreciating that it wasn't only thanks to my son that I was here, in 2010; credit was also due to my dear doc, too; and the older, this-time-listening Liz. All of them were responsible for these notes that were shaping into some kind of chronology: Jo might've been the one who'd asked the question I'd thought I'd answered, or at least neatly enough avoided, but it was the others who'd convinced me that the answers he was looking for lay within.

Come on, she calls.

Someone is humming Whitesnake's 'Here I Go Again' – '*on thy lo-o-one*'. It wasn't just Di and me who'd been drawn to Liz; Lizzie had been hurtling towards us, too. Me, especially. Oh we were alike, all right: I wasn't the only fucked-up one! In my very non-uniqueness, my ordinariness – that I'm finally owning – I was the foil her shining sought. Our spheres spun closer and closer to the charged moment of coming together as gradually separate paths merged until three random rocks were flying through space-time bare inches apart. Which couldn't last. Sucked into Liz's central orbit, Di and I had raced towards her roaring brightness.

Just A Fucking First Year: that's how I think of my students, not meaning it meanly – how could I? I'd been the JAFFYest of them all: so sure that what I was learning, the world was learning. So absolutely confident it was *my* first time that parted the Milky Way and birthed a world of stars. God, even writing about it was so self-indulgent I barely could. Forgive me, Jo: when you're the subject it all seems so much more important – and oh so serious.

That break between Grade Six and Year Seven, Di and I had hung out in each other's bedrooms labelling stationery for the year ahead and talking about Liz. Conjuring our Lizzie. It'd been my last soundtrack-less summer, filled with cicadas and the smell of cut grass. The smoke of Di's dad's incinerator wafting towards the opening ozone. We'd written to the headmistress, asking to be in Liz's year – not asking that she could be in ours – as Lizzie had suggested. Instructed, actually. Hadn't she? I played at being her, raising my voice and rolling my eyes as I faux-raved about the new books we were covering in contact: 'Oh I read that years ago. Mum has it. I mean, I kind of missed the whole love-interest stuff – she *marries*? But the red room is amazing…She really knows what it's like to be like, you know: *terror-FRIED*!'

If none of us had a choice and our friendship was an astrologically arranged marriage – would that diminish its significance, or amp it up?

She was neither good nor bad: neither the same nor different, just someone who knew me so well – and I had wanted, oh how I wanted to be so known! – that it was impossible to resist. Someone who got the mess, the contradictions: who knew you were not one thing or another. I've been so wary of that with you, Jo, given we were mother and child too – though I was always more like a big sister because of my age. But maybe that made it worse? It turned out I needn't have worried: in the blink of an eye you went from boob, to bottle, booster seat, the end of a phone, the other side of the planet and then – *pft!* – into the email ether. Now a one-way postcard away.

Have you crossed the Channel, as I write this: left Europe in your trek ever eastwards? Time-wise, are you still behind me or coming closer by the month? Living it large with a bunch of other shiny-bright young things, hiking up ruined towers and bungee-jumping into ancient ravines. Having the absolute time of your pre-adult life, as we once did – albeit so much younger and a whole lot closer to home.

Lizzie was the best friend I've never been sure I had; who'd slipped a pill on my tongue when I'd least expected it and, it'd turned out, was most receptive. So ready it was as though I'd called her up out of the dope-thick air – cowering, until she became frightening. Go on, I may as well have prompted, pop it on!

Which was how I'd finally persuaded myself to do what the doc had said. I confessed: because doing what I'd been told had worked so well for me once. Twice. It'd been the cause of everything, my saying yes. First, when the ouija board came out. Then, when we'd taken it outside – one by one ducking under that growing canopy. Remember? Oh yes, Liz nods, she remembers all right. Saying no to The Pro might've been a delayed reaction to the original drug-taking, and not the right response to the resultant situation at all. So, for a third time, I'd nodded – believing I was being offered options and choosing one. Yes. Why not swap the fog of semi-madness for the fug of medication? I might not have really believed a pill could reduce anxiety, rekindle karma and rebalance my soul, but maybe my absence of conviction wouldn't mean anything much at all.

To have spent the first trimester holding out just to give in, and – assuming I got well – prove the paid professionals had been right all along…well, what did I care? As long as I got to where I suddenly wanted very badly to be. Please, doc, help me become like everybody else, and let's pretend that asking isn't any proof I'm not.

What if I'd never been normal before? How would I go, if I had no model to return to or mirror an evolving self on? Maybe I wouldn't recognise a sane state even if I achieved it: Scaredy-cat Nat was known by her neuroses, and I feared I felt most myself when I was the self I liked least. Centred, I cease to exist, but with that freedom comes agoraphobic fear. It's a state I long for and resist. The absence of presence, which my shrink – *this* ink – was guiding me towards. To not *be* meant not having to keep my self under lock and key. Giving over control would mean no one could wrest it from me: how glorious if every thought rethought or forgot was neither a fight nor surrender! Obviously I had to take the blessed bloody pills not for the morning but months after: those already gone and those then still to come.

Doing what I knew I must, my 2087 skrying-self encourages 1987-me to trust, and stop wondering whether the this-time-legal drugs wouldn't lead me deeper into the very wood I'd run so hard from.

Having made a similarly conscious decision in 2010 – to log our original adventure – I consciously decide not to revisit it and, now spent, close this book on that story. Pad downstairs to slide the journal back between the pages of some older tome; hide that at the bottom of a leaning stack where my Jo can find it when he returns, and is ready. Or leave it, if he never is, for some future offspring to peruse.

And if I had got lost, caught in some space-time limbo-like priest's hole shored between the walls of worlds, well then, I wouldn't have been her any more and there'd be no Nat to know that she was not, now would there? Twenty-odd years later I remember thinking that (as another Nat will, some eighty years on, when the idea of an ending takes on new unabstract meaning), and tell my self – and anyone else here to hear – that the only way through was, *is*, in.

Which sends me flying back to our fateful catch-up and Liz's laughing lips. Me leaning in. And in, and in. So close I see myself reflected in her ermine eyes. Closing mine, and her kiss. Soft. *Self*-ish. Such dual feelings – of rightness, and wrongness – occupying the same space, that I am kicked out of time. And can only watch as different futures are sucked back into that one embodied act.

In a 2087 sterile room, high above a Melbourne that is no more, Nat turns the dial all the way back to 1987 – keeping one eye on the other times she's been skrying, no idea that doing so will rip her into an alternative history at the very moment of dissolution, restarting them all on the loop she's lived her whole life long. Reaching out a lifeless hand towards the two-dimensional picture the past is beaming up on the screen. Beneath the antiseptic she tastes the bite of a more basic alcohol. Beyond the halogen white light, senses the ghost of a moon.

As if in a dream, Nat pops the meniscus of probability and slides right in. Impossible! Slipping through the screensaver as if it were a curtain. Into the monitor as if the thin-film transistor liquid crystal display were water. And with the extant outbreath of death, rebirths herself in an amaranthine act.

In her mind's eye – unless it is another's, ah! and she is haunting her son's son via old notebooks he's been re-reading as he records her final thoughts – Nat roams a vast British Library of Alexandria. A virtual web of words and spells. A net, woven from twenty-six Latin characters, scrolls around her. She floats, floorless, beside infinite shelves. Runs non-existent fingers over exanimate spines.

Could she be seeing Dee's study at Mortlake, north of the London wall? Before it was ransacked when he left his home to chase angels mystical and pecuniary with Mr Kelley.

Or some memory house the Doctor painstakingly built? Perhaps to hide those three leaping days the old Gregorian calendar would've lost in the four hundred – five hundred? – years that've passed between his time and hers. The long weekend his calendar had to shed to stay in sync with the astronomical year and correct the imposition of old-style Christian time on cyclical seasons. Not that such days were anyone's to hoard, or hide in an *ars memorativa*! Listen to her: Nat's as crazy as she ever was. Just when she thought she was coming out the other end of such a sane-enough life.

This is what she's left with then, this is what she'll leave behind as she finally becomes un-one: her mad obsession, sense of possession. The thing that's ever felt the least like her – the thoughts that've felt like another's – this, it turns out, is her most particular part. In her very lack of singularity, she is singular. In her very singularity, is she *no*thing. The contradiction does her in.

Ghost-Nat lets the uploaded impressions of an infinite hive mind wash over her. So this skrying thing works both ways: in letting go she is taken over. Learning – if anything as academic as a lesson could come from being flung a slung-shot world away – that every year divisible by four is a leap year. Except for those divisible by one hundred; though centurial years that could be divided by four hundred were still leap years. Which meant 1900 wasn't and 2000 is. Or was. Or will be. *Dee!*

Nat has only a splintered second left. Soon there will be nothing to remember.

A grave has opened while she's hung on in non-space-time. A limbo like daylight-savings time – back when the seasons still changed and winter hurried evening up. She'd find herself referring retrospectively to 'real' time; then, as the new time became the real one, mistakenly relating further forward instead: so when it was three o'clock she thought 'It's really four', but actually it would've, should've been two. Until, eventually, Nat had kept sleeping only to wake naturally with the sun and realise that whichever way it went before was wrong and she was *now* living in real *real* time.

Beneath the oak Bess waits impatient. Rising, as horsemen ride up, sensing this will be when everything changes: for her, and the Empire. No thought of her dear Robert Dudley who, out of sight behind, is wedging himself into an opening in the trunk of their meeting tree. Riders not yet close enough to see. He tucks himself further in, a near-grown boy burying his face beneath its crust. As Britain welcomes a new ruler to the throne, Rob tastes bark dust in his mouth.

Which was what the first Earl of Leicester, rumoured to have once been Bess's master courtier, would remember on his deathbed decades later. When, in 1588, the Queen took up his old man's hand. Holding it the way she ever had when she wanted something. Sweetly. A finger pressing prettily into the centre of his palm.

'Remember?' she whispers. As though he had forgotten! Much as he has wanted to forget. Yes, he remembers: her. A princess, pre-crowned; them, sweethearts racing in English fields. She, whispering that he was hers, her other self and he, seeing no need to agree: the truth of it pulsing in the vivid air between them.

'I remember,' he promises with a love as sharp as winter apples. Smiling, as he should've when she'd ordered him to the tower for marrying Letty. If he had not taken Bess's jealousy seriously she might not have felt it so keenly, might've known she had no call to be so – Rob's wife was never a substitute for his Prince. Thinks her Lord, hand grown cold.

All this is in my mind: every word I've written, every dream I've dredged – pushing past Elizabethan echoes to reach my own buried memories on the other side. All, within. That's what everyone always said, and they might be right – not to mention the fact that I'm sure I contain way more besides. I know Dee's muse as well as I know – or ever knew – any of my friends, even if the only commonality between Bess and me in 2010 is gender and age.

And the only connection back in 1987 was how far we had or hadn't gone. 'Everything but,' that's what we three used to say. Until I'd done everything and, apparently, then some. Made a beautiful baby. Given up the very friendship that was all I'd had, for a relationship I didn't – and one I hadn't, yet.

Shifting on numb knees – how long have I been sitting here since slipping an odd book into a hidden nook? – I imagine Ed curled over a wax-less wick. Waiting for an unfuelled flame to spring into life. No longer not believing. He is lifting a warning finger as though he sees me, or some version of the same: his *shhh* is a message to remember as much as an instruction to keep shtum. I might be done with that past, but clearly it's not nearly done with me.

I stand, turn away from the inner vision, not wanting to see Ed walking towards a window. Not wanting to hear an earlier girl calling: '*Come on, N—!*' As he, forever, falls.

Instead I imagine, elsewhere, a hierophant's hand raised in benediction. It is as though Dee – not here, home now – is about to write what will lead us all towards some maybe seen but neither understood nor ever welcomed end. His other hand points down: connecting heaven and earth as the tarot's hanged man does with the perfect plumbline of his suspended form. Both figures, in their own ways, bridging worlds. Hadn't Liz said?

I remember Lizzie saying that in tarot, kings made things happen but the Queen made them real: we women worked like water, bringing life forth from a dormant earth. As if I needed anyone to remind me of the slumbering, sentient pool! I sense someone scribbling 'multiplication' in a margin, trying to pin down a mirror meaning in these repeated themes of reproduction and procreation with which I am threading our lives together even as my own ends, and with that…

I'm back! Remembering: John. Once upon a when, I couldn't have imagined anything ever coming between Liz and me – let alone a boy. Now I had to wonder if I weren't the one who'd opened the rift. Cracked it wide. The thought constricts. Had fatalistic thinking brought on friendship's end? (Had I, in some dark way secret from myself, wanted it? Willed it, even? My thinking that must mean it was at least possibly true.)

I am spinning through space: back and back and back. I am: dreaming – though it feels like I might be waking up, not falling into the deepest drowning sleep. I see myself repeated and divided: captured and reflected by giant glass discs rotating in space. Flung so fucking far into the past that from above the earth I see the salt-free meltwater that has slowed the advance of warmer weather, receding. Returning to an icy cap. Submerging beneath an ocean's depth. So semispheres locked in opposition – as the harsh cold northern light holds back the warm dark wet of a re-rainforested southern land – are reconnected as the tick of time untocks.

There is a sense of coming to, of almost, but not quite, consciousness. A state on the edge of states, a point on the verge of planes: a place of being-in-waiting. I, hover. I, haunt. Speaking, to myself, I sense another sometimes-self. Are my lines reeling it in? Or is it the one – *The One* – whispering these words that cleave souls together and cleft a soul apart?

Whatever there is of me, here, focuses on the image shimmering in the flickering periphery of vision. Two becoming one. Becoming three!

I home in on the circle of light.

What I see, when I look – leaping from the book, lying in the writing, launched on the screen in this remembered scene – is myself. Not *me* me, but a seventeen-year-old *she*: Nat, on her back, spread on a rock. Not lost – as I will think I am, after – but, for now, found. This is it then. That night that's ever-present. I have only to unguard an opening – let the curtain drift – for a century to disappear. Time might have passed outside, but in the constant forest it's standing still. And a child-like figure is trapped inside.

What I wonder, when Johnno makes his awkward move as carefully as he can so Nat doesn't know it's not fingers but a hard prick knocking; what I wonder, when he opens her wholly so the next day it will seem as though she is still full of him, within – and, contrarily, feel as though there's a hole in her that was not there before; what I ponder, is what it would've been like to have stayed sealed forever. What might it mean never to give up that much-vaunted but rarely really treasured prize? What if the meant-to-be moment never came?

Or came and never went and time stopped on a coital cusp?

John, I note, with an old woman's inward eyes, is not so different from the girl beneath him, really. Just another human trying to connect any way he can. But she has her head turned away to peer across the clearing at a face hanging in space. Conjured by the grass, the dope, the out-smoke and her own tendency to over-dramatise: a déjà-vued death mask. She will never know if it is real.

She will never guess that it was me!

Above that-me, then, there, is Jo's father. Had I ever really doubted it? Even when I spent the next decade semi-believing some character from history had possessed me, had I really believed I could will an apparition into being?

(And yet, here's me. The real story is hardly less fantastic.) Who John could've been is something we will never know – the answer to Jo's question no nugget of gold waiting to be conjured up and handed over.

I never knew a child would wrest me into the present. Jo and I grew up like siblings in my parent's house. And, later, roommates in our own. Willing growing selves into being. Eventually the old craziness lost its hold as I assumed second place in my own life: learning that children never love the way they're loved; accepting that was as it should be – the world would spin the wrong way if they did. Letting my old self go.

I sigh, and with a pleasure akin to sinking into a tub of precious water when skin is parched by the out-zone and muscles ache with the weight of earth's gravity, let myself stop. Begin to forget. I feel no fear, hovering on the edge of the glade: I am too aged, already as good as dead. And see how the route my life took was perfect, because it was the one taken: our course is the only navigable channel. These circumstances arise, this scenario presents itself, again and again, and even when it appears otherwise – in terms of what comes after, or went before – the notes are plucked from one lyre.

There's Ed, living on in John's son Trebonianus, who will push up against Jane's heart so she cannot breathe when she hears the news of his father's last act.

Everything already done is still to come.

It's only as I fade from the clearing – finally free, and moving on – that Lizzie emerges from the mist behind me. Stepping right through this shadow of self that my future skrying has cast back into our mutual past. How funny; it almost looks as though she's travelled here from a time further down the line than mine – turning the attention of an upgraded app to this moment as though it is a pivot point for her story too.

She wasn't the one who went mad, was she? When I became sane. She wasn't the one – on the stone, now – filled with some distant soul in a mystical act of transubstantiation? (And whose would that have been? Whose might that yet be?) The woman I became and want to continue having been – as well as the girl I once was; who has circled the clearing to watch the couple coupling from where I have been standing – wants to know not what happened then, but what is happening now. That face, which a moment ago was hanging in the clearing, it's me. Leaving. A star-filled space: two girls looking out through open eyes.

ACKNOWLEDGEMENTS

Thanks

to everyone who has, directly and indirectly, made this book: my publisher Terri-ann, for the gin, and your team(s) in and out of house; my supervisor Brenda, for firm emails on the big picture and small details

to my colleagues in academia, Tracy in particular, as well as students past and present – for helping me turn what I love doing into something I'm paid to do

to all my writing friends, but especially Nicola, Jane and Nathan, for your generosity with time and words

but mostly to my partner Peter, who has done this decade far harder than me: he's shared the worst aspects of writing a novel without reaping the reward – the absorption that gives as much as it takes.

This art has been a long time navigating, it's had its own alternate incarnations: I built it up and up – writing during nap times, while the grandparents kid-sat (thanks are due there too!), then on park benches and poolsides – before finally cutting it back in the evenings when the boys were old enough for that time to become mine.

Thank you, daniel sons, for letting me write.

And you, for reading.